"YOU DON'T KNOW HOW TO KISS, EITHER?"

Kit laughed. "You little minx—of course I do."

Encouraged by his laughter, she laid a bold hand on his thigh. "Then show me," she dared.

She heard Kit inhale sharply, but he didn't move.

Darn it, she knew he wanted to—why wouldn't he take advantage of her willingness? She let out a pretend sigh. "I guess I'll just have to find someone else to teach me, then."

"The devil you will," he grated out, and laid a hand over hers where it still rested on his thigh. "I know I'm going to regret this, but if I show you, will you promise not to pester me about it again? Or ask anyone else?"

"Of course," she said in as innocent a tone as she could manage. After all, she wasn't even sure she would like it. She just knew that with Kit, she would be safe. She closed her eyes and pursed her lips, raising her face to his.

"Not like that," he said softly.

She opened her eyes. "No?"

"No," he said as he gently cupped her check in his hand and looked deep into her eyes. "Like this . . ."

Dear Romance Readers,

In July 2000, we launched the Ballad line with four new series, and each month since then we've presented both new and continuing stories set everywhere from medieval England to the American West—the kind of passionate, romantic stories you love best, written by the most gifted authors. At the back of each book, we'll tell you when you can find subsequent books in the series that have captured your heart.

First up this month is Pam McCutcheon, with the first installment of the charming new series *The Graces*. A fairy godmother is a very good thing for three sisters who need a little help when it comes to romance—and the women who pitch in, beginning with the **Belle of the Ball,** have quite a few ancient, and highly effective, secrets up their sleeves! Next, Golden Heart finalist Laurie Brown presents *Masquerade,* as a British operative meets the woman who steals his life story for her potboilers—and captures his heart in the process. Will he learn **The Truth About Cassandra?**

Talented newcomer Caroline Clemmons takes us to the sweeping Texas plains as she begins the story of *The Kincaids,* and introduces us to a man determined to find **The Most Unsuitable Wife**—who soon discovers a passion he can't resist. Finally, Marilyn Herr explores the paths taken *In Love and War* as a hard-headed man and an equally spirited woman caught up in the dramatic French and Indian conflict decide to follow **Where the Heart Leads.** Enjoy.

Kate Duffy
Editorial Director

The Three Graces

BELLE OF
THE BALL

Pam McCutcheon

ZEBRA BOOKS
Kensington Publishing Corp.
http://www.kensingtonbooks.com

ZEBRA BOOKS are published by

Kensington Publishing Corp.
850 Third Avenue
New York, NY 10022

All Kensington titles, imprints and distributed lines are available at special quantity discounts for bulk purchases for sales promotion, premiums, fund-raising, educational or institutional use.

Special book excerpts or customized printings can also be created to fit specific needs. For details, write or phone the office of the Kensington Special Sales Manager: Kensington Publishing Corp., 850 Third Avenue, New York, NY 10022. Attn. Special Sales Department. Phone: 1-800-221-2647.

First Printing: January 2003
10 9 8 7 6 5 4 3 2 1

Printed in the United States of America

Thanks to Karen Fox and Yvonne Jocks for letting me play with their characters; to Mo Webster for giving me feedback on the manuscript at the last minute; to Angel Smits, Laura Hayden, Paula Gill and Deb Stover for ongoing feedback and support; and to Linda Kruger for spearheading the effort. Couldn't have done it without you, guys!

One

Colorado Springs, 1882

Belle Sullivan sighed as her mother fussed over her and her two sisters, all lined up for inspection in the front parlor. Belle just wanted to get through this ordeal with the minimum of bother, but it was not to be. One would think they were being presented to Mama's idol, Queen Victoria, for heaven's sake, instead of merely waiting for a few young men.

"Oh, Belle." Bridey Sullivan clucked her tongue in frustration as she straightened Belle's bodice and tugged futilely at the wrinkles in her close-fitting skirt. "How do you ever expect to catch a husband looking like that?"

Belle shrugged. She'd heard it all before, in endless detail. Her rusty red hair was too unruly, her complexion too freckled, and her manner too tomboyish.

Belle cared little for her appearance. All she wanted was to stay in the bosom of her family for the rest of her life, but Mama was determined to kick all of her baby birds out of the nest—so long as the new nest was lined with the best feathers, of course. But now that Belle was nineteen and without a beau who might turn into that most coveted of possessions—a husband—Mama was becoming frantic. She obviously saw this outing as an opportunity to rectify that situation.

Not that Belle was totally opposed to the idea, especially since the young man who had asked her out was Christopher "Kit" Stanhope, the second son of a viscount. A remittance man who seemed to do nothing but idle about, he was scorned by the hardworking self-made men of Colorado Springs, but the women found his aristocratic upbringing, education, and refined ways irresistible.

And Belle was no exception. When Kit Stanhope had asked her to step out with him, she'd been thrilled that such a handsome man, fribble though he might be, was interested in her. She had long admired him from afar, thinking him the most attractive man of her acquaintance, but assumed she could not catch his interest.

But somehow, she had. Perhaps he was one of those few discerning men able to see beyond appearances.

"She doesn't care how she looks, Mama," Charisma declared. At eighteen, Charisma came in for her share of Mama's attention, too, though with her height and sleek strawberry-blond hair, her appearance was usually without fault. Always blunt, Charisma added, "And I don't know why you should either."

Mama looked horrified. "Not care? Where would you girls be if I didn't care about your futures?"

Happy and a whole lot better off, Belle thought, but unlike Charisma, Belle knew better than to say it out loud.

Obviously trying to distract their mother, Grace,

the youngest member of the family at seventeen, twirled around the parlor, looking like a glowing candle in her new dress and bright red hair. "I think we all look lovely," she exclaimed.

But where Grace went, disaster was sure to follow. The Sullivans, used to her clumsiness, deftly rescued one urn and two figurines as Hurricane Grace whirled by. They were unable to catch two more knickknacks, but they hit the plush carpet and didn't break. In fact, that was why the carpet was there in the first place—because of Grace's little accidents.

"Oh, do be careful, Grace," Mama exclaimed as she replaced a figurine on a table. But Grace's attempt at distracting their mother didn't work, and Mama returned stubbornly to her favorite subject. "Do you want to dwindle into old maids like Miss Keithley? Living alone in that huge house all by herself with nothing but cats and no husband to call her own?"

"It doesn't sound so bad . . ." Belle muttered. At least Miss Keithley went about in society, had a place of her own, and didn't have a mother nagging at her constantly. Besides, Belle liked cats.

Mama whipped around to glare at her. "Now, you listen to me, young lady. You have it a whole lot better than I did in my day."

Belle exchanged rolling eyes with Charisma and Grace and pretended to listen, but they'd heard it all before. Mama had grown up poor as the daughter of an unlucky silver miner in Leadville. She'd married another miner, Patrick Sullivan, for love, but the early years of their marriage had been troubled by poverty and hardship.

When Patrick had finally hit the mother lode in the Grace of God Mine six years ago, Bridey had vowed to ensure her three daughters would never have to live the harsh life she'd had to endure. Once the mine was producing ore at a steady rate and didn't need Patrick's constant presence, she'd insisted on moving their small family to Colorado Springs. Having heard tales of the city they called Little London, Mama was eager to join the British aristocrats and denizens of polite society and leave her past far, far behind.

But though life was certainly easier for the Sullivans, Mama's ambitions to become a leading light of society hadn't panned out. Papa's indifference to the trappings of wealth hampered her, and though Mama had worked hard to overcome her own humble origins and lack of polish, she just tried too hard.

Undeterred by her lack of success so far, she had decided to focus all her hopes on her three daughters. Through them, she hoped to achieve the status she longed for. And to Mama, the height of success lay in obtaining an invitation to the annual Founders' Day Ball in July. If not for her, then certainly for one of her daughters. But since only the elite of Colorado Springs were invited, Belle feared Mama would never get her wish.

"I'm doing this for you," Mama finished as she tried unsuccessfully to smooth Belle's wayward curls. "You'll be much happier married to men of breeding and substance, I assure you."

"But you married for love," Charisma protested. "Why shouldn't we?"

Belle stifled a grin. Trust Charisma to blurt out the unvarnished truth.

Mama bristled. "Mind your tongue, girl. Of course you should marry for love. But remember, it's just as easy to fall in love with a rich man as it is a poor man."

Charisma frowned. "But—"

Belle cut her off with an elbow to her side. There was no use arguing with Mama on this subject. At this rate, they'd never get out of here. "Oh, I'm sorry," Belle said sweetly. "My elbow slipped. Did I hurt you?"

Charisma glared at her but took the hint and kept her mouth shut.

"Well," Grace exclaimed, "I'm looking forward to this drive. When will our escorts arrive?"

It was the right thing to say, for it finally distracted Mama. Relaxing into a smile, she said, "You have plenty of time, girls. First, I want to tell you a story. Come, sit down."

They all seated themselves, taking care to make sure Grace was sandwiched between them and far from any breakables—not an easy task in the fashionably cluttered parlor.

"Did I ever tell you the story of how your father proposed?"

The girls shook their heads. They'd heard plenty about the hardships, but very little about the more pleasant moments in the early years of their parents' marriage.

"Well, it was in the Garden of the Gods, the very park you're visiting this afternoon." Mama clasped her hands together, and her eyes turned uncharacteristically dreamy. "I was very much in love with your father, and he seemed to feel the same way about me, but he wouldn't declare himself. So, when several of us went to Colorado Springs on a visit and stopped off in the Garden of the Gods, I tried to ignore him and concentrated on the rock formations. I found all of them interesting, but the Three Graces formation just . . . spoke to me."

"What did it say?" Charisma asked with a grin.

Mama quelled her with a glance. "I placed some wildflowers at their feet and wished with all my heart that your papa would ask me to marry him. He proposed to me then and there," she said with a wistful sigh. "That's why you're named for the Three Graces."

The girls exchanged glances. They'd known who they were named for, but had never heard why before. "I thought their names were Greek and hard to pronounce," Grace said.

"Well, yes," their mother admitted. "But I named you for what they represent—beauty, charm, and grace."

Poor Mama. She had chosen entirely the wrong names for her daughters. Plain Belle had no beauty, forthright Charisma lacked charm, and Grace was . . . somewhat less than graceful. But it was a sweet story, and Belle said as much. "Why are you telling us this now?" Belle knew her mother well enough to know she had an ulterior motive.

"Well, offering flowers to the Three Graces and making a wish for a husband worked for me. Maybe it will for you three, too."

"You want us to ask for husbands from a bunch of rocks?" Charisma asked incredulously.

"Well, it couldn't hurt," Mama said. They all knew Charisma too well to be offended by her bluntness, even Mama.

"But we'll look silly," Belle protested. "Besides, we don't have any flowers."

"You will," her mother said with confidence. "Your escorts are bound to bring you posies."

"What if they don't?" Grace asked.

"Oh, they will. I reminded them myself."

Belle groaned inwardly. It was rare enough for a young gentleman to call on one of the Sullivan girls—more than once, anyway—but Mama's interference would make it even worse.

"What did you say to them?" Belle asked, feeling humiliated already. "Did you embarrass us?"

"Of course not. I simply reminded them of their responsibilities as gentlemen."

So, she *had* embarrassed them. Oh, dear. What would Kit Stanhope think of her? "Oh, Mama. How could you?" It was the first time such an eligible young man had invited her on an outing, and she felt awkward enough already.

"Well, I have to be sure my girls are treated right, don't I? I know what's due you, and they're going to treat you like proper ladies or I'll know the reason why."

And, to Mama, being proper ladies meant being escorted by proper gentlemen. Though Mama considered Kit Stanhope the catch of the town, Charisma's and Grace's escorts were just as acceptable. Charisma's intended beau, young George Winthrop, was the son of a wealthy rancher, and Harold Latham had a secure future in his father's bank.

Belle and her sisters sympathized with their mother's ambitions and, though they didn't entirely understand why those goals were so important to her, they loved her and wanted to make her happy. However, they had met with too many rebuffs from the people Mama was most anxious to impress and preferred to spend time with those who weren't so hoity-toity.

But they didn't want to let their mother down, so they had agreed amongst themselves to do everything in their power to make the outing a success. For once, they hoped to please her.

"We'll do our best to make you proud, Mama," Belle promised, and Charisma and Grace nodded their agreement.

"Including the flowers and the wish?" Mama asked.

Belle exchanged resigned glances with her sisters and spoke for the three of them. "Yes, Mama. Even the flowers and the wish." After all, what could it hurt?

The knocker sounded then, announcing the arrival of their escorts. Sudden queasiness attacked Belle's midsection. What could she do or say to such a distinguished young gentleman as Kit Stanhope? Belle knew she couldn't capture the heart and hand of such an illustrious figure, but could she make Mama proud?

The gentlemen were shown into the parlor, and Belle's heart beat wildly in her chest as she beheld her partner for the day. With his slightly wavy white-blond hair, bright blue eyes, high cheekbones in a patrician face, and erect carriage and air of confidence, Kit Stanhope looked every inch the distinguished British gentleman. And even Belle could tell his dress was the height of fashion.

He smiled with a slightly mocking air as his gaze swept her, and for once, Belle wished she had paid more attention to her appearance. Oh, dear. Maybe Mama was right—maybe such things did matter.

In fact, all three gentlemen looked splendid, and Belle felt positively dowdy beside them. She and her sisters wore the best money could buy—their mother made sure of that—but they didn't have the inbred ability to carry it off quite so well.

And, just as Mama promised, the gentlemen had brought posies. When Kit bowed slightly and presented Belle with his floral offering, she couldn't help but remember that Mama had practically forced them to bring the flowers, and it robbed the moment of any pleasure she might have felt. Belle stole a glance at her sisters. From their expressions, it seemed they felt the same way, and the moment turned awkward.

The silence was broken by Charisma, of course, who declared bluntly, "Shall we go? I'd like to see the rock formations, especially 'Kissing Camels' and 'Seal Making Love to a Nun.'"

Mother looked horrified and quickly corrected her, giving Charisma a stern look. "No, dear. The *proper* title is 'Seal and Bear.'"

George looked pained at his companion's bluntness, and Belle felt her spine stiffen. Nothing put her back up more than someone who criticized her family. "An excellent idea, Charisma," Belle said smoothly. "We shouldn't keep the horses waiting."

"Yes, let's go," Grace declared. Suiting action to words, she stepped out briskly and promptly trod on Harold's foot. When he bent over to clutch at the offended appendage, Grace whirled in remorse and caught him in the eye with her elbow.

Harold let loose with a yelp and Grace apologized profusely as she backed away—right into a knick-knack-laden table. With the ease of long practice, Belle and Charisma covered for her by surreptitiously righting the table and steadying Grace.

Though Harold now looked as fully pained as George had earlier, Belle figured he had cause. But

Grace was so horrified that Belle murmured, "It's all right—just a little accident. Come, the horses are waiting."

The others helped smooth over the incident and it was a subdued, if slightly wary group, who arrived outside—unscathed for the most part. A carriage awaited them, and Kit handed Belle into the front seat while the others seated her sisters in the back. Then Kit drove while George and Harold rode alongside.

It was a good arrangement. During the drive to the Garden of the Gods, Grace was unable to inflict any more damage on poor Harold, and Charisma's distance from George made her less likely to offend him by blurting out anything untoward.

But Belle was so concerned about keeping an eye on her sisters and their escorts' reactions that she gave very little attention to her own companion. All she knew was that he looked wonderful and smelled even better—all manly and woodsy. It was a pity they hadn't had a chance to converse much, especially since she just adored his upper-crust British accent, but perhaps she could get to know him a little better once they reached their destination.

They finally came to a stop, and as Kit helped her down from the carriage, Belle felt a little thrill course through her at his touch. She glanced shyly up into his handsome face to see if he felt the same and saw nothing but aloof politeness.

Darn—she hadn't made any sort of impression at all. Well, maybe it was time to let her sisters fend for themselves. They were big girls now and shouldn't need Belle to watch after them.

Belle hadn't paid much attention to her

surroundings, but she did now as Charisma declared, "Why, it isn't a garden at all."

Belle looked around. No, it couldn't be considered a garden, though there were a few wildflowers here and there. Instead, huge rock monoliths in odd shapes thrust up from the earth, towering high above them. Some were gray but most were made of red sandstone, the rusty color providing a vivid background for the green spring foliage. The result was slightly otherworldly and utterly breathtaking.

"Haven't you been here before?" Kit asked.

"No, we haven't," Belle said. At first, it seemed odd that they hadn't. Then she realized that anyone who knew Mama wouldn't wonder at it. Mama rarely let them leave the confines of the town, declaring there was nothing of interest beyond the borders of Little London. Except the real London, of course.

George smiled at Charisma a bit superciliously and said in a pompous tone, "So you haven't heard the story of how it was named?"

When Charisma shook her head, he added, "Local legend says that when two men were looking over the gardens, one man was so impressed, he said he thought it might make a good Milwaukee beer garden. But the other declared that it was a garden fit for the gods, and the name stuck."

A beer garden? Belle wrinkled her nose. How prosaic.

"Highly doubtful," Harold scoffed. "M'father says it's more likely the fanciful name was invented to lure people to this area."

George and Harold erupted into an argument, each defending their version of the story. Not knowing anything about it, the girls stayed silent, but Kit soon broke in and turned the men's anger aside with a joke. Then he added, "Since you two seem to know so much about the park, perhaps you will educate the rest of us?"

Belle watched in admiration as his ploy worked. Soon, George and Harold were outdoing each other in pointing out the various formations, including "Elephant Attacking a Lion," "Eagle With Pinions Spread," and "Cathedral Spires."

When they began to recite various improbable legends associated with the rock formations, Belle was reminded of their promise to Mama. When a suitable break in the conversation occurred, she asked, "And where are the Three Graces?"

George pointed to a set of three elegant, fingerlike spires of varying heights that reached toward the sky.

Belle nodded. "Would you gentlemen excuse us for a few moments? There's something we promised our mother we'd do."

Charisma rolled her eyes but managed to control her tongue until Belle led her two sisters away from the young men. "Do we really have to do this?" her outspoken sister complained.

"Oh, don't be such a fussbudget," Grace said as she tripped over a rock. But she managed to right herself without mishap. Luckily for Grace, her mishaps usually injured others and not herself. "Don't you want to see where Papa proposed to Mama? I think it's romantic."

"I think so, too," Belle said. "Besides, we promised Mama."

"Oh, all right," Charisma complained. "But I think it's silly."

"Really?" Grace said with a grin. "Even after seeing how handsome our escorts are? Doesn't it make you wonder what it would be like to be married to one of them? Just a little?"

"Well, perhaps just a little," Charisma confessed.

"Then it's not so silly, is it?" Grace said in triumph.

No, it wasn't. Especially since Belle hadn't been able to stop wondering what it would be like to be married to Kit Stanhope, to feel his strong arms around her, to touch her lips to his. . . .

Yes, his lips. Soft but firm, Kit's lips were very expressive and Belle had often found herself staring at his mouth as if mesmerized. Perhaps it wasn't such a bad idea to make a wish after all.

They made their way to the base of the formation and looked up at the rocks in awe. "So this is what we're named for," Belle murmured.

Grace stilled. "They're so grand . . ."

Charisma nodded, agreeing for once. "Inspiring."

For a moment, they simply stood there in silence, staring up at the same Three Graces who had watched as their father proposed to their mother. And this was where they were supposed to leave their flowers and wish for husbands of their own.

Could Belle dare wish for someone like Kit Stanhope? With his breeding, elegance, and charm, he could win any girl. Could she hope he might favor her?

As they stood there, each thinking their private thoughts, Belle realized that, through a trick of geography, they were able to hear their escorts' voices clearly.

"Is that George I hear?" Grace asked.

Belle nodded and the men's voices became even more distinct.

"Careful, Latham," George said with a laugh. "You're as clumsy as your date."

Seeing Grace's stricken expression, Belle said, "Maybe we should—"

Grace waved her to silence with a fierce look. "I want to hear this."

". . . never seen anyone as *un*graceful as Grace Sullivan," Harold Latham said with a bitter laugh. "One needs armor to survive an encounter with her. Too bad she doesn't live up to her name."

Not to be outdone, George said, "What about my date? Do you know of anyone *less* charming than Charisma? I don't think she's ever had a thought she hasn't voiced."

Charisma's expression turned blank, but her emotions were revealed in the pain in her eyes. Compassion for her sisters filled Belle, and rage toward the men who had hurt them. She swung away from the Three Graces, prepared to do battle, but her sisters held her back.

"No," Grace whispered. "We can't let them know we heard."

"She's right," Charisma agreed. "It would be too embarrassing."

Since when did Charisma care about that? She must really be hurting. Belle wrested herself free and heard Harold say, "And what about your date, Kit? Belle is certainly no beauty."

Belle froze, knowing she had to hear Kit's reply yet dreading it. Surely he didn't care about appearances . . . did he?

He paused for one of the longest moments of Belle's life, then drawled, "No, I'd have to say she's the most homely woman of my acquaintance."

Anguish filled Belle, but she continued to torture herself by listening.

George laughed. "So why did you invite her out?"

"I expect it's for the same reason you did," Harold said. "Because her mother paid us handsomely."

When Kit and George agreed, agony pierced Belle. How foolish she'd been to think that aristocratic Kit Stanhope would ever look twice at plain Belle Sullivan. Why, her mother had to *pay* him to even consider going out with her.

But through the pain came steely determination. She'd never forgive him for this. Or Harold and George either. They could say anything they liked about Belle, but the cads had hurt her sisters. Just look at them. Grace wore an expression of horrified anguish, and though Charisma was standing proud and defiantly straight, moisture shone in her eyes.

Charisma dashed a tear away. "They're only saying the truth. Everyone knows it."

Grace's bottom lip quivered. "I know, but . . . did they have to be so cruel?"

"They didn't know we were listening," Charisma said in their defense.

"How dare you speak up for them?" Belle demanded. Grace might be clumsy, but she was the sweetest person Belle knew. And though Charisma was outspoken, she was incredibly generous and kind to those in need. Couldn't the men see that?

Apparently not—all they saw was the superficial. Determination stiffened Belle's spine. No one insulted her family and got away with it. "Why, I'd like to—"

She checked a throttling motion when she realized she was strangling the posy Kit had given her.

"You'd like to what?" Charisma asked.

Flourishing the flowers in Kit's direction, Belle declared, "I'd like to shove this posy up his nosy."

Just as she'd hoped, that made them both laugh. Laughter was a wonderful way to ease their heartache, but how did she go about easing her own?

"I'd pay money to see that," Charisma declared.

Grace's eyes rounded in astonishment. "You're not really going to do it, are you?"

"No," Belle said reluctantly. "If I did, Mama would do far worse to me."

"Not that she deserves any consideration after what *she* did," Charisma declared.

"I agree, but we did promise to make an offering to the Three Graces and make a wish."

A mischievous light suddenly appeared in Charisma's eyes. "That's true—but we didn't promise what that wish would be." She boldly laid her bouquet at the foot of the sandstone monolith, but her tone was uncharacteristically wistful. "I wish I lived up to my name. I wish I had charm."

Grace copied her, saying, "Me, too. I wish I had true grace."

Belle sighed, feeling forced to go along as she laid her flowers alongside the others. "And I wish I were beautiful." Though she knew in her heart that all she really wanted was a chance to get even with the men who had hurt them so.

Her true wish was for revenge.

As the three Sullivan girls returned to their waiting escorts with brave smiles, the Three Graces looked down from Mount Olympus and considered their wishes.

"Shall we?" Aglaia asked.

Thalia pondered for a moment. "We did grant their mother's wish twenty years ago. I know we haven't done anything like this in such a long time, but . . . they were so heartbroken. I think we should."

"We will," Euphrosyne declared. Cocking her head, she asked, "Though shall we grant their spoken wishes . . . or the unspoken ones?"

They exchanged delighted smiles. Oh, the possibilities. . . .

Two

Kit Stanhope watched the door close behind the Sullivan sisters and sighed. They had been very subdued on the ride home, and he strongly suspected his loose-tongued conversation with Winthrop and Latham had been overheard.

Unfortunate. He hated to offend young ladies, no matter how gauche or inept they might be. But he had been more concerned with keeping favor with the men who might be able to help him find an investment than he was in minding his tongue.

Harold Latham grimaced. "Well, we survived. Barely. I don't want to go through that again."

George grinned. "Yes, but think what a great story it will make."

As the two plotted aloud how to drag the Sullivan sisters' names through the muck of public opinion, Kit listened in appalled silence. What had he done? He must rectify this immediately.

And as Harold turned to him looking for approval, Kit realized he had just the means to do it.

Though these Americans might boast of their egalitarian society and say they honored the self-made man, the truth was that many still stood in awe of British aristocracy. And there in the city known as Little London, they still looked to the members of the substantial British population as the supreme arbiters of good taste.

"Surely you jest," Kit drawled, drawing on his most cultured tones.

Appearing uncertain, Harold asked, "What do you mean?"

Though he shouldn't have to instruct them on such a basic tenet of gentlemanly behavior, Kit nonetheless undertook the task. "Why, no gentleman would sully a lady's name in such a manner."

George snorted in disgust. "Ladies? Hardly. It wasn't that long ago that the Sullivans lived in a shanty town in Leadville."

"And, like many others, they have done a fine job of overcoming their circumstances," Kit said, subtly reminding the two that their fathers had shared similar humble beginnings. "Besides, by honoring them with an outing, we have declared to the world that we think them our equals." Letting that sink in, he added, "There may have been some doubt before, but by your actions you have, in effect, *made* them ladies."

He let them ponder that for a moment. Apparently impressed by their own power, they nodded slowly.

With a heightened air of importance, George said, "Yes, I suppose we did. It wouldn't be such a good idea to turn about and denounce them now that we've made them, would it?"

"Not at all," Kit agreed.

"Quite right," Harold put in, not to be outdone. "Why, it wouldn't be the gentlemanly thing to do."

Kit bestowed approving smiles upon his unwitting students. "Well, that's settled, then. Shall we move on to the club?"

Harold and George agreed eagerly, so they made their way to the El Paso Club, a refuge where a gentleman might have a smoke and intelligent conversation in an atmosphere of privacy and refinement.

Kit stopped by the desk to pick up his mail and stuffed the two letters in his pocket as he joined Harold and George in a corner. After a few moments of desultory conversation, the two young men moved off to join their cronies, leaving Kit to his own thoughts.

Damn, but he missed England. Back home he wouldn't have to explain the concept of gentlemanly behavior to his friends—it was bred into them practically from birth.

Then again, back home he was considered a wastrel and a cad.

His gut twisted in remembered pain. Being ordered to leave home had been the low point of his existence. Worse, he had been judged guilty of ungentlemanly behavior without even a chance to defend himself. Too proud to beg for the trust he had more than earned, Kit had accepted the judgment of his father and older brother and had left England for America, there to become one of the many expatriate British younger sons who received a remittance from home on a regular basis.

But unlike many others who wasted their inheritance in drink, sport, and gambling, Kit had vowed to show his family they were wrong about him and put his quarterly funds to good use. Unfortunately, he had yet to find an investment suitable for a man of his upbringing and limited capital that wasn't designed to part a gullible remittance man from his money. Not to mention the unexpected drain on his resources in the form of one John Daltrey.

And here came the bastard now.

Kit slid deeper into the shadows, hoping to go unrecognized, but it was a forlorn hope as the figure he dreaded made his way over to Kit's corner.

"Stanhope, how are you?" the man declared in a falsely convivial tone.

The familiar sounds of home in the man's accent should have soothed Kit, but they had exactly the opposite effect coming from this man.

Kit nodded. "Daltrey." His tone was not welcoming.

Daltrey took a chair, uninvited. "Why, is that any way to greet an old friend?"

"Of course not." They might have grown up together on neighboring estates, but that didn't make them friends. "And if I run across an old friend, I'll be sure to greet him suitably."

Daltrey clasped a hand over his heart. "You wound me," he declared soulfully, though his eyes glittered with malice.

"Cut to the chase, man," Kit said. "What do you want?"

"Oh, just a little loan, like always."

"Loan, hell. It's nothing more than blackmail." It wasn't as if the man planned to pay him back.

Daltrey shrugged. "Call it what you will, but I find myself a bit short."

Kit ground his teeth, wondering what the hell Daltrey found to spend not only his own generous allowance on, but Kit's as well. "I haven't any—you took it all. And I won't have any more from home until the end of June." A month away.

"So, what are you living on, then?"

"My wits," Kit snapped. "You might try it." That is,

if he weren't sadly handicapped by the lack of them.

"Tsk, tsk," Daltrey said with a malicious smile. "Mustn't get me angry, you know. Why, I might tell the folks here exactly why you left England."

"It's a lie," Kit snarled. "Someone else sired a bastard on that girl."

"So? What does the truth matter? And who do you think they'll believe? You . . . or me?"

Unfortunately, Daltrey was right. Americans were only too ready to believe the worst of remittance men, especially since so many of them deserved the bad name they received. Men like Daltrey.

Kit shrugged, pretending a nonchalance he didn't feel. "Go ahead—spread your lies. I don't care. You can't get blood from a turnip."

"Resorting to clichés now, are you?" Daltrey studied him closely. "You must be desperate."

Kit shrugged again, really uncaring this time. Why not let him spread his lies? Though Kit had been careful to keep his dealings aboveboard so he could find a good investment, it would come to nothing if all his money went to a blackmailer. He wouldn't be able to invest it anyway.

"You mean that, don't you?" Daltrey asked in surprise. "You must really be feeling the pinch. Well, I won't bother you again until the end of the quarter, but then you'd better be ready to open your purse wide." With a smirk and a mock salute, he left.

Kit scowled. No matter how difficult it might be, he couldn't give up without a fight. He had to find some way out of this mess—short of disposing of Daltrey—permanently. Though that solution was beginning to feel more and more tempting. . . .

No, though the world would be better off without Daltrey, the local authorities were bound to frown upon his murder. And though Kit had thought of taking off for parts unknown many times, he feared it wouldn't serve. Daltrey would probably just follow him.

Besides, Kit had invested quite a bit of time in making friends and—he hoped—future business acquaintances in this town. And he'd heard stories about the wild frontier. He really didn't want to start all over somewhere else—at least here it was civilized. So, he had to find some other way to rid himself of Daltrey . . . or find another way to make money.

Suddenly remembering his letters and hoping one might have news about a potential investment, Kit pulled them out of his pocket. The first contained a small bit of pasteboard announcing the arrival of a new dressmaker in town—a Madame Aglaia, formerly of Athens, who promised elegance, distinction, and above all discretion. "Miracles performed daily," she claimed.

Baffled as to why the woman had singled out a bachelor to receive her advertisement, he shoved the card into his pocket and opened the other letter.

This one was from home. Kit read it eagerly, hoping for news of family and friends, but was soon frowning over its contents. His father, disappointed that Kit had nothing to show for the nine months he'd been in America, was demanding an accounting. If Kit didn't show some progress and return on an investment by the end of the next quarter in September, his father would disown him and cut off his funds.

Kit crumpled the letter in his fist and swore. Damn it, how could he make progress when he was beset by blackmailers and liars? Especially in only four months?

His first inclination was to tell his father to go to hell and take his money with him, but Kit enjoyed his comforts too much. Besides, Daltrey wouldn't believe his father had cut him off. And if Kit didn't turn over some cash promptly at the end of each quarter, Daltrey would spread his lies far and wide.

Then again, it *would* be nice to have his own source of funds, independent from his family, so he wouldn't have to answer to anyone else. But how could he make a lot of money, fast? The most common routes were gambling or mining, but Kit dismissed those options out of hand. They were too subject to chance and the whims of fate. That left only one solution—marriage to an heiress. He felt far more confident of achieving success in that arena. If he could stomach it.

Kit sighed. It wasn't the way he had planned to choose a wife. He had hoped someday to find a woman of wit, beauty, and breeding who would be a good companion and a lover, someone he could share his life with. But it appeared it was not to be. Marrying an heiress was quite likely the only way he could survive.

Unfortunately, he had just grievously insulted his most likely prospect—Belle Sullivan. And she would no doubt denigrate him to her *nouveau riche* friends, leaving him with no marriage prospects whatsoever.

Kit sighed. An investment was still his first choice for solving his problems, but he might have to resort to marriage in the end.

There was nothing else for it—he would have to apologize.

At supper after their disastrous trip to the Garden of the Gods, the girls were all uncharacteristically silent, and Belle picked at her food with no appetite. She had no desire to recount the events of the day despite her mother's eager probing, and it appeared Charisma and Grace felt the same way.

It was clear Mama knew something had gone wrong but couldn't figure out what it was. Their father, Patrick, was equally baffled. "So, what's the matter with you all, then?" he asked. "Usually, you're all nattcrin' on like a flock of magpies so a man can't get a word in edgewise."

"Nothing, Papa," Belle murmured.

"The devil there isn't. Why, I want to know why me girls are pulling such long faces this evening, and I want to know right now." He turned a stern glance on their mother. "Bridey?"

Their mother winced. Though she'd been born Bridey and that name had been good enough for her until she moved to Colorado Springs, she now preferred to be called by her second name, thinking it sounded more elegant. "It's Marie, dear," she reminded her husband for the millionth time.

Patrick scowled. "It's Bridey you were born, and Bridey you'll be 'til your dying day. And there's no sense pretendin' otherwise. Now, tell me what's botherin' me girls."

On the defensive, Bridey protested, "I'm sure I don't know. They won't tell me. All I know is they had a perfectly lovely outing planned with some fine young gentlemen, but when they came home, they would do nothing but mope."

"Fine young gentlemen, eh?" He speared Grace with a sharp glance. "Did they go beyond the line with ye?"

Poor Grace had been so subdued, she hadn't broken a single thing all afternoon. "No, Papa," she said quietly.

Belle could understand Grace's silence. She didn't want to tell her parents what had happened either—it was too humiliating. When Papa turned his eye on her, Belle sighed. "They were perfect gentlemen," she confirmed.

"Ha," Charisma uttered, as if the exclamation had burst its way free without her consent.

Papa turned to Charisma then. "Well, I know you'll give it to me plain with no bark on it, sweetheart. Tell me, how did the young men act ungentlemanly?"

Apparently, Charisma could hold it in no longer. "It wasn't what they did, Papa, it was what they said."

Their father's face turned stony. "And what was it they said?"

Even Charisma lost some of her bravado under that steely stare. "They said . . . they said . . ." She didn't seem to be able to get it out, until once more the words burst forth as if of their own volition. "They said Belle was plain, Grace was clumsy, and I—I was not charming."

Somehow it didn't sound as bad phrased that way, especially since Belle distinctly remembered Kit Stanhope using the word "homely" to describe her.

But her parents seemed suitably horrified anyway. Mama gasped and Papa slammed his silverware down on the table. "How dare they! They said this to yer faces?"

Apparently emboldened by their parents' reaction, Charisma said, "Well, no. We overheard them."

Papa seemed a little mollified, yet puzzled. "I don't understand. If they thought so little of ye, why did they ask ye out in the first place?"

Belle and her sisters' eyes all turned to Mama, silently accusing.

Patrick's face turned even more stony. "Bridey, what have ye done?"

"Nothing," she insisted defensively. "Is it a crime to want your daughters to do well in life?"

"What did ye do?" he persisted.

"Well, I might have encouraged the young men to ask them out . . ."

"Ha," Charisma exclaimed again. "Papa, she *paid* them to invite us."

Shocked silence reigned for a moment at the supper table, and all the hurt came flooding back. Belle's eyes filled with tears, and she suspected her sisters' did as well.

Papa surged to his feet, his voice implacable. "Bridey Marie, I'll see you upstairs. Now."

As her parents left the supper table, Grace turned to Charisma and whispered, "Did you have to say that?"

"Why shouldn't I?" Charisma asked, unrepentant. "It was the truth, wasn't it?"

They all turned silent as they heard Papa raging at Mama up in their room. Belle couldn't make out exactly what he was saying, but she knew the gist of it. When they fought, which wasn't often, they usually argued about Mama's desire to join the ranks of society, whereas Papa had no patience with a desire to climb the societal ladder. And since Mama had just crossed one of Papa's lines, there would be Sam Hill to pay.

"It's not her fault," Belle said.

"What?" Charisma exclaimed. Even Grace looked surprised at Belle's assertion.

"Mama was just trying to do what she thought was best for us." Before Charisma could say anything else, Belle added, "Oh, I don't agree with what she did either, but she was well intentioned. She didn't know how rude they would be."

As Charisma and Grace digested that, Belle added bitterly, "Winthrop, Latham, and Stanhope are the ones to blame." Especially Kit Stanhope who looked like such a paragon and acted like such a cad. The fool didn't realize what he was losing— Belle would have made him a wonderful wife. "And I'm going to get revenge on the threesome for all of us," she declared.

"Threesome?" Charisma said scornfully. "More like three scum."

Liking the sound of that, Belle said, "Yes, the threescum. I'll make them regret they were ever born."

Grace's mouth rounded in astonishment and Charisma looked intrigued. "Really?" her outspoken sister asked. "How?"

"I don't know yet, but mark my words, they'll rue the day they insulted the Sullivan sisters."

The next day, Belle was still wracking her brain, trying to come up with a way to make Stanhope and the others pay, when she heard Kit was at the door wanting to see her.

In the back parlor, Belle turned to her sisters, wondering what to do. Papa had stormed off last night, vowing to sleep at the mine, and Mama had left earlier to do some shopping.

Belle's first inclination was to have Kit Stanhope whipped from the door—she was sure Charisma would be happy to oblige—but curiosity overcame her anger, and she asked the housekeeper to show him into the front parlor in ten minutes. With Grace and Charisma in attendance, she would be adequately chaperoned.

Just as curious as Belle, her sisters agreed to sit in on the conversation. Seating them on either side of her to give support, Belle said, "Be still, Grace, so you won't break anything. And Charisma, I want you to keep your lip buttoned."

Unfortunately, there was nothing Belle could do about her own looks, but she wanted to give him as little ammunition as possible for making disparaging remarks about her family.

When Charisma would have protested, Belle added, "He insulted *me*. I'll handle it."

Grace and Charisma nodded. Since Belle was the eldest, the other two usually followed her lead, especially since she came up with the best plans.

And with anger and righteous indignation to steel her spine, Belle felt completely and utterly capable of handling one measly remittance man. But when he was shown into the parlor, she realized she had forgotten how devastatingly handsome he was.

Kit Stanhope took her breath away with his sheer presence. His striking blue eyes, the clean lines of his high cheekbones, and above all, his soft, sensitive mouth made her want to melt in a puddle right then and there.

Shame washed through her at the thought. This man and his friends had hurt her and her sisters. He had to pay.

He nodded at Belle. "Miss Sullivan," he said in his lovely British accent, then greeted her sisters. "Miss Charisma, Miss Grace." Glancing uncertainly at Grace and Charisma, he said to Belle, "May I draw you aside for a moment? I have something . . . private I need to say."

"No," Belle said baldly, borrowing from Charisma's repertoire. She wasn't about to give up the support of her sisters. "Anything you have to say to me you can say in front of them."

He nodded but remained standing since she hadn't asked him to be seated. She didn't plan to, either. Let him stand there and stew.

"I've come to apologize," he said with a rueful smile.

That simple twist of his mouth made longing surge inside Belle, but she ruthlessly repressed it. It was absurd to be so affected by the sight of a man's lips, especially one who had given her so much pain. She simply wouldn't have it. "Oh?" she asked simply, giving him plenty of rope to hang himself.

"Yes, I"—he glanced sheepishly at her sisters—"I fear you all overheard a conversation not meant for your ears."

"We didn't eavesdrop," Charisma exclaimed in protest. "Your voices carried clearly."

Belle shot her a quelling glance, silently ordering her once more to keep her mouth shut, then turned a cold face to Kit. "Yes? Go on."

"It is as I feared, then. You did overhear." His eyes turned as soft as his mouth. "I do most humbly apologize. I know the others said some unflattering things about your sisters, and I fear I said something equally uncomplimentary about you, Miss Sullivan."

"You said I was homely," Belle blurted out before she thought, then cursed her own unruly tongue. She hadn't meant to let him know how much it hurt. Her sisters moved a fraction closer to her, as if to give her support.

"Did I?" he murmured. "It was quite rude of me, wasn't it?"

"You can say that again," Charisma declared.

For once, Belle was thankful for Charisma's bluntness. Kit's soft-spoken words, gentlemanly demeanor, and that darned sense-stealing mouth of his were working powerfully on Belle's resolve. She lifted her chin, unwilling to trust herself to say anything.

"In my defense, all I can say is that I was carried along by a sort of jovial camaraderie and I said things I shouldn't. Things I didn't mean."

Belle didn't believe a word of it. "If you didn't mean it, why did you say it?"

He spread his hands helplessly. "It's lowering to admit it, but I was trying to impress my companions, so I played along with them, hoping to earn their favor by agreeing with the topic under discussion."

Unfortunately, that topic had been the shortcomings of the Sullivan sisters. But why did this man who seemingly had everything feel the need to impress such callow young men? "Then your friends have a poor idea of suitable conversation topics."

Kit nodded and another rueful smile graced his lips, sending her heart racing. "I can't argue with you there, though I wouldn't call them friends."

"Then what would you call them?"

"Er, potential business partners, perhaps?"

Ah, that explained the desire to impress them. She had heard Kit was a bit strapped for cash. "And when your . . . potential partners spread this all over town, how will you react then?"

From the sudden stiffening of her sisters, Belle realized that was the key question for them. They didn't give a hoot anymore about George or Harold—just how word of this would get about town.

"I don't think you need worry about that," Kit assured them. "They understand it wouldn't be the gentlemanly thing to do."

Since when were George and Harold concerned about being gentlemen? But the answer was staring her right in the face—since Kit Stanhope had told them how to behave, no doubt.

Well, that was one thing in his favor, especially since she felt Charisma and Grace relax in relief beside her. "Thank you for that at least." Even if no one else did, she knew where to bestow the credit.

But that didn't mean she forgave him. And so she let him know by the haughty expression on her *homely* face.

Kit cocked his head and regarded her with a beseeching expression. "I wouldn't have you angry at me for the world. What can I do to make it up to you?"

"Can you make me beautiful?" she asked dryly. And was satisfied at the surprise in his eyes.

He recovered quickly, though. She had to give him points for that. "But I'm sure you are beautiful—where it counts, inside."

"Hogwash." But it was a gallant try, even if he didn't believe a word of it.

Charisma turned to her with an arrested expression. "That's not a bad idea, you know."

"What?"

"Why not use him to make you beautiful? If any-one can do it, he can."

All three girls turned to regard him with specu-lative expressions, and Belle saw panic in his eyes before he quickly suppressed it.

"Oh, could you?" Grace asked, regarding him as if he were a miracle worker. "She really is beautiful on the inside, just like you said. She just needs a lit-tle help on the outside."

Belle felt her face flame and hushed her sister, but waited eagerly for Kit's reply nonetheless.

The British peer, refined product of hundreds of years of breeding, took Grace's question seriously and regarded Belle with a critical eye. "Well, yes, I think it can be done," he said slowly. Then, with more gallantry, he added, "It wouldn't be all that difficult. But I'm afraid I haven't the time to put into the project just now."

By this time, Belle shrewdly guessed he really meant money. "I'll pay you," she blurted out. Inside her head, revenge scenarios played themselves out. If she were beautiful, she could ensnare the three-scum in her web, then throw them aside like the scoundrels they were. That would serve them right.

But Kit Stanhope was one of those three. Could she use the very man in her revenge scheme that she planned to get revenge upon?

Delighted by the irony, she felt her mouth curve in a smile. Oh, yes, she definitely could.

And Belle had no doubt she could pull it off. She'd always been able to accomplish whatever she set her mind to—ask anyone in her family. It was just that her appearance had never been important to her be-fore. But if it would get the revenge she sought, she'd

primp and pose enough to please even Mama. And
she might even be able to obtain an invitation to
Mama's coveted Founders' Day Ball.

Besides, if Mama was so determined to marry
her off, maybe an improved appearance would
help attract a man Belle could love, not just one
who pretended to like her for her father's money.
Yes, she definitely liked this idea.

Kit looked taken aback by her proposition, so Belle
named a figure—a high one. She could easily afford
it out of the monthly pin money she never spent.
When Kit hesitated, Belle quickly doubled it, knowing the success of her transformation would depend
on this handsome Englishman. Not just to make her
look presentable, but to get her into the parties and
soirees necessary to put her plan into effect.

"Of course, this is strictly a business proposition,"
she added, lest he think she was interested in him
personally. She had been, of course, but that was
before. Now she wouldn't have him on a bet.
"Well?" she challenged.

He looked thoughtful. "What exactly would this
entail?"

Belle thought about it for a moment. "I suppose
you'd need to help me learn how to dress well, do
something with my face and hair, squire me around
to the snootiest parties . . . and make me irresistible
to all men."

She added the last airily as a jest, knowing it was
impossible to wish for, and was surprised when his
mouth quirked in response. Oh dear, the man had
a sense of humor. He was going to be even harder
to resist than she thought.

He smiled, a slow stretching of his lips that
elevated his face from merely handsome to truly

sublime. "Wouldn't a woman be better for your purposes? She could also act as a chaperone, whereas with me, you would be constantly in need of one."

He had a point, but now that Belle had the idea in her mind, she was loath to let it go. "I would prefer you." Besides, he owed her. Then, realizing he might have reservations of a different kind, she added, "Of course, we would both need to be discreet. There's no sense in others knowing of our agreement." And she certainly didn't want anyone else knowing either.

"How long would this last?" he asked.

No doubt he wanted to ensure a period to their agreement. Well, then, why not ask for everything she wanted? "Just until the Founders' Day Ball in July. If you escort me to the ball, our agreement will end then." She held her breath, wondering how he would react to her audacity.

He thought for a moment, obviously still uncertain. "May I have a few days to think it over?"

Belle's hopes fell—she had hoped to get started on her transformation right away. "I suppose so."

He must have seen the disappointment in her expression, for he added, "My hesitation has nothing to do with you, Miss Sullivan. And if I agree, of course I will escort you to the ball. I just need to see how this will fit in with my other plans. I wouldn't want to give you short shrift."

Belle nodded. Again, gallantly said. But she wanted help sooner. "You said you're looking for a business partner . . . ?"

Kit raised an eyebrow, no doubt wondering about the sudden change of subject. "That's not entirely accurate. I'm looking for a suitable investment."

"Would—would it help if I obtained you an

interview with my father?" Kit looked slightly taken aback, so she added quickly, "He's very wise when it comes to money. I thought he might be able to help you find an investment."

Kit gave her a thoughtful look. "He might at that. Yes, I would be most obliged if you could arrange an interview." He paused, then added, "And I suppose I could help you with part of your plan at least." Striking a pose, he said, "Miss Sullivan, would you do me the honor of accompanying me to Dr. Bell's garden party the week after next?"

Belle smiled at him. What a perfect way to start her campaign, with a visit to the home of one of society's leaders. And Mama would be ecstatic. "I would love that," she said truthfully.

"Wonderful." Then, digging in his pocket, Kit added, "I just remembered, I received a card from a new dressmaker in town, who would probably be glad of your custom and who promises total discretion . . ."

She took the card, reading the promise there. *Miracles performed daily.* . . . "She sounds perfect," Belle said. "See, I knew you could help me."

Kit let that go without comment, then took his leave.

Belle turned to her sisters once she was sure he was out of earshot. "What do you think?" she asked, full of anticipation but not quite sure if this was the right thing to do.

"Oh, Belle," Grace said with a sigh. "He would be perfect. I hope he decides to help you."

"What if he doesn't?" Charisma asked.

Disappointment filled Belle at the thought, but it was quite possible he would refuse. "Well, I guess I shall just have to find a woman to help me then, as he suggested."

Grace nodded. "But who?"

Belle thought for a moment, then said with sudden inspiration, "How about Miss Keithley?"

"The spinster with the cats?" Charisma asked in surprise.

"Well, what's wrong with that?" Belle asked. "I heard the reason she's unmarried is because her fiancé was tragically killed on a hunting expedition, and she's remained true to him ever since." And Miss Keithley had all the attributes the Sullivans lacked. Besides beauty, charm, and grace, she had entrée to the social set that Belle needed to achieve her revenge.

"Belle's right," Grace said. "And Miss Keithley has always been very nice to us. It wouldn't hurt to ask."

"Very well," Charisma said, apparently cross because they'd disagreed with her. "But what if she agrees to help, then Stanhope says yes?"

Belle shrugged. "Then I'd have two people to help me. There's nothing wrong with that, either."

"Very true," Charisma conceded, then smiled. "You know, with both their help, you just might be able to pull this off."

Belle's heart beat a little faster. It was just because her dreams of revenge were about to come true, she assured herself. And it had nothing to do with the thought of working with one Kit Stanhope and his sinful lips. . . .

Three

The next morning, Belle was happy to discover that Miss Keithley was not only amenable to helping her, she was positively delighted with the challenge. Insisting that Belle call her Alvina, the blond thirty-year-old woman claimed she had had little to interest her in the past few years and enthusiastically began to plan Belle's transformation from an ugly duckling into a swan.

The only part Belle had left out was her plan for revenge, suspecting her new friend wouldn't approve. She had said only that she wished to attract the attention of a gentleman. Three, to be exact, but she didn't mention that either.

Now, that same afternoon, Belle sat anxiously in the back parlor with her sisters, waiting for Mama to join them so they could put their plan into effect. Belle, her sisters, and Miss Keithley had all agreed upon one thing—Mama was a liability.

Oh, Belle loved her mother dearly, but Mama simply didn't know enough about the society she was so anxious to join and she floundered about, not having anyone to guide her. If Belle was to do this properly, she needed someone who understood it—and understood it well. But she also didn't want to hurt Mama's feelings, especially since Mama was a bit down in the mouth lately after her quarrel with Papa.

Belle sighed. There was no getting around it. If she was to achieve the revenge she sought, she would have to take Mama out of the picture.

And here she was now.

Belle cast warning glances at Charisma and Grace, reminding them of their roles.

And Grace obliged. "Oh, Mama, isn't it wonderful? Belle received a gentleman caller yesterday."

Mama glared at Belle with a stern expression. "This is the first I've heard of it. What were you thinking, entertaining a man alone? You must have a chaperone at all times or your reputation will be ruined. And if you don't have a good rep—"

"It's all right, Mama," Belle assured her, cutting short the lecture they'd all heard at least a thousand times. "I wasn't alone. Charisma and Grace were with me."

Mama looked a little mollified, but not much. "You should have asked him to return when I was at home."

"But Mama," Charisma said in a guileless tone, "Mr. Stanhope didn't seem to think there was anything wrong with us receiving him."

"Stanhope?" Mama clutched at her bosom. "You mean to tell me Lord Stanhope was here?" As the second son of a viscount, Stanhope was only an honorable, not a lord, but Mama and many others persisted in calling him Lord Stanhope.

"Yes," Belle confirmed. "He came to apologize for what he said the other day."

Mama positively beamed. "Did he? I knew he was a proper gentleman. Is that all he said?"

"No, he also said he wants to escort me to Dr.

Bell's garden party the week after next at Briarhurst Manor. I told him I would ask you. May I go?" Belle waited politely for an answer, though she knew there was little chance Mama would refuse. Dr. William Bell and his wife Cora were the leaders of society in Little London.

Mama clasped her hands in ecstasy. "Of course you may go, dear child. Briarhurst Manor? Why, imagine that."

"But what shall I wear?" Belle asked. "I'm not sure I have anything suitable. . . ." Belle watched in amusement as her mother's eyes lit up. Mama had despaired of ever getting Belle interested in what she wore and to see her doing so was one of the fondest wishes of her heart.

And, right on cue, Alvina was announced, looking splendid in a pink tailored dress and a dashing toque hat. Mama looked surprised to see her, but welcomed her cordially. Belle glanced sharply at Grace, giving her sister her cue.

"Oh, Miss Keithley, welcome," Grace exclaimed, throwing out her hands and causing a lamp to teeter dangerously. Charisma righted it as Grace continued, "We were just discussing what Belle should wear to Dr. Bell's garden party."

"And have you come to a decision?" Belle's co-conspirator asked.

Belle stared down at her pale blue dress. "Something like this, perhaps?"

Alvina regarded her critically. "Hmm, bustles are going out this season and . . . not that shade of blue, I think. Do you?"

"What's wrong with it?" Mama asked indignantly. "Why, that color looks lovely on you, Belle. That is, it would if you would just take care with your dresses."

Naturally, Mama would defend the color. Since Belle didn't care what she wore, Mama had always chosen Belle's clothes. And Mama always picked those that looked best on the blonde she had always wanted to be.

Charisma regarded her sister critically. "I think Miss Keithley is right. That pale color makes her look sallow. It does nothing for her complexion."

"Nonsense," Mama said briskly. "It's the light in here."

Alvina was undaunted. "Do you think so? You know, I was discussing colors the other night at the Opera House with Rose Kingsley and Queen Palmer . . ."

Belle hid a grin as Mama perked up at the mention of the two women who had been influential in the founding of Colorado Springs. "Oh? And what do they have to say?" she asked eagerly.

"We all agreed that while a frosty shade of blue may look splendid on a blonde, it's disastrous on a redhead. The colors of nature are more suited to Belle's coloring—green, rust, brown."

"But they're so dull . . ." Mama said, obviously weighing her distrust of a spinster's judgment against said spinster's social standing.

So Belle added the clincher. "Mrs. Palmer said Miss Keithley is the most elegantly dressed woman of her acquaintance."

That did it. In Mama's eyes, the wife of the founder of Colorado Springs could do no wrong. "Well, if *she* says so. . . . We just won't buy you anything more in pale blue then. Maybe a lovely pink."

Oh, dear. That wasn't what Belle had intended

at all. She floundered about for a way to save the situation, and Alvina came to the rescue. "Belle wants so much to make a good impression at the garden party, I thought I might offer her a bit of advice."

"Well, that is very kind of you, I'm sure," her mother said, beaming. It was obvious she liked the idea of someone of Miss Keithley's social standing taking an interest in one of her daughters.

"Oh, Mama," Belle said with enthusiasm. "She offered to come with me to the dressmaker to advise me on styles, fabrics, and colors." She hesitated a moment, then added, "Tomorrow."

"Well, all right," Mama conceded. "But I'm not sure what Mrs. Pinchot will think. . . ."

"Oh, but I don't want to go to Mrs. Pinchot again." The elderly dressmaker was too influenced by Mama's taste, and Alvina had pronounced her old-fashioned. "There's a new dressmaker in town—Madame Aglaia, from Athens." Belle handed her mother the card Kit had left with them.

Mama sniffed, holding the card as if it might bite her. "And what do you know about this woman?"

"Just that she advertises she's quick and discreet—and can perform miracles, even on someone like me."

"I don't know. . . ."

"It's worth a try," Alvina said, smiling. "Since she's so new, she's probably not busy yet and can make something up very fast." When Mama still hesitated, she added, "And if we feel she won't do justice to your daughter, we will go elsewhere, of course."

Mama sighed. "All right, then. What time shall we go tomorrow?"

Oh, no, this was what Belle had feared. Mama

would insist on coming along and that would spoil everything. She cast a pleading glance at her sisters.

"But Mama," Charisma exclaimed, "Grace and I planned on going on a picnic with the Applebaums tomorrow. Does this mean we can go by ourselves?" Crafty Charisma let her eyes sparkle at the thought of attending an event unchaperoned, especially since there were so many attractive young Applebaum sons.

"Certainly not," Mama declared. "We shall just have to find you a chaperone."

"Can't you come with us?" Grace asked in a sweet tone. "Miss Keithley can chaperone Belle to the dressmaker. And we'd miss you so if you didn't come."

Belle hid a smile. In her own way, Grace was just as crafty as Charisma.

Mama wrestled with the decision for a moment, then said, "Oh, I suppose it will be all right."

When Belle beamed at her, Mama gave her an admonitory frown. "But if I don't approve of what you've chosen . . ."

"You will, Mama," Belle promised. But it was hard to hide her jubilation. The first step in her plan for revenge had gone just as she'd hoped. With any luck, the rest of the plan would go as smoothly and she'd show the threescum just how foolhardy they'd been.

No one insulted the Sullivan sisters and got away with it.

From the heights of Mount Olympus, Aglaia smiled. She had managed to get Bridey Sullivan's agreement to let Belle come to her shop with only the tiniest bit of magic on the card.

"Congratulations, sister," Euphrosyne said. "But do you think you can continue to work with so little magic? Belle is going to be a tough challenge."

They had already agreed that each would work within her own specialty. The beauty, Aglaia, would concentrate on Belle, charming Thalia would help Charisma, and graceful Euphrosyne would work on Grace. And, to keep from interfering with each other or attracting unwanted attention from the other denizens of Mount Olympus, they had agreed to work on one sister at a time.

Aglaia shrugged. "I'll have to, won't I? If we use too much, it might attract Zeus's attention and then who knows what would happen?"

Thalia shuddered. "There's no telling—he can't stand women who are less than beautiful. He might turn Belle into a heifer or something."

Euphrosyne nodded. "Aglaia has the right of it, then. We'll just have to use as little magic as possible." She grinned. "That will make it even more fun. . . ."

Kit strolled up the avenue, ostensibly admiring the view of Pikes Peak, still snow-capped this time of year. In reality, he was debating whether to get involved in Miss Sullivan's scheme.

He had been not only rash, but boastful when he'd promised he could turn Belle Sullivan into a beauty. Could he pull it off? Oh, he knew she wasn't really homely—he had been unnecessarily harsh in condemning her looks to the others. She just needed someone to show her how to make the most of her assets.

Unlike her sisters, Belle had grace and could be charming when the occasion suited. And she certainly had a great deal of backbone—look at the way she'd stood up to him. He admired self-confidence in a woman, though it wasn't one of the traits he necessarily looked for in a wife.

No, the most important trait his future wife would possess was trust. Since it was the one thing he lacked most in his life, it was the one he longed for the most.

Money wouldn't hurt either. And, though Belle Sullivan's dowry and personality were pleasing enough, he doubted he'd ever be able to earn her trust after what she'd overheard. So she was out of the running as a prospective bride, but . . . should he help her improve her appearance?

He didn't really want to take on the job her mother should have handled years ago, but he was strapped for cash. And perhaps if he helped her, she would be kind enough to introduce him to some of her wealthy friends, or at least not give them a poor account of his actions. One of them might prove suitable to become Mrs. Christopher Stanhope.

Then again, if he spent too much time on Belle, he might not be able to find the investment he needed. What to do?

As he contemplated his options, he turned up Cascade Avenue and an item in a shop window full of feminine fripperies caught his eye. Good Lord, that looked like his family crest on the handkerchief. How could that be?

Even odder, it appeared the shop belonged to the

woman who had sent him the card. Curious now, he turned into the dressmaker's establishment.

As he entered, three women turned to regard him in surprise—Miss Sullivan, Miss Keithley, and a third very handsome older brunette who must be the owner of the shop.

Feeling conspicuous in this bastion of femininity, Kit tried to bow out, promising himself to return at another time to resolve the mystery. But the owner would have none of it.

"Mr. Stanhope," she exclaimed with a smile. "I am Madame Aglaia. May I help you?"

Embarrassed now and wondering how she knew his name, he said, "It was nothing. I just saw a handkerchief in the window and wondered how you acquired it."

"Oh?" She crossed to the window and picked up the dainty lace-edged confection. "This piece?"

He glanced at it, then did a double take. "No." But there was none other in the display. Strange— it had nothing but a bouquet of forget-me-nots embroidered on it. How could he have mistaken it for his family crest?

He glanced at the other two curious women in embarrassment, then turned back to the shop owner with a sheepish grin. "That is, yes. I'm sorry, I mistook the design on it for . . . something else."

Smiling, Madame Aglaia returned the handkerchief to the display window. "I see," she said archly. Then, glancing at the two women with a smile, she made it plain she thought he was there for another reason entirely.

And it appeared Belle thought so, too. "Have you changed your mind about helping me?"

Dear Lord, was he to make a decision now? At a loss, he stuttered, "I—I—"

Miss Keithley's expression turned frosty. "What is this about, Belle? Is this the gentleman . . . ?" She trailed off delicately, making Kit wonder how she would have finished that sentence.

As Madame Aglaia moved away to provide them privacy, Belle flushed, her cheeks rivaling the color of her hair. "Oh, no," she muttered, looking anywhere but at Kit.

Kit wasn't sure what to make of it, but Miss Keithley apparently had her own ideas. "If you are using me to meet this gentleman without your mother's knowledge—"

"Not at all," Belle assured her quickly. "I didn't know he would be here."

"It is pure happenstance," Kit confirmed.

"So why did you ask if he was to help you?" Miss Keithley asked with a lifted eyebrow.

"Well, I asked him to help make me beautiful first," Belle confided. "You see, he . . . owes me a favor."

"Yes," Kit said, glad she had explained. "But since I didn't see how I could assist her without a chaperone, I declined."

"Oh? And did you consider asking her mother to chaperone?" Miss Keithley asked dryly.

She had him there. How could he explain that any successful beautification of Belle needed to be done without her mother's interference? Then, realizing Mrs. Sullivan was nowhere to be seen, he smiled. "No, for the same reason you did not."

Miss Keithley burst into laughter. "Caught," she admitted, and Belle looked relieved. "But tell me, had you planned on assisting Belle in all phases of her transformation?"

He hadn't planned anything as yet, but the hopeful expression on Belle's face prompted him to say, "If I took on the task, of course I would."

"He did offer to take me to the garden party," Belle said in his defense.

He had acted like a cad, and here she was defending him to her friend. So Belle numbered kindness amongst her virtues—another plus in her favor. But why did she keep staring at his mouth?

"And have you decided to take on the task?" Miss Keithley persisted.

"There's no need, now that you have her in hand," Kit demurred.

The woman smiled. "Nicely phrased, but there's something to be said for having a man's opinion, especially since it is a man she wishes to impress."

Belle blushed even more furiously. So that was the way of it, eh? No wonder she wanted to change her appearance. Kit felt himself relax and realized he had subconsciously feared Belle Sullivan had set her cap for him. How absurd. This independent young American was no doubt smitten with a hard-working local and would have no use for a man who depended upon money from home to survive.

He reassessed the situation. He could use the money, and if Miss Keithley acted as chaperone, there was no further impediment to assisting Belle. None, that is, but his own reluctance to act as Pygmalian to her Galatea. He waffled. Should he . . . ?

"So," Madame Aglaia called from across the room, "are we decided upon the polonaise then?"

Surely she jested. "Oh, no," Kit said, crossing the room to take the sketch out of the dressmaker's hands. "That won't suit you at all, Miss Sullivan. And it is a little out of date, don't you think? With your slender figure, the slim princess style would be much more the thing."

Miss Keithley smiled. "Exactly what I was saying."

And so Kit Stanhope found himself drawn into a conversation on dresses, fabrics, and frills. Strangely enough, he enjoyed himself. He found himself in full accord with Miss Keithley and Madame Aglaia on what would suit Belle, and it was rather fun to watch Belle blossom with animation and confidence under the attention as they all made sure to point out her assets.

Soon they had selected several suits and evening dresses that would complement her complexion and were all vastly pleased with themselves and with Madame Aglaia's designs.

"I should have the first two dresses ready in a week," the dressmaker assured them. Then, staring thoughtfully at Belle, she added, "Perhaps I could suggest a new hairstyle to accompany your new wardrobe?"

Belle touched her hair tentatively. Though she had tried to corral it in the spiral bun many women favored, it seemed her curls did not accept confinement gracefully, for they escaped wherever possible, bouncing out randomly in wiry springs. The result, Kit admitted, was a bit of a mess.

"I don't know what to do with it," Belle admitted.

"Have you tried a hair wash of rosemary and vinegar?" Miss Keithley asked.

"No, I just wash it with soap. . . . Do you think it would help?"

"Yes, I'll give you the recipe."

Not to be outdone, Kit said, "Oh, quite. It should

help tame those wild curls of yours. And, perhaps a new cut . . . ?"

"Yes," Miss Keithley agreed. "Just the thing."

Madame Aglaia smiled. "I have a bit of skill in that area myself, if I might offer my services?"

Having been very pleased with Madame Aglaia's choices thus far, they all agreed.

As they made arrangements to meet at Madame Aglaia's in a week to observe Miss Sullivan's transformation, Kit had to laugh at himself. Somehow, he had committed himself to helping Belle achieve her transformation without even realizing how it had come about.

I just hope I won't regret it.

Four

In the coming days, Kit had further chance to reflect and decided that helping Belle wasn't going to interfere with his search for an investment after all. Especially since he hadn't had much success in finding one so far.

The investments that had been recommended to him were either too risky, too long-term, or seemed suspect. He had heard that some Americans, contemptuous of the aristocracy, had taken advantage of his countrymen's lack of knowledge of these wild lands and had swindled them. Without the proper connections or know-how, Kit feared the same would happen to him and didn't want to take any chances.

Perhaps he would have more luck with Patrick Sullivan. Everything he had heard about Belle's father confirmed that he was honest to a fault and didn't put up with shady dealings. And, true to her word, Belle had arranged a meeting for him with her father.

Kit knocked on the door of the Sullivan house and was ushered into the hall. As he waited to be announced to the master of the house, he heard furtive whispers and turned around to see three red heads pop back around a corner. He smiled. It appeared he was being observed.

"Miss Sullivan?" he said softly.

Belle appeared suddenly, as if she had been propelled by unseen forces. Unseen, perhaps, but not unknown. As Belle blushed red enough to match her hair, Kit hid his smile and said, "I take it your sisters are the cause of your . . . precipitous arrival?"

"Yes," she said with a fulminating glance into the other room. She beckoned furiously for the others to join her and Charisma appeared looking rather sheepish, while Grace bounded in with a beaming smile, setting the umbrella stand rocking.

As Charisma righted the umbrella stand, Kit smiled. Life was never dull around the Sullivan sisters.

"To what do I owe this honor?" he asked in an amused tone.

"Oh, we just wanted to wish you luck with Papa," Belle said breezily.

He grinned. She might not have beauty but she certainly didn't lack for cheek. "Thank you. Shall I need it?"

The sisters glanced at each other uncertainly. "Perhaps," Charisma conceded in her blunt way. "He doesn't care much for remittance men."

Belle shushed her quickly, but Kit's heart sank. Would this prove yet another failure?

"Papa's wonderful, really," Grace assured him. "His bark is far worse than his bite."

To cover up his dismay, Kit pretended to look alarmed. "You mean to tell me he may *bite?*"

Grace giggled, and even Belle and Charisma smiled.

"No," Belle assured him. "He hasn't bitten anyone

yet." She paused, then added with a mischievous twinkle, "That we know of."

"You relieve my mind," Kit said with an audible sigh. In more ways than one. It seemed that Belle and her sisters had forgiven him for his blunt speech, or had at least decided to give him the benefit of the doubt. Could he hope they were beginning to trust him? Or that Belle, at least, would pardon him?

Glancing at Belle's hair, which seemed just as unruly as ever, he asked, "So, have you had an opportunity to try Miss Keithley's hair-wash recipe yet?"

Belle smiled ruefully. "Not yet. I thought I would try it right before Madame cuts my hair."

"I see. Well, I look forward to the transformation." It had to help—nothing could be much worse than the unruly bush of her hair as it was now.

"So do I," Belle said so ingenuously that Kit didn't suspect the barb that followed. "I'm tired of being *homely.*"

Kit winced. Perhaps she wasn't as understanding or trusting as he'd thought. "Will you ever forgive me for that thoughtless remark?"

With a bold look, Belle said, "I might. If you make me beautiful."

"I shall do my utmost," Kit promised, but had to admit privately that the task was a daunting one.

As Belle nodded, Grace said, "It's very kind of you to help Belle."

Charisma snorted. "Why shouldn't he? He's getting paid for it, isn't he?"

Too true, and Belle had already sent him some cash on account after their encounter at the dressmaker's. But right now, she looked as if she wanted to apologize for Charisma's rudeness. No doubt she was reluctant to chastise her sister in front of an outsider.

By now, Kit was getting used to Charisma's ways and knew that behind that forthright exterior lurked a kind soul. Just look at the way she defended her sisters. And though others might find her rude, Kit thought her rather refreshing.

"Miss Charisma is quite right," he said, and was gratified to see surprise in their expressions. He bowed slightly in Belle's direction. "I *am* getting paid for assisting Miss Sullivan . . . but it is also my pleasure. Seldom do business and pleasure mesh so well."

He wasn't just being gallant. There was something exhilarating about having a hand in a person's meta-morphosis. Already, Belle seemed more outgoing. All she needed was to feel good about her appearance to give her the self-confidence she required to look beautiful in the eyes of others.

Belle smiled tentatively at him, but the house-keeper returned at that moment. Giving the girls an admonitory glance, she said, "Mr. Sullivan will see you now."

As the girls scurried away, with Belle giving him an encouraging smile over her shoulder, the house-keeper showed him into the library. The room was packed with richly bound books exuding that won-derful fragrance of leather and pressed paper that reminded him of his own library at home. He even recognized some of the same titles.

As Mr. Sullivan rose from the desk to shake his hand, Kit said, "I envy you your library. You have a marvelous collection."

The older man shrugged and glanced dismissively

at the shelves. "'Twas the wife's idea. I haven't much use for book learnin' meself."

As Sullivan said that with a challenging stare and the lilt of an Irish brogue, Kit remembered that Belle's father was most definitely a self-made man. Damn—he'd put his foot in it already and the interview hadn't even begun yet.

"So," Sullivan said, waving Kit to a seat. "Me daughter said ye was wishful t'see me?"

"Yes, sir. I was hoping you might be able to steer me toward an appropriate investment."

Sullivan scowled. Ignoring Kit's question, he said, "Aren't ye the young whelp who insulted my girls?"

Kit felt the blood drain from his face. He hadn't realized the girls had told their parents of their humiliation. Obviously, Mr. Sullivan had no intention of helping him.

Well, Kit wasn't going to lie. "I'm afraid so," he admitted. "But I didn't insult all of them. Just . . . one." And if the man had his mind made up, Kit certainly wouldn't plead for understanding. Should he take his leave?

"Well, at least yer honest," Sullivan said, scratching his chin. "And I hear tell ye apologized for it, too."

The man's approving look gave Kit renewed hope. "Yes, sir," he said warily. Was this a test?

"Good. I like a man who admits to his mistakes." Sullivan fixed him with a steely stare. "But I'm not so sure I care for the men ye call friends."

"Latham and Winthrop?" Kit said mildly. "Oh, I wouldn't call them friends, exactly." And just what was Sullivan's objection to such callow youths?

"No, not those witless pups. I'm speakin' of men such as John Daltrey. Folks around here say you spend a bit of time in his company."

Kit felt contempt curl his lip. "Not by choice. He's no friend of mine. We were merely neighbors back in Sussex—grew up on neighboring estates." No need to go into more than that.

Sullivan nodded in understanding. "That's all right, then. A man can't always choose his neighbors."

Kit relaxed a bit. "True, though I often wish I could."

Sullivan leaned back in his chair and regarded Kit from under bushy eyebrows. "So, what was yer offense?"

"I beg your pardon?" Kit asked in frigid accents.

"Most men o' yer stripe were kicked out of England for one transgression or another. What was yours?"

"I made no transgression," Kit said stiffly. Being booted out didn't mean he was guilty.

Sullivan nodded, but Kit wasn't sure the man believed him.

"So, what is it ye want of me?"

"Well, sir, I have a bit of money." Money he had squirreled away when he first arrived in this country, money that Daltrey knew nothing about. "I'd like to put it to good use, but I've no wish to be taken for a fool. Most men hereabouts say you're an honest, discerning man, and I thought you might be able to suggest an investment."

"Hmmph. Most of yer compatriots waste their money on sport, women, and song."

Too true. But it was all they knew. The class and primogeniture system in England was so skewed, only the eldest son was taught estate management and had an established purpose in life. Since it was no longer possible to purchase army commissions, younger sons had little choice of honorable occupation other than the clergy. For those not so inclined, any taint of the shop or actually sullying one's hands to make a living was frowned upon as not respectable. Hence, they occupied their time in the way they knew best—in dissipation.

But Kit knew what Sullivan's reaction would be to this, so he forbore to offer an excuse for his countrymen. "Some do waste their money that way," he admitted.

"But not yerself, eh?"

"No, sir." Not if he wanted to regain his good name at home.

"Well, good. What have ye looked at?"

"I've eliminated gambling and mining."

Sullivan raised his eyebrows at that. "Minin' too dirty for ye?"

"Too risky," Kit corrected, but had to admit his father would most definitely find it too dirty and not at all respectable.

"Aye, 'tis that." Sullivan scratched his chin again. "How about ranchin'?"

It was the way many of his countrymen had tried. But how could he phrase this so as not to offend? "I've heard it's difficult to find an honest seller."

That was putting it mildly. He'd heard horror stories of Englishmen being sold diseased cattle or worthless so-called grazing land. With no expertise in the area, Kit found it too chancy as well.

But Sullivan just nodded and thought some more. "Well, now, the city's growing. They'll be needin' more businesses and stores afore long, to keep up with the demand of the womenfolk fer all them fancy gewgaws and modern conveniences. A man who gets in on the ground floor of somethin' like that might make himself a tidy fortune."

Kit shook his head regretfully. "I'm sorry, but I could never engage in trade." His father would definitely not approve.

As soon as he uttered the words, Kit wished he could take them back—he sounded so pompous. And, from the expression on Sullivan's face, that was exactly how he saw it as well.

"Well, young man, if yer afraid to get yer hands dirty, I don't know how I can help you."

Kit could have kicked himself. But explaining would only make it worse. How could he tell this very honorable and well-regarded gentleman that the gentry considered his occupation and those of his friends beneath their notice?

He took a stab at it anyway. "That wasn't what I meant, I assure you. It's just that my father—" How to put this without sounding condescending?

"Yer father wouldn't approve of his son hobnobbing with us lesser folk."

Now he'd insulted the man. "I'm sorry, sir, I didn't mean to—"

"Never you mind," Sullivan said with a shushing motion. "I've an idea that's exactly what yer father would say. And, to tell ye the truth, it speaks well of ye that ye want to please him."

Needed to please him was more like it, but Kit let the man believe what he wanted. Instead of responding, he merely shrugged.

Sullivan shook his head. "Ye have a puzzle there, son. I tell you what—I'll think on it and let ye know if I come up with something respectable and not too uncertain."

"Thank you, sir," Kit said with sincerity and took

his leave. Though he had hoped for more, at least it might not be a total loss. And one thing was for certain—he was leaving with a great deal more respect for Patrick Sullivan. Not only was the man honest, but he was shrewd and obviously cared for his family . . . which was more than Kit could say about his father or older brother.

As he exited the library, Kit heard scurrying sounds, then a loud "psst" coming from the hall.

With a smile, he peered into the hall, and just as he suspected, Belle was there, this time without her sisters. Belle certainly didn't let convention dictate her actions. Oddly enough, he found it intriguing.

"What did he say?" Belle asked.

Kit glanced down at his hat and said dryly, "You mean you didn't listen at the door?"

Her face flamed, confirming his guess. "Well, yes, but I couldn't hear everything."

Just what had she heard? And, more importantly, what had she inferred from it? In any case, Kit decided to satisfy her curiosity. She would no doubt learn all the details from her father anyway. "He promised to keep his eyes open for an investment for me."

"Good," Belle said with another one of those odd looks at his mouth. "I'm sure he'll find something. And if he doesn't, I will," she declared.

Was that a promise or a threat? With the best grace he could, Kit thanked her and left the house. It seemed the only investment anyone had found for him was in spending his time on Belle Sullivan. Even that had yet to show any dividends—significant ones anyway.

He twisted his mouth in a wry grin. But one thing

was for sure—it had afforded him the only true amusement he'd found in this land so far.

Belle could barely contain her excitement. Today was the day Kit and Alvina would make her beautiful. And she had a good start on it already. Yesterday afternoon, she had tried the rosemary and vinegar hair wash. Though it had smelled rather odd and made her hair feel even stranger, once it dried, it had left her hair very soft. And not only had it tamed her wiry curls, but it had slightly changed the color of her hair—for the better, she thought. Instead of a rusty red, it now appeared auburn, a much more acceptable color in her eyes.

Eager to see what else could be done with it, Belle entered Madame Aglaia's a little early for her appointment. Luckily, the dressmaker had no one else in the shop except for Alvina, who had arrived early as well.

"Miss Sullivan, how wonderful to see you." As before, the beautiful dressmaker greeted Belle as if she were a longtime friend.

Smiling, Belle said, "Oh, I know I'm early. I'm just so excited to see what might be done with my hair."

Madame Aglaia smiled, an expression full of satisfaction. "Ah, I see you have a head start on it already. Lovely, just lovely."

Alvina agreed, marveling about the improvement.

Belle beamed. "Yes, it's so much nicer now. What style do you think will look best on me?"

"Come, let's look, shall we?" The dressmaker urged her to a room at the back of the establishment that was set up with a dresser and mirror, and a small table that held a number of sketches from *Godey's Lady's Book.*

Madame Aglaia had Belle unpin her hair and regarded her thoughtfully. "It is too bad the Titus is no longer in style. The short curls would suit your piquant little face."

Piquant? No one had ever said anything so nice about her appearance before. Belle felt herself flush. "I don't mind. Mama would be horrified if I cut my hair that short anyway."

"And short hair is really not the thing," Alvina said ruefully as she sorted through the sketches.

Then she and Madame Aglaia seized upon the same drawing at the same time. "Perfect," Alvina declared, as the dressmaker nodded. "You must have a fringe, Belle."

But Belle wasn't so sure. "I don't know," she said doubtfully, studying the drawing of a woman with short, feathery locks framing her face. "Don't you think a fringe would look a little . . . fuzzy on me?"

"Oh, no," Madame assured her. "Well, it might have looked so before, but now that your hair is so improved, it will have the effect of soft curls around your face, highlighting your best feature—your eyes."

"My best feature?" Belle repeated in wonder. She hadn't even known she *had* one.

"Yes, my dear," Madame said with a smile. "You have lovely eyes—such a pretty shade of pale green—and the way they sort of slant up at the corners is very appealing."

"I have pretty eyes?" Belle repeated in wonder. "Why has no one told me so?"

"Because they never noticed them before," Alvina said. "Not with your hair the way it was. Oh, do try this style, Belle. And you must use a sort of braided, pieced bun in back, to give it more interest, instead of that boring spiral thing."

"Well, if you say so . . ."

Madame Aglaia smiled. "We do. But I don't want to alarm you when I cut the front of your hair shorter than you're used to." She draped a piece of cloth over the mirror and set to work on Belle's hair, with comments and advice from Alvina.

At first, Belle was a little nervous, but realized she certainly couldn't look worse than she had before. She had to trust these two experienced women to do what was best for her.

Once Madame Aglaia had finished cutting and arranging her hair, Alvina declared it perfect, but they still wouldn't let Belle see it yet. Nor would they let her look in the mirror as they had her try on one of her new ensembles—a lovely ball gown in a vivid shade of green that had a lower neckline than she was accustomed to.

Kit had arrived by now, but they kept him cooling his heels in the other room while Belle finished her toilette under the watchful eyes of her mentors.

Then, once they were satisfied with her appearance, they sent her out to see Kit.

Belle held her breath, hoping for stunned admiration.

What she got was a nod and a cool assessment. "Good choices," Kit said. "The hair suits you and the dress color lights up your face. Very nice."

Nice? Her spirits sank. She had hoped for breathtakingly beautiful. Oh, dear. This wasn't going to work. How could she ensnare the threescum if she couldn't even get them to notice her as a woman?

Quickly, she found a mirror and stared at her reflection to learn the worst. Yes, there was definitely an improvement. The soft curls around her face gave her an elfin look and enhanced her eyes. And the dress made her complexion look as if it had a healthy glow instead of the sallowness she had become accustomed to. But . . . it wasn't what she'd hoped for, and her disappointment showed in her expression.

"What's wrong?" Alvina asked. "Don't you like the way you look?"

"Oh, yes," Belle said, knowing how hard her friends had worked to make her look *this* good. "But I was hoping for . . . something more."

"You're quite pretty now," Alvina assured her.

Pretty? Perhaps, but not stunning. "Yes, I suppose . . ."

"Very pretty," Kit agreed. But though his lips formed compliments, the admiration didn't quite reach his eyes the way she had hoped.

Belle didn't want to be ungrateful, but she didn't know how to put her dismay into words without hurting their feelings. So she picked on a minor point instead. "But my freckles . . . can nothing be done with them?"

"Short of covering them with cosmetics . . . ?" Madame Aglaia ventured.

Regretfully, Belle shook her head. It wouldn't do. Mama would definitely not approve.

Madame shrugged. "There are freckle creams available, but none are very effective. The best preventative for freckles is to ensure your skin is covered when you go out into the sun."

And so Mama had said—Belle should have listened.

Kit cocked his head and regarded her thoughtfully. "Your freckles aren't the real problem, are they? What is it?"

He was too observant. Belle hemmed and hawed, but finally blurted out, "You promised to make me beautiful. . . ."

She should have known better. Who could expect plain Belle to turn into a *femme fatale* overnight? The raw material just wasn't there to begin with.

"Ah, I see," Kit said, though he exchanged puzzled glances with Alvina. "Do you fear the gentleman whose attention you wish to capture won't be impressed by your improved appearance?"

Frankly, yes. And her fears were obviously not unfounded. Just look at Kit's reaction—it hadn't made a parcel of difference in how he looked at her or treated her. She nodded.

"Shouldn't he like you regardless of how you look?" Alvina asked.

In an ideal world, yes. "He hasn't yet," Belle said bluntly.

"Just who is this man you're trying to impress?" Kit asked, looking as if he'd like to set the man straight right then and there.

"I—I'd rather not say." Belle had no intention of letting him know that, in actuality, there were three men whose attention she wanted to attract, including Kit Stanhope himself.

"It's no use," Alvina told him. "I haven't been able to pry the name out of her."

Kit looked a little peeved, but Madame Aglaia said, "It isn't so much that you want to be beautiful, then, but that you want to be popular . . . sought after . . . irresistible?"

"Well, yes," Belle admitted. "Isn't it the same thing?"

Madame smiled. "Not necessarily."

Alvina and Kit looked struck by her statement. "Madame has a point," Kit said slowly. "Beauty alone is not nearly enough—not if you wish to take the town by storm. You need to be *interesting.*"

"Yes, that's it," Alvina concurred excitedly.

Interesting? That sounded promising, if Belle could just figure out what it meant. "But how?"

Madame Aglaia shrugged. "Experience, mystery, allure, Parisian polish . . ."

Belle's spirits fell. "I haven't any experience, I can't go to Paris, and it's difficult to suddenly become mysterious or alluring when the people around here have known me for years."

"Perhaps," Madame said with a mysterious smile. "Perhaps not."

"What do other women do to be interesting?" Belle asked.

"They have the vapors. . . . " Kit said doubtfully.

Alvina shook her head. "No, that won't serve. We have too many invalids in town as it is. They're not . . . interesting."

Very true. And Belle didn't want to be the object of pity, for heaven's sake.

"Perhaps an exotic perfume," Madame suggested.

"Yeees," Alvina agreed. "Something musky and redolent of forbidden pleasures."

Belle blushed at that, but though she protested, she really liked the sound of smelling like a man's hidden desire. She glanced at Kit, wondering how he felt about it.

"A good start," he said, "but perfume is not enough. She needs something . . . special."

"Special?" Belle repeated, not sure what he meant.

"Yes, something that sets you apart from the

others. Something that only you can do well." He turned to her expectantly. "So, what can you do well?"

"Nothing." Nothing that would help in a ballroom, anyway.

"Then we shall have to find something," Alvina declared. "Perhaps she wears only green, or carries outrageous parasols, or . . . sports the most dashing hats around."

"Now you're thinking," Kit declared. "What have you in that line?" he asked Madame Aglaia.

She smiled mysteriously, almost as if she'd been waiting for them to reach this point in the discussion. "Just a moment. I have the very thing." She rummaged in a back room and came back with a beautiful hand-painted fan that complemented the dress Belle wore. "Here, try this."

Belle obediently opened it and fanned herself.

"No, no," Madame said gently. "Like this." Standing in front of Belle, she showed her how to cover her lower face and peek out over the fan with just her eyes showing. "Now, look mischievous," she whispered.

As Madame moved away, Belle did as she instructed and gave Kit a saucy look over the lace-edged fan.

His stunned expression and Alvina's gasp of pleasure gave her a thrill.

"That's it," Alvina whispered. "Why, your eyes look positively enchanting."

"Indeed," Madame agreed with a self-satisfied smile. "With the fan, you are a lady of mystery, a saucy minx . . . a coquette. You must carry a fan with every ensemble—each one more beautiful than the last. Don't you agree, Mr. Stanhope?"

But Kit was still staring at Belle with his mouth open. A thrill coursed through her. Oh, my, was this all she needed to capture his attention?

And the rest of the threescum, too, of course, she added hastily to herself.

"What?" Kit asked Madame distractedly. Then, turning from Belle, he wiped a hand over his face and said, "Oh. Yes, the very thing. Um, do you know the, uh, language of the fan, Miss Sullivan?"

"Well, no," she admitted, lowering the fan, a little disappointed he had recovered so quickly. She knew it couldn't be that easy. "What's that?"

"A way for women to convey their feelings to men without words. I learned to interpret it when I was in Paris last year with my sisters, but I don't think it has reached this continent yet."

Alvina nodded. "I've heard of it, but don't know much about it."

"Then we shall make Miss Sullivan an expert," Kit declared with a smile. Turning to Belle, he asked, "What do you think? I shall be most happy to teach it to you."

Belle raised the fan once more to cover her self-satisfied smile. "It sounds wonderful." And she watched in wonder once more as Kit didn't seem to be able to take his eyes off her. If her untrained use of the fan had this sort of effect on him, she definitely wanted to learn more.

No, she reminded herself sternly. Her goal was not to capture Kit's attention, at least not yet. She needed to take care of George and Harold first.

And with this fanciful little weapon, she might just have the ammunition she needed to make her dreams of revenge come true.

Five

As arranged, Kit went to Madame Aglaia's the next day to meet Belle, but this time Miss Keithley was regretfully unable to join them. Kit had convinced Belle that Madame would provide sufficient chaperonage to satisfy even her mother and reminded her they couldn't waste any time—there was only a week left until her debut at the garden party.

All in all, Kit was very pleased with himself. Between the three of them, they had managed to find a way to make Belle provocative and intriguing. Why, she had even piqued his interest there for a moment or two.

But only for a moment. It was Belle, after all—his student and employer. It wouldn't do to be attracted to her.

As Belle arrived, Madame escorted them to the back room once more for privacy and stayed to play duenna.

Belle was wearing one of Madame's creations—a rust-colored, tailored dress with a matching jacket that made her look sophisticated and grown up, quite unlike the Belle he had met just a few short weeks ago. She sorted through the fans Madame had laid out for their inspection and looked up at

Kit uncertainly. "Does the type of fan matter? There are so many. . . ."

Madame had provided a large selection, including lace-edged fans, painted fans, Chinese fans, embroidered fans, and feathered fans. And they came in a variety of sticks ranging from mother-of-pearl to fretted ivory, sandalwood, and cedar.

"No, the only requirement is that it feels comfortable in your hand," Kit assured her.

She nodded and selected a painted fan with ivory sticks that matched her dress. Kit suggested she open and close it a few times to assure herself she could do so with ease. She did so, then asked eagerly, "What now?"

"Before Mr. Stanhope teaches you the language of the fan, perhaps I could give you a few pointers on how to use it," Madame said with a smile.

"But I've been using one all my life." So saying, Belle demonstrated by flipping it open and fanning herself.

Kit hid a smile as Madame shook her head in mock reproach. "That is all well and good if all you wish is a small breeze, but the discerning lady uses a fan as an extension of her hand . . . an expression of her emotions."

"I don't understand," Belle said.

Since it appeared Madame knew exactly what he had in mind, Kit suggested she show Belle.

"Very well." The dressmaker picked up a fan from the selection. "To get a gentleman's attention without touching him, you might use it thus." She tapped imperiously on his sleeve with the folded fan. "Or, if you are displeased with him . . ." She opened the fan, then snapped it shut at the end of Kit's nose in a very effective demonstration of pique. Too effective—Kit suppressed an urge to finger the slighted appendage.

"You might use it as a more decorous way of pointing at an object of conversation . . . " Madame made a graceful arc with her hand as she held the fan with feigned nonchalance, but it quite clearly ended up pointing directly at his chest. "Or as a way of displaying ennui." The fan now drooped languidly from her wrist.

As Madame continued to wield it in demonstration, the bits of paper and wood seemed almost alive, and Kit realized he had been wise to solicit her assistance. The woman had a master hand with the fan and Belle would do well to learn from her.

And Belle seemed to be an avid pupil as she watched Madame Aglaia with stunned fascination. "Oh," she exclaimed breathlessly, "is this the language of the fan?"

"Not at all," Kit told her. "Madame is merely demonstrating the basic mechanics of expressing emotions with the fan. I'll show you the language later. For now, why don't you try some of the gestures Madame showed you?"

Eagerly, Belle tried it. At first, her attempts were too broad, almost a caricature, but with Madame's excellent training and Kit's encouragement, she soon caught the knack of it and wielded the fan with grace and elegance. She was so obviously delighted with herself that her face became animated and her eyes sparkled.

My Lord, she is lovely like this, Kit realized. As she cast him a saucy look over the top of the fan, he said, "Don't move—hold that position a moment."

Then he whisked her around to face the mirror. "Do you see what I see, Miss Sullivan?"

Belle caught her breath in a gasp and reached out toward the glass to touch it tentatively. "Oh, my. Is that me?" She spun around and gave him an impulsive hug. "Oh, yes, this is what I wanted. Thank you!"

Having an armful of the soft and slender Belle Sullivan and being enveloped in the musky, heady perfume they had chosen for her acted powerfully on his senses. Suddenly, he no longer saw her as a pupil, but as a sensuous and desirable woman. His arms closed instinctively around her and he longed to draw her even closer. But reason returned just as swiftly.

This wouldn't do at all. He jerked away from her embrace, then hastily turned his panicked retreat into a bow toward Madame Aglaia. "I think you should, er, give credit where credit is due."

Madame gave him an arch look that said she wasn't fooled, but Belle didn't seem to notice as she gave Madame an equally enthusiastic hug.

See? his conscience chided him. *She was just treating you like an uncle or an older brother—not as a prospective lover.* So why had she felt so soft and yielding in his arms?

Kit groaned inwardly. He had done his job only too well—the gauche but endearing Miss Sullivan had somehow turned into an accomplished coquette with no knowledge of the power she held over men.

Or at least, he hoped she was unaware of her power. If she ever learned, heaven pity the man she had set her sights on, for he was doomed.

"Mr. Stanhope, are you all right?" came Belle's concerned voice.

Lord in heaven, he must have stood there, thunderstruck, like a fool. Pulling himself together and straightening his waistcoat, Kit said, "Ah, yes. Of course. I was merely . . . woolgathering."

Belle gave him an odd look but seemed to accept his explanation. "Will you teach me the language now?" she asked with an impish peek over her fan.

Trying to ignore her appeal, he said, "Ah, yes. I have it right here." He pulled a piece of paper from his pocket and handed it to her. "I've written it all down—all you need to do is follow this."

Belle looked disappointed. "Aren't you going to show me?"

Definitely not. He wasn't sure he should be anywhere in her proximity until he had himself under control once more. Ignoring Madame's small, all-knowing smile, Kit said, "You don't need me—it's all right there."

"Oh, but I do need you," Belle said with a small motion of her fan to his arm to stay his movements—a very feminine gesture that had just the effect she wanted.

He swallowed hard. She learned quickly—and all too well. "I just realized—perhaps it isn't such a good idea for you to be spending so much time in my company . . ."

"But why not?" she asked, disappointment showing on her countenance.

"Your . . . intended may not like it," he said desperately.

"Oh, pooh," she said with an airy wave of her fan. "He'll never know—unless you tell him."

"Someone may talk."

"Who? Madame? Miss Keithley? I don't think so."

"Of course we won't," Madame assured him, her

amused expression showing that she knew he knew that and that he was grasping at straws.

"But . . . your mother may find out, and then where would we be?"

Belle waved that away as well. "Oh, she won't. And even if she did, she thinks *you* can do no wrong. Besides, you promised to help me."

Kit didn't remember agreeing to any such thing, but his own actions had condemned him. By taking on the task of improving Belle, he had made a tacit, unspoken promise. And he was a man of his word. "Very well," he said with a sigh. "I shall show you the language of the fan."

But I'm not going to enjoy it.

Belle's lessons proceeded as promised, but she didn't enjoy them. Kit did his part and dutifully taught her the language of the fan under Alvina and Madame Aglaia's chaperonage, but it was less fun than she had hoped and more tedious than she had imagined.

She learned to show pleasure, displeasure, curiosity, and a variety of other emotions with the fan, but none seemed to have a significant effect on him. Worse, she never saw that glint in his eye again—the one that showed he had some awareness of her as a woman. Instead, he drilled her over and over again until she swore she could perform the moves correctly and gracefully in her sleep.

But once she was totally conversant with the proper movements and their meaning, they had realized that in order to be effective, others would have to learn it, too. So they devised a plan to put into action tonight at a musical soiree at Miss Keithley's.

Charisma and Grace watched her eagerly in her bedroom mirror as she dressed for the evening. "You're so beautiful tonight," Grace exclaimed.

Belle laughed. She did look elegant in the new evening dress, and it was a becoming shade of dusty blue. "Not quite, but I shall endeavor to be interesting and hope it does the trick."

"I'm sure it will," Charisma said with conviction. "I just wish we could go with you tonight to see your triumph."

"I do, too, but it was hard enough to get Mama to let *me* go."

Grace bounced on the bed, completely disheveling the bedding. "However did you manage to convince Mama not to accompany you?"

"Well, since Mama and Papa are still at odds because of what she did to us, all I did was tell Papa that I feared she would embarrass me."

Charisma frowned. "Do you think they'll ever reconcile?"

"Oh, I'm sure they will," Belle said with an airy wave of her hand. "They always have before."

"But it's been so long . . . " Grace said with a forlorn look.

"And Mama has never done anything so horrible before," Charisma reminded her. "But Belle is right—they'll come around."

"I hope you're right," Grace said. Then, regaining her usual sunny spirits, she asked, "What can we do to help you with tonight?"

Belle smiled at her sister's enthusiasm. "Would you like to help me choose a fan?"

"Oh, may I?" Enthusiastic now, Grace searched

through the assortment Madame Aglaia had sent over and plucked one out of the group with sticks of lightweight wood covered with blue silk and tipped with small white feathers. "Oh, use this one, Belle. It's so pretty—it looks like a bird."

Grace fluttered it around the room but was so intent on flying her "bird," she didn't see the footstool. Naturally, she tripped over it, but Belle and Charisma, with the ease of long practice, were there not only to break her fall, but to keep her from breaking anything else.

"Oh, I'm sorry," Grace said as she righted herself and quickly inspected the fan that had hit the floor in her hand. "But look, the fan is all right."

She flourished it at Belle, who took it and held it against her dress. The blue silk complemented the hue of her gown, so she said, "All right, Grace, the 'bird' fan it is."

The maid arrived to let Belle know her father was waiting, and Grace hugged her. "Good luck tonight. Have fun."

"Yes," Charisma added. "And remember everything so you can tell us all about it when you get home."

"I will," Belle promised. Until recently, the girls had pretty much been inseparable, but with Belle's metamorphosis and plan for revenge, that had necessarily changed so that Belle now did more and more things without her sisters. She knew that eventually they would all find lives of their own away from each other, but it still made her sad.

But she couldn't let those emotions spoil this evening. She shrugged off her melancholy and went downstairs to where Papa was waiting to escort her to the soiree. Mama was conspicuously absent—her way of letting her displeasure be known.

But Papa filled in admirably, even complimenting Belle on her appearance. "Ye look lovely tonight, me girl."

Belle hugged him. "Thank you, Papa." She was nervous about this evening and it helped to know she was looking her best.

As he handed her into the waiting carriage to drive the short distance to Alvina's, he asked, "Now, are ye sure ye want to mess with all this folderol? 'Tisn't just to please yer mother, is it?"

"Oh, no," she assured him. Though she could understand why he asked. In the past, she had resisted any suggestion of dressing up and going out, hating to mess with all that folderol, as he put it. "I'm having fun, Papa. And Miss Keithley is so nice—she's done so much to help me. I want to do this, and I'm sure I'll have a wonderful time."

"Well, I guess yer growin' up, then," he said with a hint of sadness.

She hugged him, suddenly wishing things could stay as they were forever. But that wasn't possible . . . or desirable, either. "I'm afraid so, but I'll always be your daughter . . . and I'll always love you."

The carriage stopped and her father said gruffly, "See that ye do." But he gave her an extra hug as he escorted her out of the carriage to Miss Keithley's door.

Miss Keithley promised to see her safely home, and he left Belle, albeit a little reluctantly, in the woman's care.

Alvina smiled and drew her into the house. "Your father seems like a very nice man," she said with a touch of inquisitiveness. Though Mama had tried her best to push her way into society, Papa had never entered into her sentiments, so few people knew him, except for those he worked with. As a result, people were curious about him.

"He's wonderful," Belle assured her, then stopped to pet a tortoiseshell cat who had leapt up onto a chair to inspect her.

"I'm glad you like cats," Alvina said with a smile. "I know many people confine their pets when they have guests, but my two are part of the family, and I hate to shut them up. Besides, they like having guests as much as I do."

"I love animals," Belle assured her. "What are their names?"

"The one you're petting now is Sheba, and the black cat at your feet is Cleopatra."

Belle bent to give Cleopatra some attention, too. "My, what grand names."

"They're very grand cats," Alvina assured her with a twinkle in her eye.

A knock sounded, startling Belle, who suddenly remembered why they were there tonight.

"Are you nervous?" Alvina asked.

"A little," Belle admitted, clutching her fan like a lifeline. It felt like a whole flock of tiny birds had taken up residence in her stomach, flying in agitated circles. A great deal depended on this evening. Was she up to it?

She'd better be, for her time was at hand.

Their first guest was shown into the salon and Belle relaxed when she saw it was Kit, then became nervous all over again. As Alvina went to check on her preparations, Belle felt suddenly very aware of Kit Stanhope. He was so handsome in his dark evening dress, with his fair hair shining in the lamplight and his lips looking so very inviting as he greeted her with a smile.

Stop dwelling on his mouth, she told herself sternly. What was it about a simple pair of lips that could hold her in such thrall? She refused to dwell on it and raised her gaze to concentrate instead on another feature—his eyes.

Hmm, those cool blue eyes were too assessing, too knowing . . . too disconcerting. It was safer to focus her gaze somewhere in between . . . like his nose. Yes, that was better. Patrician-looking though it might be, a nose was much less intimidating than eyes, much less dangerous than lips. A nose was . . . safe.

"Miss Sullivan?" Kit said with a quizzical smile. "Are you all right?"

"Of course," she said, though she kept her gaze from straying from the area of safety.

He fingered his nose in puzzlement. "Is there something wrong with my nose?"

Feeling herself flush, Belle looked away. "No, of course not. You look wonderful." Magnificent, even. Then, to change the subject, she asked, "How do I look?" and turned slowly for his perusal.

Kit nodded as she turned. "Very nice." He commented favorably on her hair, the style of her gown, and its color.

Belle supposed she should be gratified, but he was treating her more like a horse under inspection than a prospective flirt. If he tried to check her teeth, she swore she'd bite him.

Annoyed, she wondered how in Sam Hill she could get him to fall in love with her so she could spurn him if he persisted in treating her like a filly for sale. She wanted to stamp her foot in frustration, but it would ruin the whole image she was trying to project.

"Whose neck is that, I wonder?" Kit asked with amusement in his tone.

"What?"

"The way you are abusing that fan, I thought you might have a particular person's neck in mind . . . ?"

Belle suddenly realized she had been unconsciously opening and shutting the fan with unwonted force. Closing it once more with a snap, she laughed nervously, then slapped him playfully on the arm with it, albeit a little harder than she had intended. "No, of course not. I'm just nervous."

He winced. "Well, perhaps you should find a way to calm yourself before you break the fan . . . or my arm."

She couldn't help it—she tittered out of pure embarrassment. Oh, dear. He must think her a simpering fool. With her face overly warm now, she snapped the fan open to use it for its more mundane purpose—cooling her face—and saw a small white feather waft loose and float down to the carpet.

Sheba pounced upon the prize, and Belle wondered whether to acknowledge the small incident, but decided to pretend it didn't exist to avoid further embarrassment.

Unfortunately, more white down caught her eye as she realized there were three tiny pieces of fluff on Kit's sleeve. Oh, no. She must have deposited them there when she whacked him on the arm.

Calculating quickly how to remove them from his pristine black jacket without calling attention to her *faux pas*, Belle moved closer to him and said, "I just need a little time to get over my nervousness. I'm sure I'll be fine soon."

With a reassuring and rather firm brush of his arm, she swept the feathers off his sleeve . . . only to see Cleopatra leap up to swat at the three tufts as they wafted slowly down.

Mortified, Belle quickly drew Kit's attention away. Between Grace's handling and her own mangling of the poor fan, it was no wonder the feathers must have come loose. She just hoped it would survive the night and their plan without shedding too much or looking too bedraggled.

She didn't have much time to worry as Alvina returned and the other guests began arriving. They had all been carefully chosen for this evening to fit in with their plan—just enough people to spread the word about Belle's transformation, but not enough to intimidate her in her first public appearance as the new, improved Belle Sullivan.

And as she made the rounds of the small party, she was gratified to hear quite a few compliments, especially from George Winthrop and Harold Latham. She had hoped they would find her attractive and become smitten so she could exact her revenge, but they were acting a bit odd—as if she were somehow their protégée. They even seemed to be taking credit for her blossoming.

The situation seemed to amuse Kit, but it annoyed Belle. How could she make them fall for her if they treated her like a favorite niece whom they patted on the head and sent off to play? She would just have to find a way to change their attitude.

As the evening progressed, Belle tried to keep her use of the fan strictly controlled, but she used it naturally as she spoke and found herself shedding feathers everywhere. Unfortunately, the cats followed her everywhere as well, no doubt looking upon her as the source of the new fun toys or wondering when the bird in her hand would light somewhere within reach.

Good grief, with her feline escort and shedding fan, how would she be able to carry out her part of the plan? With exasperation, she surreptitiously fanned another loose feather out of sight and saw Kit approaching her with a glass of punch.

"I thought you might be parched," he said and handed her the punch with one hand as he deftly snatched a piece of loose fluff from the air with the other, then placed it in his pocket as if it were a perfectly ordinary occurrence.

Belle accepted the punch gratefully, wondering if she should ignore his action with as much aplomb as he had just shown, but as she opened her lips to speak, she gestured with the fan in her hand and a small feather landed on her lip.

Well, this is impossible to ignore. She couldn't very well stand there with a feather sticking out of her mouth and pretend it didn't exist. Fleetingly, she considered swallowing the evidence, but that was just too disgusting to contemplate.

She raised her gaze to Kit and saw him watching her dilemma with unholy amusement in his eyes. "Having a *fowl* time of it, are we?" he drawled.

Oh, who was she fooling? Snatching the feather from her mouth and tossing it to the cats, she wailed, "I'm molting. . . ."

He let out a bark of laughter. "I know." But he didn't seem to be able to say anything further as he struggled to hold his mirth in check.

"What shall I do?" she whispered fiercely. "I can't

go through with the plan looking like I've just had a dust-up with a flock of chickens."

He grinned, setting his cool blue eyes alight with humor. "Er, if you would allow me?" She nodded in resignation as he removed one piece of down from her hair and another from her shoulder. Then he added in a low tone, "Miss Keithley and I noticed your . . . predicament, and she's gone to get you another fan."

"But how will we make the switch? Surely everyone's noticed the fan I have." How could they miss it?

"All you have to do is follow my lead . . . and don't swish it about so."

"All right," she said with a sigh and let the fan dangle down to her side, resolving not to use it again. "What are you going to do?"

But Belle never learned what he had planned because Sheba, finally seeing her prize within reach, leapt up to knock the fan out of Belle's hand. It went flying just like the bird it resembled . . . right into Cleopatra's pouncing paws.

Belle couldn't help it—she let out a surprised scream, which unfortunately drew everyone's attention. In horror, Belle watched as the cats briefly fought over their prey, then ripped it in two. With a triumphant growl, Sheba sat glowering at the crowd over her severed half while Cleo made off with the other. Stunned silence reigned as Cleopatra darted over to Alvina and laid the mangled fan at her mistress's feet.

Belle knew she should be mortified, but the cat looked so absurdly proud of herself, she couldn't help it—she burst into laughter.

And the tension in the room suddenly disappeared as everyone followed suit. "I'm so sorry,"

Alvina said, though her eyes were twinkling merrily. "Let me replace it, please."

"There's no need," Belle said with a laugh. "Just give it a decent burial."

Everyone laughed again. Thank heavens the amusement was at the situation and not at her expense.

"No, I insist on replacing it," Alvina said. "Just a moment."

Alvina signaled a maid to deal with the fatally wounded fan, and as she rushed off to find a replacement, Kit whispered, "You handled that very well."

Belle rolled her eyes. "Thank you, but I hope that wasn't the plan you had in mind."

"No," he said with a devilishly charming grin. "But it worked admirably. Now no one will question Miss Keithley providing you with a new fan."

Alvina came back with a pretty painted one, sans feathers, and whispered to the two of them, "Now seems like a good time, don't you think?"

Belle gulped. "I guess so. . . ."

"You'll do just fine," Alvina promised her, patting her hand and drawing her into a small group that contained the most notorious chatterbox in town— Millicent Mattingly.

"My dear, that was so amusing," Miss Mattingly gushed in a piercing tone without a trace of condescension. "I vow, you will become the talk of the town."

"Oh, I hope not," Belle demurred. Not that way, anyway. And since she seemed to have most everyone's attention, she deliberately looked at Kit and opened and shut her fan with a snap.

On cue, Kit approached the group with a hand held over his heart. "Miss Sullivan, you wound me."

Belle pretended to ignore him as Alvina said her lines. "But how, sir? She said not a word."

He appealed to Miss Mattingly. "But didn't you see, she accused me of being cruel."

"Why, no," the gossip said. "She said no such thing."

"Perhaps her lips did not, but her fan did."

"Her fan?" Now Millicent Mattingly looked intrigued. "How is that possible?"

Pretending to ignore her question, Belle looked coquettishly at Kit over her fan and improvised. "It is no more than you deserve, sir, for being so unkind as to distract me long enough so that Sheba was able to snatch the fan from my grasp."

A smile tugged at the corner of Kit's mouth as he bowed slightly and said, "I do apologize for not being more vigilant, but I had no notion Madame Sheba was so inclined. Will you forgive me?"

Belle smiled at Kit and let the fan speak for her as she closed it and let it rest on her right cheek in the sign for "yes."

Kit grinned. "Splendid."

Miss Mattingly stared at both of them and said in her penetrating voice, "But she said nothing. How did you divine her answer?"

"Have you not heard of the language of the fan?" Kit asked. "It is all the rage in Paris."

Belle smiled to herself. Millicent Mattingly's loud voice had caught the crowd's attention, and they all looked intrigued at Kit's statement.

"Paris? Do tell us all about it," Miss Mattingly urged.

"Not I," Kit demurred, "but Miss Sullivan seems quite expert. . . ."

Miss Mattingly turned her eager stare on Belle. "Oh, will you show us?"

"I don't know . . ." Belle said. Kit and Alvina had agreed she should appear reluctant, but now that it was time for the curtain to go up, Belle found her reluctance was no act. She had a bit of stage fright.

"Oh, please do," Alvina coaxed her, just as they had rehearsed. And several others chimed in with their agreement.

So, Belle allowed herself to be persuaded and the men rearranged the furniture under Kit's direction to put Belle at the center of a semicircle.

Kit gave her an encouraging nod and said, "Come on, show us."

Belle calmed herself, remembering that this was the first stage in her plan to exact revenge. With a small quaver in her voice, she said, "There are thirty or so messages you can send with a fan."

But as they all watched eagerly, even approvingly, to learn the latest trend from Paris, Belle relaxed and felt her voice return to normal. Mischievously, she stared directly at Kit and transferred the fan to her right hand. "This gesture means 'You are too willing.'"

They all laughed and Belle felt herself relax even more. Staring at George now, she deliberately dropped the fan. "This means 'We shall be friends.'"

George smiled and retrieved the fan for her. "I hope so," he said and returned the item with a gallant gesture. "Please, continue."

She held the closed fan to her heart and gave Harold a meaningful look. "This position signifies 'You have won my love.'"

Harold flushed and Belle realized she held a powerful weapon here. No longer did the threescum regard her as an object of pity or scorn, or even avuncular condescension. Now, with this little fan, she held their very emotions in her hand.

But though Harold and George seemed fascinated, Kit merely looked amused. So Belle diverted herself by flirting with the other two, staring directly into their eyes as she demonstrated such moves as "Do not forget me," "I love you," or "I always long to be near you."

To punish Kit, she favored him with "I hate you," "Do not be so imprudent," and "I love another."

The rest of the guests seemed amused by these tactics, but Kit was becoming less and less so. Who cared? She was having fun, and no one was taking her seriously anyway . . . except, she hoped, for George and Harold.

After she was done, everyone was eager to try their skills at performing or interpreting the latest fad, and Belle was thoroughly satisfied. Though the evening had started out a little rocky, she had achieved exactly what she had set out to do—gain acceptance in the society the threescum thrived in.

She smiled. Tomorrow, word of her success would be all over Colorado Springs and Belle Sullivan would become a force to reckon with.

Six

The afternoon following Belle's successful debut, Kit left his lodgings at the Colorado Springs Hotel and walked up Pikes Peak Avenue to meet her at the dressmaker's as planned.

Last night, Belle had done them all proud, even better than they'd hoped. He had never been quite so amused in his life as when he watched her try to ignore her cloud of feathers and attendant cats, but she had handled it with unexpected aplomb.

So why did the triumph seem so flat? He ought to be happy that he was giving Belle value for her money—and seeing return on *some* investment, at least. But he didn't quite feel as good about it as he had hoped. Could it be because the pupil seemed to have outstripped the tutor?

Once Belle had faced her own roomful of eager students, her endearing schoolgirl traits had vanished and she had suddenly turned into a beguiling coquette. One, moreover, who had singled him out for some outrageous set-downs. The minx.

He smiled at the memory. Ah, could that be the problem? Was he piqued that she had flirted with those callow youths and not him?

No, he had seen through her game, so that

wasn't it. He supposed he had just wanted a little more . . . appreciation of his efforts.

Suddenly, his musings were interrupted by two men who hailed him. "Lord Stanhope," they called.

Kit sighed in resignation as he recognized the callow youths in question—Harold Latham and George Winthrop. He had given up on trying to convince them he wasn't a "lord." They apparently enjoyed numbering a British peer amongst their acquaintances and it wasn't worth the effort to convince them to address him otherwise. He smiled and nodded as they approached.

George grinned at him with a knowing leer. "Quite an entertaining evening last night, eh?"

Kit stiffened. Was he making fun of poor Belle and her feathers? "Yes, I enjoyed myself."

"Indeed," Harold said with a smitten air. "I've never seen Miss Sullivan in such fine form. Why, she was positively bewitching."

Kit smiled tightly as he realized his apprehension was unfounded. Latham and Winthrop seemed full of admiration for the woman they had so recently condemned as beneath their notice.

"We did well there," George said with a smug expression.

Puzzled, Kit said, "I beg your pardon?"

"You know, bringing her into fashion and all." George puffed out his chest. "When we acknowledged her as a lady, it must have been just the thing she needed to improve herself."

"I . . . see," Kit said slowly. Did they really believe they had that much to do with Belle's transformation? Apparently so, since Harold appeared just as proud of himself as George. Dryly, Kit added, "You don't know your own power. . . ." Truly.

Harold laughed. "But she really gave *you* what-for last night, didn't she? Guess you didn't make quite as good an impression on her as we did."

Good Lord, was that really what they thought? Couldn't they see Belle had been teasing him? Punishing him, no doubt, for not falling under her spell the way all the other gentlemen had.

But if they couldn't see it, he wasn't going to correct their misconception. "I am devastated," he drawled.

George clapped him on the back in one of those hearty American gestures of bonhomie. "Well, I guess she just prefers plain old Americans to a fancy man like you."

Kit wasn't quite sure how to answer that bit of rudeness, but fortunately Latham and Winthrop wandered off then, congratulating themselves and each other on how well they had brought Belle into fashion.

Kit grimaced, but it was his own fault, really, for putting the idea into their heads in the first place. He tried to resume his walk up the avenue, but a pair of women rode by in their carriage and called out a greeting—Miss Mattingly and her bosom friend, Miss Gaither.

Kit nodded politely to them and would have kept on walking, but Miss Mattingly had the driver pull over and called out in her shrill voice to beckon him over. "Mr. Stanhope, how nice to see you."

Kit murmured some pleasantries, and Miss Mattingly said, "I was just telling Miss Gaither about the soiree she missed last night. It was most diverting— do tell her how amusing Miss Sullivan was. I don't think she believes me."

Though Kit was sure Miss Gaither thought no such

thing, he solemnly confirmed Millicent Mattingly's version of the events and continued to do so as Miss Mattingly enthused about Belle and her amazing language of the fan.

Millicent tittered and gave him an arch look. "It was most instructive to watch the way in which she used the fan to captivate most of the men in the room. Don't you agree?"

Kit allowed as how he did, wondering how he could pull himself away politely before he had to endure much more of this gossip's retelling of the previous night.

Millicent used her own fan in awkward imitation, and Kit spotted an opening. When the closed fan paused by her left ear, Kit pretended he had read the message, "I wish to get rid of you."

Bowing, he said, "I beg your pardon. I didn't wish to offend. I shall leave at once." Then, trying not to laugh at the surprised expression on Miss Mattingly's face, he strolled on as fast as he could politely do so.

Miss Mattingly called out, "Oh, dear, I didn't mean— Do wait, Mr. Stanhope."

Kit pretended not to hear, though how anyone could imagine he could miss her penetrating voice was a mystery.

"Oh, dear," she said to her friend in what she no doubt thought was a low, confiding tone. "Poor Mr. Stanhope. Insulted both last night and today—by two different women. I declare, the poor man must be feeling terribly slighted."

Kit walked faster. Good Lord, were all the residents of this town so unobservant? Did they really think Belle's needling last night was anything more than teasing?

Apparently so. Either that, or he was the one who

had misinterpreted her actions. Could it be she really was angry at him? He frowned. Surely he couldn't be *that* far off in his interpretation . . . could he?

As he neared the shop, another male voice hailed him. Kit sighed in resignation. Colorado Springs had never seemed smaller.

He turned to see who it was and found John Daltrey grinning at him. Kit stiffened, unsure whether to be annoyed that his blackmailer had tracked him down, or happy that this was one person, at least, who wouldn't rib him about the events of last night.

"What do you want?" he asked, not bothering to be civil.

Daltrey ignored his question. "Hmm, humiliated by women, are you?"

So he'd heard that, had he? Kit grimaced. Of course he had—everyone in a two block radius had no doubt heard Millicent Mattingly's piercing voice. "Nothing of the sort," Kit said stiffly.

"Really?" Daltrey drawled, apparently not convinced. "And who was the other woman who slighted you?"

"No one. She was mistaken." Kit's eyes narrowed, and he wondered why he was bothering to explain. "It's none of your concern, anyway."

Daltrey shrugged. "Perhaps not. But there's a young lady back in Sussex you left feeling more than a little slighted. . . ."

His innuendo made Kit's temper flare, but he kept it in check here on the public street. He didn't bother to deny the slander again—he wouldn't give Daltrey the satisfaction.

But enough of this verbal sparring. "What do you want?"

"Oh, nothing," Daltrey assured him, oozing

insincerity. "Say, when do you get your quarterly allowance again?"

"Soon," Kit said through gritted teeth. "Don't worry, you'll get your money."

"Oh, I'm sure of that," Daltrey said with a wolfish smile. "Tell me, how are you managing to eke out a living if your pockets are as empty as you claim?"

"I manage."

"I see. With the help of a woman, perhaps?"

Kit felt a tic start in his left eye. "What are you getting at?" he demanded tightly. Had the man somehow learned of his agreement with Belle?

"I hear you are spending a great deal of time at a certain handsome dressmaker's establishment . . . ?"

"You shouldn't believe everything you hear." But though Kit relaxed, he was concerned nonetheless. It was obvious Daltrey didn't have any more details or he wouldn't be bent so obviously on a fishing expedition. But if anyone should learn Kit was meeting Belle there secretly, her reputation would be ruined.

"The dressmaker seems a bit long in the tooth for you," Daltrey admitted. "But do you think she might be interested in hearing of the young lady back in Sussex?" Daltrey watched Kit's face avidly for his reaction.

"I doubt it," Kit said with a raised eyebrow, allowing a bit of amusement to color his tone so Daltrey would believe he was far off the mark. "She isn't the type of woman who would listen to scurrilous gossip."

"*Every* woman listens to gossip," Daltrey said with an insincere smile.

Knowing he had to give Daltrey something or the man would continue to dig and find out what was really going on, Kit sighed heavily. "If you must

know, we are related. She is my mother's second
cousin's daughter."

"I never knew the Stanhopes had a Greek connection."

"We don't speak of it," Kit said curtly.

Because it didn't exist. . . .

"Ah, a poor relation, then," Daltrey said wisely.
"So why bother to visit her?"

Kit cast about for a reasonable explanation. "She
and my mother have always corresponded faith-
fully," he lied without a shadow of remorse. He also
hoped Daltrey would get the implication that
Madame Aglaia, being in his mother's confidence,
would already be fully cognizant of Kit's reason for
residing in Colorado Springs. Though he hated to
appear vulnerable in front of this blackmailer, Kit
let longing show in his voice. "It's the only way I
hear news of home."

Daltrey's lip curled in contempt. "Very well," he
said, obviously annoyed that he was balked of his
fun. "But I'll expect to see some cash as soon as you
get your quarterly remittance—or the rest of Little
London will hear of your disgrace."

Hear the lies, he meant, Kit thought with annoyance. "Of course," he said. Conscious of the curious
looks of passersby, he schooled his features so as not
to betray his feelings and took his leave.

He continued up the short walk to Madame
Aglaia's and debated whether to go in. Was Daltrey
still watching? Kit couldn't risk a glance to see. But
just in case the man was still lurking about, Kit
passed the dressmaker's, then made his way down
a side street and approached the shop at the trades-
man's entrance in the back.

Madame opened the door readily enough, but

not without giving him a silent question in the form of a raised eyebrow. As Kit joined her and Belle in a back room, Madame said, "What was that all about?"

"Yes," Belle said with curiosity before he could answer. "Who was that handsome gentleman we saw you speaking with? Is he the reason you're late?"

"Yes," Kit said shortly. Daltrey was to blame for many things, Kit's tardiness the least of them. "That . . . man," he refused to call him a gentleman, "lived on a neighboring estate back home."

"Oh," Belle said with a smile. "Is he a friend of yours?"

Kit scowled. "No. John Daltrey is a scoundrel and a wastrel. I suggest you stay far, far away from him."

"But why?" Belle asked, sounding all innocence. Innocence Daltrey would have no hesitation in shattering, given the opportunity.

"He was trying to find out why I've been spending so much time here at Madame Aglaia's." He turned to the dressmaker with an apologetic expression. "Your pardon, ma'am, but I told him we were related and you corresponded regularly with my mother."

Madame smiled. "Quite all right. It won't do me any harm to be thought a shirttail relation of the Stanhopes." She glanced askance at Belle. "And it might do some good elsewhere . . ."

Thank heavens the woman understood. "Exactly."

"I don't understand," Belle said. "Why did you tell him that?"

"To preserve your reputation," Kit said baldly. Madame nodded and Belle looked back and forth between the two of them with confusion. "Is it in jeopardy?"

"It might be if John Daltrey learned I was meeting you here secretly."

"Oh, I see," Belle said in a small voice.

He hoped she did. Her reputation was her most precious possession. "I think it would be best if Miss Keithley continued as your sole instructor."

"Because of this?" Belle asked incredulously. Then, with a thoughtful expression, she added, "No, it's because of last night, isn't it? But—"

"Of course not," Kit said with more annoyance than he had intended. Did everyone think him a simpleton? "You were a hit—a wild success with the entire party."

Belle flushed. "Well, except for the feathers, maybe . . ."

Madame laughed. "I heard about the feathers. I had no idea the fan was so flimsy or I would never have sent it over."

"But I treated you abominably," Belle admitted to Kit with a sheepish grin.

"Think nothing of it," Kit assured her. "I don't."

"Then why do you no longer want to teach me?" she asked, obviously puzzled.

Several reasons, but only one that he could voice. He felt a little foolish that he was developing an affection for his pupil, and worried that Daltrey would make her a target for additional blackmailing schemes. He gave her the only reason he could voice. "To protect you."

Then, before she could object again, he added, "Besides, you were quite the success last night. You don't need me. Miss Keithley and Madame Aglaia can lend you any assistance you might require in the future. It's best if we aren't seen together."

"But you promised to take me to Dr. Bell's party . . . and to help me until the Founder's Day Ball," she protested.

"After your success last night, you should have no problem finding someone to escort you," Kit assured her.

"But I'm comfortable with *you*. I don't want anyone else."

Kit wasn't sure he cared for the word "comfortable." It sounded entirely too . . . domesticated for his peace of mind. "You'll manage."

"No, I won't," she said crossly. "Besides, you promised."

Madame Aglaia moved between them as if to referee their bout. "He's quite right, Miss Sullivan. Your reputation is of utmost importance."

Then, before Belle could protest once more, Madame turned to Kit and placed a hand on his arm. "But don't you think you are being overly cautious? You have been most circumspect and I'm sure no one suspects anything untoward. And I should certainly set them straight if they did."

Somehow, though Kit didn't quite know how it came about, he found Madame's arguments entirely logical and reasonable. He wavered. "I don't know. . . ."

Madame continued her insidious persuasion. "There's no harm in simply escorting her to events, is there? Especially if you are chaperoned by Miss Keithley."

"I suppose not. But—"

"And honestly, as long as you are discreet and

chaperoned at all times, there's no harm in your meeting her here, either. Is there?"

"You have a point," Kit admitted. Though he wasn't quite sure how she had made him change his mind. All she had done was touch his arm, and his resolve had become putty in her hands. Then again, could it be that a part of him didn't want to leave off helping Belle so soon?

Belle clapped her hands in delight. "Good."

Feeling he needed to reclaim some of his manhood, Kit added, "But only until the Founders' Day Ball. That's the limit of our agreement."

"All right," Belle agreed with a smile. "I'm sure that's all the time I'll need. . . ."

Her expression turned so calculating, Kit's eyebrows rose. What did she have in mind now? And what poor soul was the object of her schemes?

Later that evening, Aglaia met with the other two Graces to review her progress. "That was a close one," Aglaia said. "I had to use just a jot of . . . persuasion to convince him to stay on."

"Yes, we saw," Thalia said. "But I hope you-know-who wasn't paying attention."

"It was only a little magic," Aglaia said, defending herself.

Euphrosyne nodded with a graceful movement. "But why did you bother? He was right, you know—he could harm her reputation."

"But don't you see?" Aglaia said. "They are so obviously perfect for each other."

"Perfect?" Euphrosyne repeated. "Why, he thinks her a schoolgirl, and she wants him for nothing but revenge."

Thalia smiled charmingly. "Oh no, dear. You haven't been paying attention. They're made for each other, all right."

Euphrosyne shrugged. "I haven't really been paying attention, it's true. I'll defer to your judgment."

Aglaia accepted her capitulation with an inclination of her head. "Our main problem seems to be that Daltrey person. Did you hear what he called me? Long in the tooth!"

Thalia patted her hand. "You're nothing of the kind. You're barely three thousand years old, dear. And, of course, as the Grace of Beauty, you're the most beautiful of us all. Why, he hasn't even seen you. He just made a totally unfounded assumption."

Somewhat mollified, Aglaia said, "Perhaps. But I don't trust him. I think I'm going to do a little sleuthing and see what I can learn about him." And Zeus help the man if she learned he was interfering in her matchmaking, for surely no one else would.

On the morning of the garden party, Belle lay in bed, reluctant to get up. She'd been having the most marvelous dream and wanted to savor it awhile longer. She'd been the belle of the ball on Founders' Day, and her revenge on Harold and George was successful. They were so humiliated, they couldn't show their faces in public.

In a satisfied glow, she had danced with Kit, thrilling to the feel of his arms about her, and watching him stare down at her in besotted admiration. Unable to resist her glowing beauty, he had whirled her out to a secluded balcony and kissed her.

Belle held her fingers to her lips in remembered

bliss. Though she had never experienced the feel of a man's mouth on hers, she had an excellent imagination. In the dream she had almost swooned in delight when she had finally felt those marvelous lips on hers. . . .

But mixed in with the delight had been savage triumph as she prepared to spurn him and exact her revenge. Thankfully, she had woken before she could put that part of her plan into effect.

Thankfully? What was she thinking? Kit Stanhope might have helped her find beauty, but she still owed him for that unkind remark of his.

He apologized for that, and very nicely, too, her conscience chided her.

But he was also one of the threescum who had hurt and humiliated her sisters. She nodded decisively. For that, he had to pay.

Unfortunately, though her plan to ensnare Harold and George was coming along nicely, Kit seemed immune to her charms. Oh, there was that one moment with the fan, but he had recovered all too soon. And when she had tried to punish him by making him the object of her scorn in the fan lessons, he seemed more amused than annoyed— not exactly the mien of a would-be lover. Perhaps she needed to take a different tack, find another way to get revenge.

Hmm, where was he vulnerable? In this investment scheme of his? No, that was out. She didn't know anything about that sort of thing. Besides, that was his livelihood. He had hurt her emotionally, not fiscally. It was only fair that she repay him in kind. Hmm, Kit also seemed to be wary of that man she had seen him talking to. What was his name? Oh, yes—Daltrey. Maybe she should make a few discreet inquiries about him.

A knock on the door jolted her out of her musings, but before she could say anything, her sisters barged in.

Charisma placed her hands on her hips and regarded Belle with reproach. "What are you doing still in bed? Have you forgotten about the garden party today?"

Belle laughed and threw back her covers. "No, I didn't forget. I was just daydreaming."

"About what?" Grace wanted to know.

"Oh, the wish I made in the Garden of the Gods," Belle said breezily. She didn't want to share the dream kiss with her sisters.

Grace bounced onto the end of the bed. "Your wish came true—do you think ours will, too? Oh, I hope so."

"But my wish hasn't come true yet," Belle said, puzzled.

"Yes, it did," Grace insisted. "You're beautiful now."

"Oh, that wish." Belle laughed. "Well, that may be what I said out loud, but what I really wished for, inside, was revenge on the threescum."

"Oh," Grace said, sounding deflated. "But do you think the Graces are supposed to grant the wish you voice or the one you keep secret?"

"Neither," Charisma said scornfully. "You don't really believe a bunch of rocks are going to grant our wishes, do you?"

Grace pouted. "Well, it's looking pretty good for Belle so far."

Before the conversation could degenerate into an argument, Belle said, "I won't get anywhere unless I get dressed soon. I need to look ravishing today." It was necessary to put stage one of her plan into effect.

"All right," Charisma said briskly. "And we dismissed the maid so we can help you."

They assisted Belle in choosing and donning a lovely dress in a shade of russet that lit up her face, then helped her put her hair up in the becoming new style Madame had recommended.

"What fan will you use today?" Grace asked.

"Well, it better not have feathers," Charisma said with a laugh.

"Definitely not," Belle agreed. "Why don't you choose something, Charisma?" Charisma couldn't do worse than Grace, and her sisters did like being a part of Belle's new social life.

Charisma sorted through them and held one up. "Look, here's a painted fan with strong cedar sticks, and the colors go with your dress." Ever practical, she opened and closed it several times. "Looks sturdy enough to survive one small garden party—and no feathers or other loose adornments."

"Sounds perfect," Belle said, and took it from her. "There, I'm ready. How do I look?"

She twirled around for her sisters who assured her she had never looked better.

"Good—I hope Harold and George agree with you." And Kit, too, she added to herself.

"What are you going to do to them?" Charisma asked.

That part was still a little unclear. She just had to wait and see what opportunities presented themselves. "I don't know, but I'll think of something." Her plan had gone very well so far, and she had no doubt it would continue to do so.

They trooped downstairs just as Kit and Alvina

arrived. As Belle joined her friends in the small closed carriage, she found herself seated next to Kit, crowded up against his side in the close confines. How odd—it made her tingly all over. She had never felt like this when she sat next to her father.

The longer she sat there, the more she realized she was enjoying the sensation. Sitting this close, with her arm and leg pressed up against Kit's, Belle suddenly realized how very tall he was . . . how very firm. And he smelled wonderful—manly and woodsy.

As he conversed with Alvina, Belle had the oddest urge to reach out and touch him. She wanted to caress the muscles beneath his arm, see if his thighs were as hard as they looked beneath the taut material of his trousers, feel those mobile lips against hers. . . .

Oh, dear. It was getting warm in here. With her free hand, Belle applied the fan vigorously.

Alvina looked at her with concern. "Are you all right? You look a little flushed."

"Yes, yes, of course. I'm just warm, that's all."

"Are you nervous?" Kit asked.

"A little," Belle admitted. It was certainly a good excuse for her strange reaction. And, since it was the first time she was actually entering society— Alvina's small soiree didn't count—she had every right to be apprehensive.

"Don't worry," Kit said, patting her on the hand as if she were a foolish child. "You laid the groundwork very well at Miss Keithley's, so we have no tasks for you to perform at this party. All you have to do is enjoy yourself."

Well, he might not have any plans, but she did.

Vague ones, true, but with the language of the fan, she hoped to get at least one third of her revenge taken care of today. And at the same time, perhaps she could find a way to make Kit Stanhope stop treating her like a child.

Belle continued to scheme and fan herself as Kit and Alvina carried on a conversation about people Belle didn't know. Then, as Belle cooled and slowed her vigorous hand movement, the picture on the fan caught her eye.

Oh, dear. Was that what she thought it was?

She spread it out surreptitiously and took a good look, staring in rising horror at the scene depicted. Some exacting artist had painted Adam and Eve in the Garden of Eden . . . unclothed . . . in full frontal anatomical detail.

Oh, my, was that what a man's nether parts looked like? Did Kit have one of those?

Belle snapped the fan shut and felt her face heat in embarrassment, then had to fight an urge to peer into Kit's lap to see if she could discern an answer to her question.

"Are you all right?" Alvina asked.

Belle jumped in startlement. Was her guilt written all over her face? Did Alvina know she was imagining Kit naked? Did *Kit*?

"I'm fine," Belle managed to say.

But she wasn't fine. She was nowhere near fine. In fact, she was positively frantic. Everyone at the garden party would have heard about her language of the fan by now and would be expecting her to use this . . . this . . . lewd instrument.

But how could she flash bare breasts and bare . . . other things in the faces of the social elite of Colorado Springs?

She couldn't, of course. Abruptly, her plans changed. Forget trying to exact revenge today. Instead, it was imperative she find a way to get rid of her shocking fan.

The only question was, how was she going to do it without causing undue comment?

Seven

As they drove to the garden party and Kit conversed on mundane topics with Miss Keithley, his mind was occupied with another matter entirely. His search for a suitable investment had proven difficult, so it appeared he would have to take another look at finding a wife, preferably an heiress. It might be the only way to salvage his future.

This garden party would be a good place to start shopping, especially since he had been wrong to think Belle might help introduce him to her *nouveau riche* friends. Surprisingly, he had discovered that Belle had few friends other than Miss Keithley, Madame Aglaia, and himself.

It wasn't that she was standoffish, it was just that she seemed wholly content within the bosom of her family. She and her sisters were so close, she had little need for outside friendships.

He envied them that. His own family had never had that sort of closeness. If they had, he probably wouldn't be in this mess in the first place.

And, to tell the truth, he would give a great deal to experience it for himself. A tiny voice whispered in his ear, *You can have that if you marry Belle. . . .*

No, that wouldn't do. She had made it very clear that she was trying to capture the attention of a specific man at this garden party. And though Kit wouldn't balk at trying to win her away from another man if he felt she was the perfect future Mrs. Kit Stanhope, the fact was, he wasn't sure at all.

Oh, Belle had the liveliness of spirit and mental agility he desired in a wife, but she lacked the one thing he found truly important—trust. His stupidity at the Garden of the Gods had seen to that.

He sensed a continued reserve in her though he had long since apologized for his ill-advised remark. No doubt she still nursed a grudge for being called homely. He winced at the memory. No wonder she didn't trust him enough to tell him the name of the man she was trying to impress.

And though he was rather enjoying the feel of her soft body pressed up against his side in the carriage, he felt her tense every time they were thrown against each other, as if she couldn't bear his touch.

Yet another reason why Belle wouldn't serve. Kit sighed. He'd just have to pay attention at the garden party and find a young woman who would.

The carriage stopped, and Kit sensed a marked increase in Belle's tension. "Are you sure you're all right?" he asked.

"Of course," she said, but there was a slightly alarmed expression on her face.

He lowered his voice as Miss Keithley exited the carriage. "Are you certain? You needn't do this if you don't wish to."

Belle seemed to waver, but said, "I'm just a little nervous."

He felt sure it was more than that, but obviously, she wasn't about to say more. Nodding, he helped her out of the carriage.

As she walked away, he noticed a tassel protruding

from beneath the cushion where she'd been sitting. Curious, he tugged on it, and pulled out her fan. Belle must really be nervous if she'd left this behind.

"Excuse me, Miss Sullivan," he said with a smile as he held it out to her. "You seem to have forgotten this."

She looked at it in disgust but made no move to take it.

He continued to offer the fan, wondering why she was regarding it as though it were a venomous snake. "I found it in the cushion. You must have dropped it by accident."

"Yes, yes, of course," she said with a forced laugh. She took it from him gingerly, as if she were afraid it might bite.

How odd. What was she thinking? Did she fear a repeat of the other night? "I don't think you need to fear feathers flying today." He looked around. "And there don't seem to be any cats present."

Though there *were* an abundance of boisterous children, dogs, goats, and other livestock in attendance. All in all, a typical party at Briarhurst Manor.

"I know," she said, but she still clutched her fan in a death grip, as if she were afraid it might fly off without her. But when she glanced around and her gaze rested on the animals, her gaze turned speculative.

Now what was going on in her agile mind?

Since Miss Keithley seemed to have been appropriated by a gaggle of her friends, Kit remembered his duty. "Have you met our hostess?" he asked. When Belle shook her head, he led her over to Cora Bell and introduced them to each other.

Mrs. Bell clasped her hands together. "Oh, how

marvelous," she exclaimed. "Another Bell. Are we related, dear?"

Though she was one of the leading society hostesses, Cora Bell was a bit scatterbrained. Kit hid his amusement as he watched Belle try to mask her confusion.

"No, I don't think so," Belle said warily. "My family comes from Ireland."

"Dr. Bell comes from Ireland, too," Cora enthused. "We probably are related and you just don't know it."

Belle glanced up at Kit, evidently looking for a clue on how to answer, but he could do nothing but grin at her.

"I suppose it's possible," Belle said with a weak smile.

"Marvelous," Cora Bell said. "And I have heard wonderful things about your language of the fan. Will you demonstrate it for us later?"

Belle blanched and said swiftly, "Oh, no. I couldn't."

"No?" Cora looked as surprised as Kit felt.

Belle certainly seemed to enjoy showing her prowess the other night. What was wrong?

Belle recovered quickly. "I mean . . . it would be impolite of me to monopolize your guests."

"Oh, nonsense," Cora said, waving away her objection. "I'm sure everyone will be thrilled to see it. No more excuses, please. You simply *must* demonstrate for us."

He didn't think it was possible, but Belle looked even more wan than before. "Later, perhaps?" she asked, making it sound more like a plea for a pardon than a graceful acquiescence. But she gripped her fan so tightly that her knuckles had turned white.

"Of course." Cora waved her arms regally. "Now, go have fun."

Kit drew Belle away. "What was that all about?" he murmured for her ears alone as they strolled one of the paths.

"I don't know," Belle said, placing her hands behind her back as if she were hiding something. "She's a bit dotty, isn't she?"

Kit raised an eyebrow. "You're deliberately misunderstanding me. I meant, of course, what's wrong with you?"

Belle stiffened. "I don't know what you mean." She glanced down at her clasped hands, more to avoid his gaze than anything else, he suspected.

Odd—her hands were empty now, but she'd been holding the fan just a moment ago. . . . Glancing back the way they had come, Kit spotted the missing accessory under a bush alongside the path. "Ah, you've lost your fan again." He retrieved it for her quickly, but when he handed it to her, she looked annoyed instead of thankful.

Could it be the loss of her fan was deliberate? Curious now, Kit resolved to figure out exactly what was going on.

As they walked the garden paths and chatted with the other guests, Kit noticed that Belle didn't even attempt to use her fan as she had learned. Even when people asked her to demonstrate her knowledge, she put them off with a vague promise to show everyone later or used someone else's fan.

In the meantime, she kept her own firmly closed . . . except when she tried to lose it.

It became an unspoken game between them. Belle would drop the fan when he wasn't looking, then he would find where she had secreted it. Each time he found it and presented it to her, she received it with more and more ill grace.

Though it amused him, he would have stopped the game if she weren't so adamant about insisting nothing was wrong.

Damn it, why won't she confide in me?

Then a new player entered the game. A woman whose name he didn't catch stopped Belle. "Ah, Miss Sullivan. I hear you are a connoisseur of fans, as am I." The woman spread her fan, saying, "This is a Paris original, with a series of charming French vignettes painted on it."

Belle dutifully admired it, but when the woman asked, "May I see yours?" Belle blanched.

"Oh, no," she said. "It's nowhere near as splendid as yours."

The woman raised her eyebrows, still friendly. "That doesn't matter. I am interested in all manner of fans." She reached for Belle's. "I see your sticks are made of cedar. Is it painted?"

Belle moved the fan out of the woman's reach, placing her hands behind her back firmly but unmistakably. "Yes, it is, but you don't want to see it."

"I don't?" the woman asked, looking a little insulted now. "Why not?"

"Because . . . because my sister painted it," Belle said quickly. "I carry it because she made it for me, but it is quite hideous. Really, I wouldn't want to offend your eyes with such a sight."

Losing interest now that she had learned the fan was a poor homemade article, the woman wandered away.

Kit glanced down to ask Belle once more what was going on and noticed that she had angled her body so that her back was toward a rather large, shaggy white dog. He smothered a grin when it became obvious she was twirling the tasseled end in a rather obvious attempt to entice the dog to make off with it.

But, unlike Miss Keithley's cats, the dog wasn't interested in feminine fripperies. Not when there was food around. He sniffed the breeze and bounded away, in search of more edible treats, no doubt.

Kit grinned and reached behind her to take her fan. "Why don't you just dip it in some sauce and feed it to the goats?"

For a moment, Belle looked as if she was actually considering the idea, but as he started to open it, she snatched it out of his hands and looked away. "Why, what do you mean?"

Taking her chin gently between his fingers, Kit turned her face up to meet his gaze. "What's wrong with the fan?"

She lowered her eyes. "Nothing."

"You're not very good at prevarication, you know."

She tried to act indignant. "Are you calling me a liar?"

He wasn't having any of her distractions. Giving her an admonitory look, he said, "The truth, please. Why are you trying to get rid of it?" He cast about for a reason. "Does it have a hole in it? Is it tearing like the other one?"

"No, it's quite sturdy," she said with annoyance he sensed was directed more at the fan than himself.

"Does it not open properly?"

"It opens just fine," she snapped.

Annoyed now himself, Kit said, "Can you not trust me for once? You're paying me to advise you on how to get along in society. To do that, I need to understand why you're acting so oddly."

"I'm not acting oddly," Belle protested, but her heart obviously wasn't in it.

Sensing she was weakening, Kit said, "May I see the fan, please?"

Belle clutched it tightly in both hands. "No, it's too . . . embarrassing."

His eyebrows rose. Now they were finally getting somewhere. "Why is it embarrassing?"

She flushed. "I . . . it just is."

He held out his hand. "May I see it?"

Her blush deepened. "I don't think that's such a good idea."

"It's all right," he assured her softly. "I'm not easily embarrassed."

"Perhaps you're not," she exclaimed, "but I am!"

He continued to hold out his hand, and she sighed. "All right, but I don't want anyone else to see it." Looking both ways, she was evidently satisfied they were unobserved, for she pulled him into a secluded bower and reluctantly placed the fan in his hand.

Very curious now, Kit opened the fan and hid a grin. The nude figures depicted there had no doubt given the sheltered Belle quite a shock. Especially since both figures seemed extraordinarily well endowed.

He glanced at Belle in mock admonition, though he spoke in a low tone to keep them from being discovered there in their hiding place. "I'm surprised at you, Miss Sullivan—carrying such a lewd instrument. And you say your sister made this?"

Belle slapped his arm and he couldn't help but laugh.

"Stop that," she hissed. "You know I didn't choose it on purpose—Charisma picked it out. And before you say anything else, I'm sure she didn't notice the picture either. Quit laughing and help me get rid of it."

He tried to control his mirth. "How? Shall I find a goat and give him a treat?"

"No," she said reluctantly. "With my luck, he'd chew off everything but the . . . the pertinent parts and drop it in Mrs. Bell's lap. Can't we just lose it in the bushes?"

"And chance some child coming upon it unaware and getting an eyeful of those, er, pertinent parts?"

"Oh, I suppose not," Belle said, crestfallen. "What shall I do with it, then?"

Kit slid it up his sleeve until it was out of sight. "Why don't I just keep it for you until after we leave?"

"Fine. In fact, keep it forever—I don't want anything else to do with it."

"Very well, then. Shall I see if I can procure another for you?"

"No," she said, sounding irritable. "It's already ruined my plan."

"Plan? What plan is that?"

Looking aghast, she said quickly, "I mean my day. It's ruined my day." In an obvious attempt to change the subject, she added, "If Mrs. Bell wants me to demonstrate the language of the fan, she'll just have to lend me one. Or perhaps I can borrow Alvina's. What do you think?"

He thought she was trying to change the subject. What was she up to? And what part did she expect him to play in her schemes? "What plan?" he persisted.

She hesitated, then said with an airy wave of her hand, "Oh, you know. My plan to become a beauty and take the town by storm."

It almost rang true, but not quite. Obviously, she was lying again. In the privacy of their screened abode, he grasped her chin once more and turned her gaze to face his. "Why don't you tell me the truth?"

She glanced down and away though her chin was still caught in his grasp. When she moistened her lips, he sensed another lie coming. Moving closer, he muttered, "Can't you trust me for once?"

Damn, that came out more plaintive and with more intensity than he had intended. Belle's gaze flew to his, and her eyes opened wide in surprise.

Kit shuttered his eyes immediately, not wanting her to know how much her trust meant to him. But her face was so near and her skin so soft . . . He couldn't help but let his fingers wander to caress her chin, to cup her cheek in his hand.

He stared down at her and found her gazing at his mouth in wonder, her lips slightly parted. Her very kissable lips . . .

He leaned down to capture those lips with his but froze when he heard a rustle in the bushes. He jerked away. Dear Lord, what was he doing? This was Belle, his student. He was supposed to protect her virtue, not harm it.

He stepped back and glanced around, wondering if they'd been observed. The bushes rustled some more, then opened to reveal the dog they'd seen earlier, triumphant now with a chicken leg in his mouth. The dog gave them a wary look, then veered away and ran off once more.

Kit relaxed. But his relief was short-lived as he

realized how badly he could have compromised Belle. Unforgivable.

"I beg your pardon," he said swiftly. "That should not have happened."

Belle wouldn't meet his gaze, but he could see that her fair, freckled skin had reddened, and not from the sun, he would wager.

Gesturing toward the path, he said, "Shall we join the others?"

"Of course," she said and stepped out briskly.

Kit berated himself. Not only had he almost gone beyond the pale, but Belle's antics had distracted him so much, he had wholly forgotten his original purpose here—to search for a potential wife. Intending to rectify that omission immediately, he steered them toward a large group of people.

Luckily, the most attractive of the local heiresses, Miss Helena Downs, was present. As were Belle's most persistent suitors—Latham and Winthrop. The moment Belle's swains descended upon her, Kit took the opportunity to drift closer to Miss Downs.

The heiress was very shy, but by dint of gentle questioning and with the help of her friends, he was able to discern that her passion was opera and she planned to attend Colorado Springs' new Opera House next week with her parents. Pleased with this bit of intelligence, Kit promised to see her there and made his way back to Belle.

Latham and Winthrop were still hovering, doing their utmost to capture her notice. Belle looked pleased by the attention, but the abortive motion of her hands made it obvious she missed having a fan in them.

Wickedly, Kit thought about offering her the one

up his sleeve, but knew she'd never forgive him if
he did.

Suddenly, he saw her stiffen. He moved closer to
discern her problem, and there was a sudden silence
as the two men regarded Belle with expectation.

"Did I come at a bad time?" Kit drawled.

"Oh, no," Belle assured him, though two bright
spots of color showed on her cheeks. "They were just
explaining their role in bringing me into fashion,
and offered to do the same for my sisters." She gave
Kit a brittle smile. "Charisma and Grace are in such
need of it, you see."

He did see. But obviously, these two clods didn't.
Insulting Belle's sisters was one sure way to get her
back up. "Ah, but I'm sure your sisters need no
help from anyone. They are charming originals just
as they are." And his raised eyebrows dared Latham
and Winthrop to disagree.

Finally realizing their *faux pas*, the two hurriedly
agreed with Kit, speaking almost simultaneously.
"Oh, yes, charming." "Original." "Just as he said."
"Quite." They practically tumbled over each other
and their own tongues in their haste to get the
assurances out.

Belle gave them a tight smile and they must have
felt forgiven, for they hurried off before she could
change her mind.

Kit turned to share his amusement with Belle but
she was looking peaked and holding one hand to
her head. "Are you feeling quite the thing?"

"No, I think I have a headache."

And Kit knew exactly who had caused it—the
idiots. "Shall we leave, then?"

"I don't know—I don't want to curtail your

enjoyment, and Mrs. Bell did ask me to demonstrate the fan. . . ."

"I'm quite ready to leave if you are," Kit assured her. He beckoned Alvina over. "Shall I make our excuses?"

"Yes, thank you."

But as they drove home, Kit recalled how skill-fully Belle had deflected questions about her "plan." He didn't believe her protestations for a moment, of course—she was still a poor liar.

Just what was she up to?

Belle had put her sisters off yesterday after her return from the garden party, pleading her headache as an excuse. But now that it was morn-ing, they descended upon her bedroom, demanding an explanation.

Belle tried to ignore them by pulling the covers over her head, but Charisma ruthlessly pulled them away.

Grace bounced on the bed, making the bed and everything else in the room quake and quiver. "What happened yesterday?" she asked eagerly. "Did you get revenge on one of the threescum?"

Belle just moaned, reluctant to leave her com-fortable bed and confess to failure once more.

"I doubt it," Charisma said dryly, placing her hands on Grace's shoulders to stop her bouncing. "Or she would have gloated already. Something went wrong, didn't it?"

Since Charisma accompanied that observation with a poke in Belle's side, Belle was hard put to ignore her. "Oh, all right," she said crossly, sitting up to glare at her sister. "Yes, something went wrong—with that fan you picked out for me."

Charisma raised an elegant eyebrow. "What was wrong with it? It looked sturdy enough to me."

"Oh, it was. Too sturdy."

"What happened?" Grace asked, wide-eyed.

"Charisma forgot to look at the picture."

"So?" Charisma said.

"So it was a scene of Adam and Eve . . . unclothed." She lowered her voice and gestured vaguely below her waist. *"Explicitly* unclothed."

"Really?" Charisma asked with a twinkle in her eye. "Where is it? I'd like to see what a man's—"

"Don't you dare say it," Grace interrupted her with a shocked look. "Or I'll tell Mama."

"Don't be silly," Charisma scoffed. "I was just going to say I'd like to see what a man's . . . parts look like." She turned a curious gaze on Belle. "What *do* they look like?"

"Well, I'm not going to tell you," Belle said vehemently. She could just imagine herself trying to describe that odd appendage she'd seen only too briefly. "And I don't have the fan anymore—I got rid of it. You'll just have to wait until you're married to satisfy your curiosity."

"Spoilsport," Charisma muttered.

Belle was unmoved. "Well, if you'd looked at the fan before you gave it to me, you'd know by now." And Belle would have been spared the embarrassment.

Charisma cast a speculative glance at Belle's box of fans. "I wonder . . ."

"Keep your wondering to yourself," Belle said, jumping out of bed to snatch up the box and shove it under the bed. She had to do something to protect her sisters from the strange, warm, tingly sensations such pictures evoked.

Or was it the thought of Kit's parts that made Belle feel that way?

No matter, she shouldn't be thinking of Kit that way, anyway. "And from now on, I'll choose my own fans, thank you very much."

Charisma shrugged, pretending indifference. But Grace looked concerned. "Maybe you should give up on the idea of revenge altogether."

Belle had been thinking that, too, until her encounter with Harold and George yesterday. Why, they had the nerve to repeat their assertion that Charisma was overly bold and Grace too clumsy. Worse, they had suggested that all her sisters needed was a little guidance from them to be accepted in society. The scum.

Belle scowled. She didn't want to tell her sisters that and upset them all over again. Big sister Belle would take care of it for them. "No, I'm definitely going to get revenge."

"But how?" Charisma asked. "Do you have a plan?"

"Sort of. Stanhope invited me to the Opera House next weekend. I'll just have to put the first phase into place then."

"Really?" Grace asked. "You're going to the opera with Mr. Stanhope? How exciting."

Belle had thought so, too, when he asked her in the carriage on the way home. That is, until he made it sound like yet another lesson in her ongoing attempts at refinement. "Not really," she admitted. "It's just part of the job for him." She looked at the bedside clock. "And I'd better get ready—I'm supposed to meet him and Miss Keithley at Madame Aglaia's in an hour and a half."

"And Mama is expecting us to go shopping with her this morning," Grace said.

So they left Belle alone to stew over her failure and plan her next foray into revenge. She anticipated no problems in bringing Harold and George to heel, but Kit was another matter.

Yesterday, she'd almost thought she'd had him. He'd been so close, so tender, so on the verge of kissing her.

Her heart beat faster at the memory and she had a strange fluttering in her middle. She'd been so eager to experience her first kiss . . . especially when he lowered that wonderful mouth toward hers. Then he had jerked away, darn it. Just when things were getting really interesting. . . .

Every time it seemed he was getting close to falling under her spell, something happened to make him back away. Frustrated, she wondered why the man had so much self-control . . . and how she could break it. She longed to be in his arms, feel his lips against hers, get a peek at him without his clothes . . .

Oh, dear. Where had *that* thought come from? It was that horrid fan—it had put these strange ideas in her head. Belle consoled herself with the assurance that she wanted Kit falling for her only so she could spurn him, punish him for his rude remarks.

She slumped in relief. Yes, that was it. After all, he was one of the threescum.

But unfortunately, Kit had been distracted at the party after he had wrenched himself away from her . . . and he had paid a great deal too much attention to Miss Downs. Frowning, Belle wondered what Helena had that she didn't. Why had Kit left Belle's side to be so attentive to such a quiet little mouse? If Belle knew the answer to that question, it might help her capture all of Kit's attention for herself.

Was it the girl's meekness? No, he seemed to enjoy their spirited discussions. Belle considered and discarded a dozen different attributes, then finally realized Miss Downs's one outstanding charm—her milk-white complexion.

Belle slumped in defeat. She might as well give up—she'd never be able to achieve such beautiful coloring with these freckles.

Or could she? Grinning, Belle realized she needed to have a private talk with Madame Aglaia.

After Alvina arrived and the two of them made their way to Madame Aglaia's, Belle wondered how she was going to pull Madame aside to discuss the delicate subject of cosmetics. She didn't want to broach the subject in front of Alvina and Kit—she doubted they'd approve.

She needn't have worried, however. Kit was already there, and he immediately engaged Alvina in a discussion of what Belle should wear to the opera, leaving Madame to apologize profusely for having sent Belle such an inappropriate fashion accessory.

"I should have checked the fans more carefully," she mourned.

"It's all right—no harm done," Belle assured her.

"Oh, no, Mr. Stanhope told me how very mortified you were. Please, is there anything I can do to make it up to you?"

Belle smiled. "Well, as a matter of fact, there is." Pulling the dressmaker aside, she said, "Do you remember our earlier discussion about my freckles?"

"Yes, of course. But I think they're quite attractive. Are you certain you wish to be rid of them?"

Madame was just being kind. "Positive." When the dressmaker continued to look skeptical, Belle added, "The gentleman I'm interested in seems to prefer young women with white complexions, free of blemishes."

"I see," she said doubtfully. "But if you're unwilling to use cosmetics, I'm not sure there's anything we can do."

"Well, I'm not wholly averse to the idea . . ." Belle trailed off with a significant glance at her other two mentors, hoping Madame would get the idea.

Apparently, she did. "Ah, I see. Well, if you wish to be discreet . . ."

Belle nodded vigorously. She wanted to have a freckle-free face, but didn't want the cosmetics to be so obvious that she gained a reputation for being fast. "I do."

Madame looked thoughtful. "Then it would be best to try it under the soft, forgiving light of gaslight, instead of the bright sun."

"That sounds like a good idea," Belle said. "What did you have in mind?"

"There is a product I've heard of. . . . I should be able to procure it before your evening at the opera."

Belle beamed at her. "Oh, thank you, Madame. You're a life saver." With a complexion like Miss Downs's, Belle was sure to capture Kit's attention.

"Well, it's the least I can do after providing you with such inappropriate fans," Madame said, patting her hand. "Shall we join the others now?"

Belle nodded, and as she approached Kit and Alvina, Kit called her over to hold a length of cream-colored satin against her face. "She would look lovely in this, don't you think?" he asked.

Unexpectedly, an answer came from the doorway.

"Oh yes, indeed," Bridey Sullivan gushed as she surged into the room with Charisma and Grace in her wake. "Lord Stanhope, you are so perceptive. That would suit my little girl right down to the ground."

As Mama enthused over Kit's taste, Belle cast her sisters a horrified, questioning look. By dint of shrugs, wiggled eyebrows, and waving arms, they managed to convey that they had nothing to do with this. That they had, in fact, tried to dissuade Mama from coming in here.

Kit stiffened and Belle felt hot with embarrassment. Mama would ruin everything.

Even now, Mama was wagging her finger in Kit's face. "Naughty boy," she said with an arch look. "Arranging to meet my daughter like this. What will people say?"

Kit dropped the bolt of fabric onto the table and assumed a haughty expression. "I did nothing of the kind, Mrs. Sullivan," he said, lying without apparent compunction as Belle held her breath in dismay.

"Oh, no? Then what are you doing in a dressmaker's shop?"

Madame Aglaia stepped into the line of fire. "He was visiting me," she said quickly, continuing the fiction Kit had started. "We are in the way of being related."

"Really?"

Belle released the breath she had been holding, but Mama didn't look convinced.

"Quite so," Kit said. "And Miss Keithley asked for my opinion on the satin versus the . . . er, lace for Miss Sullivan."

"Yes," Alvina intervened. "And he was kind enough to give us his opinion."

Mama must have believed her, for her expression fell. "Oh, I see."

"But now, I must really be taking my leave," Kit said swiftly. Turning to Madame Aglaia, he said, "I'll see you another time, cousin."

"Of course," Madame said as Kit made a quick exit.

Once he was gone, Mama turned on Belle and pulled her aside to whisper, "You sly thing, you. Here you are, pretending you care nothing for catching a husband when you have cast your net for the most eligible bachelor in town."

"Oh, no, Mama." Horrified, Belle glanced at Alvina, hoping she hadn't overheard. The last thing Belle wanted was for Kit—or anyone—to think she was pursuing him.

Mama patted her hand. "It's all right, dear." She sighed in ecstasy. "It would be so nice to have an aristocrat in the family. Do what you can to attract him—you won't hear any recriminations from me."

"Yes, Mama," Belle mumbled. It was easier just to agree. After all, she had every intention of doing just that. For once, she and Mama were in perfect accord.

But Belle had an entirely different end result in mind. . . .

Eight

For a week, Belle used every method she had heard of to get rid of her freckles, from bleaching them with lemon to abrading her skin with a solution of borax and rosewater. Unfortunately, nothing worked. They just made her skin sting and smell odd, and the freckles were still there.

In her room, she slumped in dejection. She had so hoped to have white skin for this evening without the use of cosmetics, but it was not to be. If she wanted to be beautiful, she would just have to slather some concoction on her face. That is, if Madame Aglaia had been able to find one that would work.

Since Alvina had other plans for the evening, Belle had enlisted the rest of her family to ensure that Mama was too busy to accompany her to the opera, so that Madame could play chaperone.

When Madame finally arrived, she presented Belle with a fan. "I think this is what you requested."

Belle spread it open in delight. Made of large plumes of ostrich feathers, the fan opened in graceful elegance, complete with a design of a cat at the base, staring up at the feathers with a mischievous look in its eyes. Even better, the handle had a lorgnette built into it so Belle could get a better look at what was happening onstage at the opera. "Why, it's perfect," Belle exclaimed. Functional as well as beautiful. "How ever did you find it?"

Madame shrugged. "I made it myself, once I knew what you were looking for."

Not only was she a fabulous dressmaker, but she had other accomplishments as well. "It's wonderful," Belle said and hugged her. Belle was taking no chances on something being wrong with this fan, so she had vowed to check it thoroughly herself. After she did so, she said, "Now, tell me. Have you come up with something to cover my freckles?"

With a smile, Madame produced a small jar. "I have indeed."

Belle clapped her hands. "Wonderful. Shall we try it?"

"Yes, of course." Madame helped her put the cream on, saying, "When I was in France, this was called *fard blanc de bismuth*, but is known here as pearl powder."

As Belle regarded herself in the mirror of her dressing table, Charisma and Grace entered without knocking, and Charisma stared at Belle's reflection. "What do you have on your face?" she asked in horror.

Belle lifted her chin in defiance. "Madame calls it pearl powder. Don't you think it makes my complexion look better?" Belle liked the way it looked—it glowed a pearlescent white with nary a freckle in sight. And luckily, she only needed to use it on her face since her neck and chest were rarely exposed to the sun.

Grace tripped over the rug as she moved closer to get a better look, but quickly righted herself. "I don't know," she said. "You look kind of pasty. . . ."

"Not pasty," Belle insisted. "A delicate milky white, don't you think?" Just like Miss Downs.

"Here," Madame said. "Let me turn down the lights as they will appear at the opera. Now, what do you think?"

Belle thought she looked beautiful.

Charisma nodded grudgingly. "It looks better like that. Your freckles are gone, and your skin does look white—almost natural. But . . . do you have to wear that muck on your face?"

Belle gave her an admonitory glance. "Not everyone has a complexion as smooth and creamy as yours and Grace's," she reminded her sister. "Some of us just need a little help." She glanced at herself in the mirror once more, very pleased with the result. "And I do need to be beautiful tonight."

"Oh, you are," Grace assured her.

Madame raised an eyebrow. "And you will be even more so if you were to dress for the occasion . . . ?"

Belle laughed. "I guess it wouldn't do to arrive at the opera in my robe."

So, Madame helped her get dressed in the dazzling creation she had made for Belle—emerald green satin trimmed with a spangly material that sparkled as if she had captured the very stars in the sky. And with her shoulders bare and the tight corset making her breasts plump into generous mounds, she looked positively . . . feminine.

It wasn't a look she had striven for before, but Belle rather liked it. For once, she looked like a woman.

Once Madame dressed her hair up in a style that made her neck look long and graceful, Belle stared at her reflection in awe. *Oh, my.* She had never imagined she could look so wondrous.

Even Charisma nodded approvingly. "No one will call you homely now," she declared.

Grace beamed at her. "You'll have the men falling all over themselves to get to you."

Belle laughed. "You're exaggerating," she said, but she was very pleased. Tonight, surely she would capture at least one man's heart.

Maybe even two.

To ensure that Kit saw her at her best, they turned the lights down in the hall. After her sisters had positioned him for the best possible view, Belle made a graceful entrance. She paused for a moment so he could get the full effect of the vision she knew herself to be and held her breath, waiting for his reaction.

He just stared at her for a moment, apparently speechless.

Belle smiled to herself. An auspicious beginning.

"You look . . . stunning," he said. And this time, his expression matched his words as his gaze drifted down to her décolletage and lingered there.

Belle's breasts tightened in response and goose bumps covered her bare flesh. *Oh, my*, she thought again as her gaze locked on his sinful mouth. He looked rather marvelous himself. His hair appeared starkly white-blond against the rich black of his evening dress, making him look totally handsome and very sleek and sophisticated.

Her breathing quickened and she felt the tips of her breasts crinkle in response as a warm fluttering started in the pit of her stomach. Oh, dear, Kit Stanhope made her feel positively decadent.

She simply stood there, reeling with the sensations, not sure what to do next.

"Are you cold, dear?" Madame asked with a smile

and draped a gauzy spangled wrap around Belle's shoulders.

Grateful for being given something to do, Belle drew the flimsy shawl around her bare skin, trying to warm herself.

Kit's gaze lifted to her face and he seemed to come to his senses. Odd. Had her expanse of flesh had that much effect on him? As an experiment, she opened the wrap, once more revealing her décolletage. Sure enough, Kit's gaze dove back to the shadowy cleft as if his eyes were a magnet and her breasts the lodestone.

She casually closed the wrap again, and his gaze cleared once more. How interesting. She had never realized these two mounds of flesh constituted such a powerful weapon. Pleased with the discovery, she decided to consider carefully how to deploy them.

He cleared his throat. "You look . . ." He paused, apparently unable to find the appropriate word.

"Adequate?" Belle supplied with a half-smile.

He waved her words away impatiently. "You know better than that. You look . . . stupendous. Breathtaking. Extraordinary. You will eclipse all other women at the opera."

A warm glow filled Belle. It was quite obvious he wasn't merely trying to be polite and was perhaps exaggerating only a little. It was balm to her foolish pride. "Do go on," she said with a mischievous smile. This certainly made up for being called homely.

Kit's eyes laughed with her as he placed a hand over his heart. "Ah, but words fail to capture the vitality of your presence." He gestured expansively, getting into it now. "No one can hold a candle to your radiance. Your hair is a crown of fiery glory, your eyes are pools of liquid moonlight, your nose is—"

"Enough," Belle said, laughing. "I get the idea. Though I see you can be quite poetic when you try."

A smile remained upon his lips, but his eyes turned serious. "Ah, but only when properly inspired."

He leaned down to kiss her hand and Belle's heart once more thumped erratically in her chest. Devil take him—she shouldn't react so improperly to the man on whom she had vowed vengeance.

She did still want vengeance, didn't she? Yes, of course she did—for her sisters' sake.

Kit gave her a quizzical look when she withdrew her hand with a shaky breath, but he said only, "Shall we go?"

Belle glanced up, then blushed. She had been so caught up with Kit, she had entirely forgotten they had an audience. Madame was watching them with a small smile, and Charisma and Grace looked as stunned as she felt. Belle averted her gaze, not wanting them to see whatever showed in her eyes. "Yes, I think we'd better go, or we'll be late."

Charisma and Grace wished them well, and Belle left with Kit and Madame for the opera. The carriage he had rented this time was larger than the one before, and they were able to sit on the same seat without touching.

But even so, she could still feel the warmth emanating from his body, sense his decidedly masculine presence envelop her. She inhaled, loving the scent that was uniquely Kit, wishing they were alone in the darkness so she could move closer, feel his body against hers, trace those decadent lips. . . .

Madame cleared her throat, and Belle jumped in dismay. Oh, no, she was doing it again. She couldn't moon over Kit. Not if she wanted to get revenge.

He certainly seemed smitten this evening. All she had to do was open her wrap and she had him under her spell. Would it be better to make Kit her first victim instead?

The anguish that thought caused surprised her. Quickly, she rejected that idea. After all, she needed him to squire her around to the parties, including the Founders' Day Ball in July. No, Kit definitely had to be last. That meant she had to set her sights on either Harold or George tonight. Relief filled her at the thought, but she refused to speculate why.

When they arrived at the Opera House, Belle was pleased to see that Kit had reserved box seats. Now she could not only see everyone and everything, but be seen by the people who mattered.

As they seated themselves, Madame handed Belle her fan. Kit raised his eyebrows. "Feathers? You're brave tonight."

Belle smiled. "I assure you they are securely attached and I didn't let Grace anywhere near it." She spread open the plumes to display the decoration at the base of the fan. "And since this is probably the only cat we'll see tonight, I doubt I have anything to fear. Do you?"

He quirked a smile at her. "Very clever."

Belle thought so—better to make fun of herself than to be caught out when others did it to her. "Thank you."

"But no Adam and Eve?" he asked with a grin.

Belle grimaced. "Of course not. You and I are the only ones who know of *that* embarrassment."

Kit smiled but said nothing as Belle's newfound friends inundated their box, all exclaiming over her clever fan. Impatiently, she waited for Harold or George to join the rest. Where were they? If they didn't come, her plan would be ruined.

Then, finally, Harold arrived—without George for once. Smiling at him, Belle loosened her shawl and leaned forward to greet him warmly, deploying her weapons to full advantage.

Harold's gaze locked on target and Belle smiled to herself. *Bull's-eye.* "How are you this evening, Mr. Latham?"

"F-fine," he stuttered. Then his gaze rose to hers. "I thought you were mad at us. Uh, me. After the garden party?"

"Not at all," Belle assured him with an arch look over her fan. "I merely had the headache. I'm afraid I was terribly rude to you."

"Oh, no. You couldn't— You wouldn't—" His gaze lowered to her chest once more and he swallowed hard. "You look quite . . . magnificent this evening. George will be sorry he missed them." He colored and stammered out, "I—I mean you. He'll be sorry he missed *you.*"

And this was the man who had called *Grace* clumsy . . . ? Well, her revenge would be just as fitting. Belle gave him a sultry look and ran her fan along his sleeve with a little caress. "Well, I'm not sorry."

He gulped again. "You—you're not?"

"No," she assured him softly. "I've been wanting to get to know you better."

"Me, too," he said eagerly. "Get to know you, I mean."

She smiled. "Good." But activity on the stage heralded an interruption, so she gave him a regretful smile. "It appears the opera is beginning." She lowered her voice and peered at him coquettishly over the top of her fan. "Perhaps we'll see each other at the interval . . . ?"

He nodded vigorously. "Of course. The interval. See you then."

As he departed, Belle noticed that while she had been occupied with Harold, Kit had been conversing with Miss Downs again. Belle waited impatiently as the young girl flirted a bit more with Kit, then took her leave. What was going on here? Was Kit becoming interested in that meek little mouse?

It appeared that way. But why? Tonight, Belle's skin was just as white as Miss Downs's and her twin stockpiles of ammunition were far larger. It didn't seem fair that Kit should give the insipid girl more attention than he gave Belle.

As the last visitor left their box, Kit turned toward her with a questioning look. "What was that all about?"

"What?"

"You were flirting shamelessly with Harold Latham."

Belle seated herself with a huff. "Like you were with Miss Downs?"

He raised an eyebrow. "I was merely being polite."

"What makes you think I wasn't?" she challenged.

A sardonic grin graced his face. "The fact that you were displaying your . . . charms like a peacock on parade?"

"I was not." How dared he? Especially since he no longer seemed so enamored of those "charms." "I was just trying to show him how sorry I was for being rude to him at the garden party."

"*You* were rude to *him*? I—"

"Shh," she said and gestured toward the stage. "The curtain's rising." And not a moment too soon, either.

Kit sat stiffly for a moment. Then, as the opera unfolded, he spoke in a low voice to explain the story to her.

With the lights dimmed, the sound of his rich voice and the feel of his warm breath on her face and neck made her shiver with feelings she didn't understand. It was so dark in the theater now that no one would know if he leaned a little closer, pressed his luscious lips to her neck. . . .

Belle felt herself swaying toward him and stopped herself abruptly. She shouldn't let Kit Stanhope's attractiveness divert her—she must remember her original plan. Steeling herself against him, Belle leaned away and listened with only half an ear.

Kit might think the purpose of coming here was to see *Camille*, but Belle knew better. The purpose was to see and be seen. She used her lorgnette to scan the house for Harold and spotted him downstairs, gazing up at her in rapt admiration. Good—she intended to keep him that way. When Kit wasn't looking, she flirted with Harold over her fan.

Once the intermission arrived, Harold was there like a shot, offering to get her a lemonade. She favored him with a smile, wondering how she was going to get rid of Kit and Madame so she could put her plan into effect.

Strangely enough, Madame provided the ruse to distract Kit, noticing that Miss Downs had dropped one of her earrings on the floor. Kit offered to return it to her, so Belle was free to accept Harold's offer of a walk through the house.

Leaving her wrap behind, she wandered off with Harold and Madame in attendance. Once Harold had procured a lemonade for her and Madame, Belle knew she had to act quickly, before the intermission was over, especially since she had no idea how long it would last. Shivering, she said, "Oh, no. I must have left my shawl in the box. Would you be a dear, Madame, and retrieve it for me?"

Madame raised an eyebrow and Belle had the distinct impression she wasn't fooling the woman one bit, but she went off to do Belle's bidding nonetheless.

Of course, Belle had no intention of being there when she got back. Now was the time to put her plan into effect.

Surprisingly, she felt a little apprehensive.

Ridiculous—now was the perfect time to enact her revenge. Her sisters were counting on her. So, Belle strolled the corridors with Harold in close attendance, looking for a small alcove or something suitable. Spotting a small withdrawing room, she turned to Harold with a limp wrist against her brow and swayed a little. "Oh, dear, I'm feeling faint. . . ."

He looked anxious. "Should I get Madame Aglaia for you?"

What a dolt.

"Oh no," she said faintly. "But if I could just rest for a few minutes. . . ."

"Of course." He looked wildly around, then finally spotted the small room which had been in plain sight all along. "In here—will this do?"

"Oh, yes. I think so." Belle allowed herself to fall

limply but gracefully onto the small fainting couch inside. When Harold looked anxiously toward the door, she said, "Please don't leave me."

"Of course not," he said as he leaned over her protectively.

Now what? She sighed soulfully, then realized her ammunition had flattened out once she lay down. She raised herself to a sitting position, thereby bringing her bosom in close proximity to Harold's interested gaze.

He stared, transfixed, but she was becoming rather peeved with him. Would he never take the initiative? "You're so good to me," she said and laid her hand on his sleeve as she gazed up at him with a worshipful look.

"I am?"

"Positively wonderful," she assured him, laying it on as thick as she dared. "Whatever would I do without you?"

Harold gulped. "You needn't. Be without me, I mean. Let's get married."

What an ungainly proposal. She smiled, savoring the moment so she could tell her sisters all about it later. *This is for Grace.* She took a deep, satisfied breath and said, "I wouldn't marry you to save my soul."

He seemed a little confused by the disparity between her words and her expression. "You don't mean that," he said and reached for her.

She slid off the couch and out of his reach. "Oh, but I do. Who would want to marry a clumsy oaf like you?" She had a small pang of conscience—cruelty didn't come as easily as she'd hoped.

For a moment, his expression was truly priceless. Now *he* knew what it felt like to be humiliated, only she had done him the courtesy of doing it in private. She had her revenge at last.

"But you're so beautiful," he protested.

He still didn't get it. "And I wasn't worth your while when I was plain?"

Confused, he added, "That was then. This is now. I love you."

"But *I* don't love *you*," she said baldly. Nothing else seemed to be making it through that thick head of his.

His face darkened with anger. "That's not what you said a minute ago."

Before she knew what had happened, his arms were around her and he showered her face and neck with kisses.

"Stop!" she gasped out, but his only response was to grip her harder. Panic suffused her and she struggled to get away, to no avail. Fear had even paralyzed her voice—she tried to scream, but all that came out was a high-pitched "Eeeeek."

Suddenly, she saw a dark shape hurtle through the doorway and rip Harold away from her. *Thank God, it's Kit.* With one powerful blow, he knocked Harold to the floor.

The cretin just sprawled there, nursing his jaw and staring up at Kit with fear in his eyes. "I wasn't— I didn't—"

Kit cut him off with an angry slash of his hand. "It was quite obvious you were and you did. You, sir, are no gentleman."

"She wanted it," Harold said petulantly.

Kit gestured at Belle, who still stood there in shock with her bosom heaving. "Does that look like a lady who welcomed your advances?"

Belle raised her hands to her burning cheeks. She must look exceedingly disheveled.

Harold sneered. "She's no lady—"

But he broke off when Kit took a threatening step toward him. "She is far more a lady than you are a gentleman," Kit said in a murderous tone. "And if I ever hear you say anything to the contrary, I will ensure your father hears of your conduct. Am I understood?"

Harold scrambled to his feet. His face was white now, with his jaw darkening where Kit had hit him. "Perfectly," he spat out and rushed from the room.

Belle shrank away when he passed, but it appeared he was no longer interested in her, only in getting as far away as he could from Kit Stanhope and the humiliation he had just suffered.

"Are you all right?" Kit asked her. No, demanded was more like it. He was still exceedingly angry.

"I—I think so," Belle stammered out. "But thank heavens you arrived when you did."

Kit strode swiftly toward the door and closed and locked it.

"Wha-what are you doing?" Had she been wrenched from the arms of one man only to be ravished by another?

Kit stalked toward her and she backed against the wall, wide-eyed, shrinking away when he reached toward her. Then she sighed in relief when it appeared he was reaching for the gaslight above her head. But when he turned it down so there was only the faintest glow to light the area, she became nervous all over again.

"What are you doing?" she repeated in a tremulous voice, prepared to bolt for the door if she didn't like his answer. She wasn't sure she cared for this side of Kit.

"Preserving your reputation," he said in clipped tones.

Relief washed through her at his words, though they didn't make sense. "By locking me in with you?"

"No one knows you're in here with me but Harold, and I'm sure he's far away by now. I simply want to ensure no one sees you looking like this before I have a chance to get you away. We'll wait until the opera is well under way again, then leave with no one the wiser."

That made sense, and she felt the last of her tenseness fade away. "Looking like what?" She made a vain attempt to smooth the wrinkles Harold had put in her dress.

"As if you've been thoroughly debauched. Come," he said, "sit down before you fall down."

It was a good idea. Belle made her way to the couch in the dim light and Kit joined her there. But oddly, now that he had made it clear he was only there to preserve her reputation, she wished he wasn't quite so much the gentleman. She cast about for a topic of conversation, but nothing seemed appropriate in this darkened room with this virile man beside her.

Kit, though, had no such problem. "What were you thinking?" he burst out.

"What?"

"What sort of game were you playing?"

Belle stiffened. "I don't know what you mean," she lied.

Obviously impatient with her answer, he asked, "Is

Latham the man whose attention you were trying to catch?"

"No, of course not." Well, not in the way he meant.

"Then why did you lead him on?"

"I didn't," she protested, though she knew full well she had. But she couldn't admit it, for then she would have to explain why.

"You are more naive than I thought," Kit said with a sigh. "Don't you know what it means when a man looks at you that way?"

"You mean the same way *you* looked at me this evening?" Belle asked with a toss of her head. "No, tell me what it means."

Kit raked a hand through his hair. "It's not the same at all. When a man like Latham looks at you like that, he has only one thing in mind."

"What?"

"He desires you, wants you."

Well, wasn't that the point of her becoming beautiful? "What's wrong with that?"

"Nothing, if he never acts on it. But when given the opportunity you handed him, he will thoroughly compromise your reputation." Kit's voice tightened. "If I hadn't come along, you might have been ruined."

"Oh," she said in a small voice, suddenly realizing what "ruined" implied. She had been so intent on revenge, she hadn't realized the potential consequences to herself. Kit was right—she hadn't been thinking. "I'm sorry," she said in a small voice. "And I do appreciate your help. It seems I still have much to learn."

"That you do," he said in an uncompromising tone.

She didn't care for his tone, especially since she

was becoming more and more aware of him seated only inches away on the fainting couch. They were all alone in the darkened room, and he had been looking at her the same way Harold had. Didn't Kit have the faintest urge to compromise her himself?

"Perhaps you can help me understand something, then," Belle said.

"Perhaps. What is it?"

"Is kissing always so unpleasant?" She knew she was playing a dangerous game, but couldn't help herself.

"Why? Did he kiss you?"

"Well, he kissed my face and neck and landed one or two on my mouth. . . ."

"And you didn't enjoy it?"

She wished she could see his expression. "No—his mouth was wet. It was . . . unpleasant." Disgusting, in fact.

"It's not always so," Kit said softly. "In fact, when done correctly, it can be quite. . . enervating."

Her heart beat a little faster. *I knew it.* "Would you . . . care to demonstrate?" she asked, the darkness giving her an uncharacteristic boldness.

"Demonstrate?" he repeated in a choked tone.

"Yes," she said, trying to make it sound like a reasonable request. "Since you are my instructor, it seems only fitting that you should show me the proper way to go about it."

He tensed beside her, and she moved closer in encouragement. *Please, touch me.*

But Kit didn't accept her invitation. "I don't think it's a good idea," he murmured.

She was heartened by the sound of regret in his tone. "Oh, I see," she said with a sigh. "You don't know how to do it either."

He laughed. "You little minx—of course I do."

Encouraged by his laughter, she laid a bold hand on his thigh. "Then show me," she dared.

She heard Kit inhale sharply, but he didn't move.

Darn it, she knew he wanted to—why wouldn't he take advantage of her willingness? She let out a pretend sigh. "I guess I'll just have to find someone else to teach me, then."

"The devil you will," he grated out, and laid a hand over hers where it still rested on his thigh. "I know I'm going to regret this, but if I show you, will you promise not to pester me about it again? Or ask anyone else?"

"Of course," she said in as innocent a tone as she could manage. After all, she wasn't even sure she would like it. She just knew that with Kit, she would be safe. She closed her eyes and pursed her lips, raising her face to his.

"Not like that," he said softly.

She opened her eyes. "No?"

"No, like this. . . ."

He gently cupped her cheek in his hand and looked deep into her eyes. Dizziness assailed her. If his mere touch made her feel faint, what would his kiss be like? She hoped she was going to learn soon. . . .

He lowered his head and pressed those marvelous lips against her neck. *Oh, my.* Then again and again, lower. *Oh, yes.* Her bosom heaved with unexpressed emotion, and she felt the tips of her breasts tighten into hard little points.

And still he went lower, kissing his way down from the hollow of her neck to the cleft between her quivering mounds, pausing to lick her there with a flick of his tongue. *Oh, oh!*

Suddenly, she wanted more. More what, she didn't know. More kissing, more skin, more Kit. She grasped his head between her hands, feeling the urge to hold on to *something* or she feared she would spin out of control.

Then, finally, he lowered her to the couch and kissed her full on the lips—a soft exploratory caress that made her limbs melt like hot butter. His arms went around her and she held on for dear life, twining her fingers in his soft hair, holding him to her. One kiss led to another, then another, until she was breathless with the pure ecstasy of it.

She moaned and Kit raised his head. "Are you all right?" he asked huskily.

"Oh, yes. Please, don't stop." It felt so good to have him lying atop her, the hard ridge against her thigh testament to the fact that he had the same parts as the Adam on her fan.

With pale blue eyes glittering in the dim lamplight, he held her gaze with his as he kissed the swell of her breast above the dress once more. She inhaled sharply, but didn't move, sensing there was much more to come.

He kissed the other side softly, and Belle almost moaned in frustration as warmth flowed through her body. *More, I want more.*

He moved his hand to take the place of his lips, running his fingers gently across her bare skin. Then his fingers turned and she held her breath as he dipped them beneath the neckline of her gown. *Yes, yes!*

A sudden scratching sound made them both freeze. Was there someone at the door? Kit bolted to his feet and helped her to a sitting position.

Feeling as if she'd suddenly been doused with icy water, Belle quickly tried to right her clothing.

"Is someone there?" Kit called.

"Yes, it's just me," Madame Aglaia said. But, oddly, her voice came from the back of the room instead of the front.

Oh, dear. Belle had entirely forgotten about her chaperone. And so had Kit, it seemed. Darn it, Madame would have to show up just as things were getting good. . . .

There was a thud as Madame apparently ran into a piece of furniture. "Why is it so dark in here?" she asked.

Kit answered softly, "Because I didn't want anyone to know we were here until I could get Belle out safely."

"Ah, I thought as much," Madame said.

"How did you get in?" Kit asked.

"I found a back door." Madame had reached Belle by now and said in a wry tone, "Here's that wrap you wanted, dear."

"How did you know we were here?" Belle asked. Had Harold told the world?

"It's a chaperone's duty to know," Madame said vaguely. "When I saw Mr. Latham running out with a bruise developing on his jaw, I figured something was amiss." Then, turning to Kit, she added, "Don't you think you could turn the light on now that I'm here?"

"Of course." Kit went toward the light and turned it up.

Belle patted her hair a little nervously, hoping Madame would attribute any dishevelment to Harold's crude advances, since she had apparently figured out what happened.

But had she discerned what had happened with Kit as well? Belle raised shy eyes to him and was surprised to see a look of shock on his face.

"What's wrong?" she asked.

"Are you all right?" he demanded.

"Of course." Except for being a bit peeved that their kissing lesson had been cut off so abruptly. "Why do you ask?"

"Your face has gone totally gray . . ." he said hesitantly.

Madame glanced at Belle's face and gasped. "It's turned the color of ashes."

Belle's hands flew to her cheeks. Was this her punishment for acting like a wanton? No one had told her such a thing might happen. She leapt to her feet and went to the mirror over the mantel. They were right. She looked ghastly.

Kit came closer and peered at her face suspiciously, then wiped one finger across her cheek. Frowning, he said, "I thought your face looked whiter than normal this evening. You're using pearl powder, aren't you?"

Belle was so surprised, she couldn't confirm or deny his accusation. Quickly, she drew the wrap over her head to hide her face.

But Madame had no such problem. "How did you know?"

"Because bismuth, when it comes in contact with a sulfurous gas like those used in the jets in the opera house, turns a sickly gray," he said dryly. "That's why it is seldom used anymore."

"Oh, I'm sorry, dear," Madame said, increasing Belle's mortification. "I didn't know."

Belle just moaned beneath the covering of her wrap.

"Well, since your chaperone is here," Kit said, "I'll call for the carriage so we can get you home and you can wash your face." With that, he left.

Belle had never been so mortified in all her life. What must Kit think of her? First, he had caught her being compromised in the arms of another man. Then, when she had talked him into giving her a little lesson in love, he had been horrified to find he was not only kissing a girl who used cosmetics, but one who had gone as gray as a weathered board because of it.

"What have I done?" she wailed.

Cryptically, Madame said, "You really must be careful what you wish for. . . ."

Nine

Kit's pace was a little slower as he headed to Madame Aglaia's the next morning. How could he have been such a fool? He knew better than to succumb to the charms of an innocent. What he had almost done with Belle was too close to what he had been unjustly expelled from England for. Worse, he had flattened Harold for doing the same thing. How could he have acted so irresponsibly?

Just because Belle seemed to be repelled by Harold's advances and had encouraged Kit's was no justification for his actions. He relived the moment of his decision the previous night, trying to determine where he had gone wrong.

Actually, it had started the moment he saw Belle in that low-cut dress. . . .

Hers was no more daring than the gowns of the rest of the women at the opera, but for some reason, the sight of her bare flesh had sent his senses reeling. The schoolgirl had blossomed into a vibrant, entirely feminine woman. Then, when she had practically dared him to kiss her, to tutor her in the arts of love, what man could resist?

Not Kit, obviously. Though he should have. He just hoped they could remain friends after his misconduct.

He approached Madame Aglaia's establishment from the rear as had become his habit. Miss Keithley and Madame greeted him warmly, but Belle seemed not to know how to react to him. She blushed and mumbled something, then looked away.

Damn. Could the situation be any more awkward? He needed to take care of it right away, before the others wondered what had happened.

Approaching Belle, he asked, "May I see you alone for a moment?" When she looked doubtful, he added, "Just over on the other side of the room." He wanted to make it clear he didn't intend to ravish her and that she'd be in full view the whole time.

But when he had pulled her aside, she still looked uncomfortable and wouldn't meet his eyes. To wipe that look from her face, he said, "You're in much better looks this morning, Miss Sullivan. Not feeling so *gray,* are you?"

Her gaze flew to his with a surprised look. "Well, yes," she said with asperity. "But how unkind of you to remind me of my, er . . ." She trailed off, obviously uncertain how to finish the sentence.

"Adventures in cosmetics?" he supplied with a grin.

"Exactly." And though she tried to hide it, he could see humor peeking through in her eyes.

Ah, there was the Belle he knew and lov—er, liked. "Well, there was no need to resort to cosmetics, you know. I rather prefer your freckles."

"You do?" she asked in a surprised tone.

"Yes, of course. You look quite charming in them." But he hadn't come here to flirt with her again. He let his grin fade and assumed a serious expression, appropriate to the gravity of the situation. "I must apologize for last night," he said in a low voice.

Belle's gaze darted away and her color heightened. "There's no need."

"But there is. You were attacked by two men last night. The only difference is, one of them got away with it."

"That's not the only difference," she muttered with a roll of her eyes.

He ignored that aside, and chose not to think about what she meant. He glanced toward where Miss Keithley and Madame stood chatting. "Miss Keithley seems entirely unaware of what happened. I take it the word hasn't gotten out?"

Belle shook her head. "Madame said not to worry. No one knows a thing, except for Harold Latham, and he's inexplicably left town. To visit relatives in Philadelphia, they say."

"How convenient." He wondered how Madame knew they were in the clear. Then again, she was a very resourceful woman. "It doesn't matter if anyone else is aware of the events of last night or not. I am, and I hope you will accept my sincere apology. I did not act the gentleman."

She raised one eyebrow and tossed him a challenging look. "Really? How odd—you made me feel very much a woman."

Oh, Lord, what now? Panic suffused him. Had he created a monster? "Only your husband should make you feel that way," he said sternly.

Kit held his breath. It was practically a proposal. And if she insisted on marriage after his reprehensible behavior, he would have no choice but to agree. Though he was surprised to realize the thought of marriage to Belle wasn't horrible, marrying to avoid a scandal was an abysmal way to begin a life together.

She shrugged. "But other men don't think only a husband should make a woman feel that way—they seem to try to enjoy that pleasure with every woman they meet."

Did she imagine that made it acceptable? "That might do for a man, but for a woman, those same actions make the difference between a wife and a mistress."

Belle frowned, but she was too intelligent not to take his meaning—and to know he was right. She shrugged. "There's nothing to apologize for. You were just giving me a lesson, right?" She slanted him a bitter smile. "That's what I pay you for."

Ouch. "Well, I promise you, there will be no more such lessons. If any."

She frowned up at him. "But you promised."

He sighed, unwilling to go through that argument again. "Yes, I know. I promised to escort you to the Founders' Day Ball. I won't renege on that promise." And it couldn't come soon enough for him.

He started to take his leave, but Belle stopped him. "Wait a moment. I have a note for you from Father." At Kit's incredulous look, she added, "Don't worry. He asked me to drop it off at the front desk of your hotel. He didn't know I'd be seeing you here."

Kit opened the note, wondering what the man wanted. "He says he wants me to see him tomorrow morning on a matter of some importance." He blanched. "Do you think he knows?" The last thing Kit wanted to deal with was an irate father, especially when he was in the wrong.

"I doubt it," Belle said with a shrug. "He's probably found an investment for you. So," she added cheerily, "I'll see you at the house tomorrow morning."

Kit agreed, but he wasn't looking forward to it.

* * *

Kit arrived a little early for his appointment with Mr. Sullivan, but this time none of the man's daughters were in evidence, though Kit thought he heard their voices in other parts of the house. Nor was he kept waiting this time—he was shown into the study immediately.

Sullivan waved Kit brusquely to a chair as he finished with some paperwork on the desk. Once he was done, he turned and regarded Kit with a stern air. "Do ye know why I've asked ye here?"

Kit could think of several reasons, but only one he cared to voice aloud—especially when the man spoke in that uncompromising tone. Apprehensively, he ventured, "You've found an investment for me?"

"Well, no, but now that ye mention it, I just heard General Palmer is lookin' fer more investors to build a fancy hotel on a bit o' property at Pikes Peak and Cascade. Is that something ye might be interested in?"

Kit shook his head regretfully. "I'm afraid my father wouldn't approve of anything like that." It smacked too much of trade.

Sullivan nodded. "Aye, I thought as much." Then he speared Kit with a look. "Let me get this straight. Yer father just wants ye to find a good investment to see ye well established, is that it?"

"Well, yes." Provided, of course, that he found it acceptable.

Sullivan scratched his chin. "I know 'tis an odd question, but have ye thought about marryin' money to secure your position?"

"Yes, I've thought of it," Kit admitted. Though he wasn't proud of the fact.

Sullivan's eyes narrowed. "So that's why yer spendin' so much time with me daughter, eh?"

Kit swallowed hard. Oh, so that's what this meeting was really about. How much had the man heard? "No, sir. Though I've thought of marrying an heiress, I have come to realize that I cannot offer for a woman unless I have some real affection for her."

He'd learned that last evening. Miss Downs was a sweet young woman and would make some man a wonderful wife, but not Kit. Oddly, he'd discovered a romantic streak in himself. It wasn't enough to be comfortably well-off—he wanted to enjoy his wife as well. After all, they'd be spending the rest of their lives together.

He shuddered at the thought of spending any length of time with Miss Downs and her shy inanities. He'd be bored within a week, wanting to murder her within a month, and himself within two.

"I see," Sullivan said. "So what exactly *are* yer intentions toward my daughter?"

"Your daughter?" Kit echoed. He knew he sounded as inane as Miss Downs, but he used the question as a stalling tactic while his mind raced, trying to determine exactly what Sullivan had heard . . . and what the man intended to do about it.

"Yes, me daughter. Belle," Sullivan clarified, in case Kit was too thick to understand. "Me wife tells me you've been seen a lot in Belle's company."

Kit relaxed. This was just a bit of Mrs. Sullivan's heavy-handed matchmaking, it seemed, and not a prelude to Sullivan challenging him to a duel at dawn.

"Ah, that," Kit said with a smile. "There's a very good reason for that."

"And what would that be?"

Kit squirmed a little, knowing what he was about to reveal didn't put either him or Belle in a good light. "She, er, hired me."

Sullivan's eyebrows rose. "To do what?"

Kit hesitated, not knowing how much Belle wanted her parents to know. He swallowed hard. "I'm afraid I'm not at liberty to divulge that information, sir."

Sullivan stared at him for a moment, then went to the door and bellowed for his daughter. "Belle, come here. Now."

After a few moments, Belle arrived in the study looking a little flustered and quite puzzled. Her father waved her to a seat near Kit's, then stood with his hands behind his back and glared at them both. "Mr. Stanhope here tells me ye hired him. Is that true?"

Belle glanced at Kit and he gave her an encouraging nod. From everything he'd seen of Patrick Sullivan, he was a fair man, especially if you told the truth.

Belle glanced down at her clasped hands. "Yes, Papa."

"To do what?" Sullivan repeated with a scowl.

She shrugged but still wouldn't look up. "Oh, you know. To squire me around town, teach me to be a lady, introduce me to the right people."

"Is this yer mother's idea?" her father asked.

Belle's head came up then. "No," she admitted. "I didn't tell her. I didn't want her to think I wasn't confident in her teaching. But don't worry, Papa, we were always chaperoned by Miss Keithley or Madame Aglaia."

Well, almost always, Kit added to himself. But

Belle didn't seem to want to divulge that any more than he did. Thank heavens.

"Hmph. I see. But now she thinks yon Stanhope is after makin' ye an offer."

Belle blushed. "I know, Papa. I've told her it's not true, but you know how Mama is."

"Aye, I do that." He stopped glaring at them and shook his head. "Those things have never mattered to you before," he said with a puzzled look at Belle. "Why now?"

Once again, Belle wouldn't meet her father's eyes. "It all goes back to that day in the Garden of the Gods. . . ."

"When this young pup called ye homely?" Sullivan asked.

Kit winced. Was he never going to be forgiven for that thoughtless remark?

"Yes, Papa. I wanted to be beautiful, and Mr. Stanhope and the others are helping me with that."

"Is that all?" Sullivan persisted.

Belle nodded, her hands pleating her skirt nervously. "Of course, Papa. What else would there be?"

Her father stared at her for a moment as if he could pull the information from her by pure force of will, then sighed and told her she could go.

Belle escaped from the room, but Kit wasn't so lucky.

Sullivan speared him with a glance. "There's more to it she's not telling me. Do ye know what 'tis?"

Kit shrugged. "I have an idea. . . ."

"Well? Out with it, man."

"She has mentioned before that she was trying to impress a man—a particular man."

Sullivan nodded. "I thought as much. And who would that be?"

"I don't know," Kit admitted. "She won't tell me." Or anyone else, for that matter.

"Well, I expect we'll learn soon enough," Sullivan said with a smile. "Belle is a very resourceful young lady. What Belle wants, Belle usually gets."

No doubt. The question was, what the devil did Belle want?

Ten

Belle wasn't given any time to wonder if Papa had believed her because Charisma and Grace buttonholed her as soon as she left the study and whisked Belle off to her room to interrogate her.

Grace tripped over the rug but managed to land on the bed without breaking anything. "What did Papa want?"

"And why was Mr. Stanhope there?" Charisma asked. "Did he come to offer for you?"

Belle felt herself color. "No, of course not. You know that's only Mama's wishful thinking. Papa figured out that I hired Kit and wanted to know why. I explained I hired him to make me beautiful."

"Oh," Charisma said, looking disappointed. "I thought maybe that was how you were getting back at Mr. Stanhope—by having him ask Papa for your hand."

Belle hadn't realized that was how it would appear to her sisters. "No, I don't think he's quite to that point yet." But she had hopes. . . .

"So who are you going to get revenge on next?" Grace asked eagerly.

"George Winthrop," Belle said without hesitation. Charisma nodded sagely. "I thought as much."

"What do you mean?" Belle asked. Charisma looked entirely too smug, as if she thought she knew something. Which she didn't, of course. Belle had been very careful to keep her thoughts and feelings to herself of late. It was odd for her to keep so many secrets from her sisters, but there were just some things too . . . private, too special, to share.

"Well, ever since you gave Harold his comeuppance, it's been nothing but Mr. Stanhope this and Kit that. Why, one would think you had a liking for the man," Charisma drawled.

"You *have* spoken of him quite a bit," Grace said, looking uncertain.

Belle turned her eyes away from Charisma's too-perceptive gaze. "Nonsense. It's just that I've been in his company so much and learning so much from him, that I've naturally mentioned him a time or two."

Charisma snorted. "A time or two? More like a thousand times or two."

Belle gave her sister a haughty look. "Don't exaggerate. It isn't ladylike. Besides, I'm sure I've mentioned Madame Aglaia and Miss Keithley just as often."

Charisma raised an eyebrow, somehow managing to look disbelieving and challenging all at the same time. "Not quite. Why, I don't think you intend to get revenge on him at all."

"That's not true," Belle protested, though it was weaker than she would have liked.

And though Grace continued to look uncertain, she said, "Belle always keeps her word. You know that."

"Prove it," Charisma said baldly. "Do him next."

"No." Belle felt herself color. "I—I can't."

"Why not?" her outspoken sister demanded.

"Because . . . because . . . I need him to escort me to the Founders' Day Ball," Belle concluded triumphantly.

Charisma frowned. "That's true. All right then, you have a point."

Since Charisma gave a little, Belle did, too. "Besides, he'll be harder than George."

"Harder how?" Grace wanted to know.

"It'll be a lot more difficult to make him fall at my feet—he knows me too well. As the saying goes, familiarity breeds contempt."

"I don't know," Charisma said. "That didn't look like contempt in his eyes the other night when you wore that green dress. In fact, he looked quite taken with you."

Yes, he had, hadn't he? Belle suppressed a wistful smile, remembering how taken he had been—and how she had almost let him take *her*. "But it didn't last long." Unfortunately, he was more worried about the consequences of his actions than repeating them.

Darn it.

Grace looked crestfallen. "Too bad. But maybe you can find some other way to get him back."

"Such as?" Belle asked apprehensively.

"Such as this investment he's so intent upon," Charisma said. "There's something odd about that, don't you think?"

"What's odd about it?" Belle asked, honestly confused.

Charisma shrugged. "Well, it seems awfully important to him. Do you know why?"

"No. . . ." Belle had never thought to question it. But now that her sister mentioned it, Kit did seem rather single-minded about the subject.

"Charisma is right," Grace said. "And he's a remittance man. I know not all remittance men are the wastrels Papa makes them out to be, but . . . why is he living here in Little London instead of the real London?"

Belle shrugged. She didn't know the answer to that question, either.

"Well," Charisma declared, "he seems to know a great deal more about you than you do about him."

Struck by the undeniable truth of Charisma's statement, Belle nodded slowly. She had thought she knew everything she needed to know about Kit—his family background, his prospects, his lovely accent, the shape of his mouth. . . .

But, as Charisma pointed out, Kit was a mystery to her. She knew nothing of his past, his deepest aspirations, or his plans for the future. "You're right," Belle said. "I don't know as much as I thought. I really need to learn more." To get her revenge, of course.

And what was the man about, anyway, to keep such things from her when he knew her every thought so well? Steely determination filled Belle. "Yes, I need to learn more."

And I will.

Mama burst in then, triumphantly waving a folded piece of paper as if it were manna from on high. "Oh, Belle, you'll never guess what I just received," she said breathlessly.

"A personal note from Queen Victoria?" Charisma hazarded with a raised eyebrow.

Grace's eyes lit. "No, I know. The deed to a long-lost gold mine!"

Mama cast them a withering glance. "No, but it's almost as good." She took a deep breath, the paper clutched to her ample bosom, and announced, "Mrs. Cora Bell has invited us on an outing tomorrow to view the wildflowers."

"Wildflowers?" Charisma echoed with scorn. "She invited you to tootle around town looking for stray weeds?"

"Don't be impertinent, dear," Mama said, evidently too far gone in rapture to put any heat in that reprimand. "And, no, we're not going to 'tootle' around town—where did you hear such a word anyway?" Without waiting for an answer, she continued with a rapturous expression, "It's a full day excursion up Ute Pass toward Cripple Creek. They say the wildflowers grow in great profusion up there."

Grace smiled. "That sounds wonderful. I know how much you've wanted to meet Mrs. Bell."

Belle agreed. Mama sounded so happy, happier than she'd been in a long time, especially since she and Papa still weren't speaking. "I'm so happy for you, Mama."

"Oh, the invitation's for you, too," Mama assured her. "And she's arranged for Lord Stanhope and Madame Aglaia to accompany us. Isn't that marvelous?"

"Yes, marvelous," Belle agreed with a significant glance at her sisters. Just the opportunity she needed to learn more about Kit.

"Well, hurry then," Mama said, fluttering her hands in agitation. "There's so much to do. We must decide what to wear, what to bring, what to say . . . and we only have twenty-four hours left."

Only twenty-four hours in which to come up with a plan to get Kit alone and get some answers from him. Belle just hoped it would be enough.

* * *

The Three Graces met for tea on Mount Olympus and Euphrosyne poured a cup with an air of elegance many envied. "Really, Aglaia, haven't you granted Belle's wish yet? I'm anxious to get started on Grace but have to wait until you and Thalia are done with Belle and Charisma."

"It's taking a little longer than I thought it would," Aglaia admitted.

Charming as always, Thalia sipped her tea and asked, "Why is that? Her wish seems very straightforward."

Aglaia shook her head. "It's not as easy as you think. Her wishes are so muddled."

"You mean because she wished aloud for beauty but silently for revenge?" Euphrosyne asked.

"Yes," Aglaia said thoughtfully. "I'm doing my best, but I'm not quite sure which of her wishes to help her with—the wish she voiced, the unspoken wish in her mind, or the wish she holds deep in her heart. . . ."

Thalia raised an eloquent eyebrow. "Is there really any choice?"

Aglaia sighed. "No, I suppose not. You're quite right. The answer is very clear."

Arranging it, however, would be much more difficult.

The next morning, the closest Belle had come to a plan was to enlist Madame's help to learn more about Kit. Luckily, the dressmaker arrived early to bring Belle a new walking dress she had just completed.

Mama was in raptures over the sunny jonquil outfit with its matching lace fan and parasol. Clasping her hands together in ecstasy, she declared, "You'll be the very vision of spring. Do help her dress, won't you, Madame?"

"Of course," Madame Aglaia said with a smile and accompanied Belle to her bedroom.

Madame was already dressed for the outing herself, in a stunning outfit of royal blue that made her dark hair and olive skin look radiant.

"You look beautiful," Belle said wistfully. No matter how well she dressed, Belle would never have one-tenth the sophistication and poise this woman displayed with such ease.

"Thank you, dear. And so shall you when we have finished dressing you."

As Madame Aglaia chatted about the upcoming outing, she seemed so unsurprised by her invitation that it made Belle wonder. "Did you . . . do something to arrange this outing?" Belle asked once she was finally dressed.

Madame tugged at Belle's cuff and eyed the rest of her dress critically. "Me? Of course not. Whatever gave you that idea?"

She sounded so innocent, Belle couldn't help but believe her. But . . . "Aren't you surprised you were invited?"

"Not really. Somehow, the word has gotten out that I am a sort of cousin to Mr. Stanhope, and my shop has suddenly been besieged with women coming to ascertain my social standing."

Belle was taken aback at the news. Feeling contrite, she said, "Oh, no. I'm so sorry."

Madame's eyes twinkled. "I'm not. It's been very good for business."

"But how is Mr. Stanhope taking it?" Belle didn't think he had envisioned this sort of thing when he had casually passed Madame off as a distant relation to protect Belle's reputation. "Is he angry?"

Madame smiled. "No, he appears rather amused by the whole thing."

Of course. The man never seemed to react the way she thought he would. He was truly a man of mystery. "Madame, I wonder . . ."

"Wonder what, dear?"

"I know you're not really related to Mr. Stanhope, but . . . how much do you know about him?"

Madame raised an eyebrow. "About as much as you do, I suppose. Why do you ask?"

Belle tried for a nonchalant shrug, but suspected Madame wasn't fooled. "Oh, no reason in particular. It's just that he knows so much about me, and I've just come to realize I know very little about him."

"And you would like to use this outing as an opportunity to get to know him better?" Madame guessed shrewdly.

Really, the woman was positively uncanny at times. "Yes, but I'm afraid Mama . . ." Belle trailed off, not wanting to be disloyal to her mother by finishing that sentence.

"Your mother won't be a problem," Madame promised. "You'll see."

Madame's prediction came true. Though Mama gushed over Kit when he arrived to escort them, she didn't have much time to embarrass Belle before they met the rest of their party—a half dozen or so open carriages with twice as many people—at the edge of town.

Mrs. Bell caught sight of them and beckoned

them over to introduce them to the other occupant of her carriage, Mrs. Thurgood. "So glad you could make it," she said to Madame Aglaia. "I've admired your gowns so often. It is really true you are related to the Stanhopes?"

It was blunt, but asked with such sweetness that one couldn't help but forgive her.

"It isn't for me to say," Madame demurred, casting a mischievous glance at Kit.

Kit nodded gravely, though there was a twinkle in his eye. "I am certain the Stanhopes would be honored by such a connection."

"I should have known you wouldn't say," Mrs. Bell declared, but seemed somehow satisfied that they had confirmed their relationship. Then she turned her attention to Mama. "So glad you could come as well, Mrs. Sullivan. I've enjoyed your lovely daughter's company so much and, you know, I think we might be related."

"Do you?" Mama seemed surprised but pleased.

"Yes, I'm sure of it," Mrs. Bell declared. "Come, you and Madame Aglaia must sit in our carriage so we can discuss the matter."

Mama looked torn. "I don't know. I wouldn't want to leave Belle alone with Mr. Stanhope. . . ." But it was obvious she very much wanted a tête-à-tête with the leader of Little London society.

"Oh, pooh," Mrs. Bell said and airily waved away Mama's objections. "The young people will be quite all right by themselves. After all, they're in an open carriage and won't be out of our sight the whole way, now will they?"

"I suppose not," Mama said doubtfully, though it was obvious she was more than willing to be persuaded.

Mrs. Bell beamed. "Madame will tell you it's all right, won't you?"

Madame smiled. "Yes, of course. I don't see how anyone could have any objections if Mrs. Bell doesn't."

That was all Mama needed. With a beaming smile, she agreed and Kit assisted her and Madame Aglaia from his carriage to Mrs. Bell's without Mama apparently giving her daughter another thought.

Soon, Mama and Mrs. Bell were chattering away as if they were bosom friends, trying to determine if they were related or not.

As the carriages pulled out, Belle shook her head in disbelief. "Only Mama would find Mrs. Bell's reasoning that we are related totally logical."

Kit laughed. "Well, at least it will keep them occupied for the remainder of the trip."

"Good," Belle said with a significant look at her escort. "I wanted to catch you alone." And thank goodness the other members of this little excursion were too far away to hear their conversation.

"Oh?" Kit said, and suddenly the atmosphere was charged with meaning and undertones that Belle only half understood.

She felt her cheeks warm and spread her simple fan to cover her face so that no one else could see the betraying color. She didn't totally comprehend how to play this flirting game of words and hidden meanings, but she was willing to try. Gazing coquettishly at him over the top of her fan, she felt a betraying flutter in her middle as she said archly, "I think you grasp my meaning, sir."

"Ah, but I think I don't," Kit said. "And don't try

to play off your tricks on me—I'm the one who taught them to you."

Closing her fan with a snap, Belle gave up on the idea of flirting. She sighed. Kit was just too prosaic sometimes. "I meant only that I wished to talk to you. Alone."

"And what exactly does that gleam in your eye portend? Should I worry?"

He sounded amused, but Belle chose to take his words differently. "That depends." She raised an eyebrow. "Do you have anything to worry about?"

Kit flashed her a half-smile. "Not that I know of. Unless you are referring to the other night . . . ?"

"No, of course not," Belle said. "We agreed not to speak of that night." But that flutter appeared once more in her middle at the memory.

"Oh, is that what we agreed to?" Kit said softly, though his eyes were on the road.

Well, that was certainly the impression Belle had come away with. Though, to be honest, she didn't remember them arriving at any conclusion except that he would still take her to the Founders' Day Ball. And, much as Belle enjoyed reliving the joyous moments when Kit had held her in his arms, she was afraid to hear his version of the events for fear he hadn't enjoyed them as much as she had.

"Well, if we didn't agree to it, we should have," she said with asperity.

"Whatever the lady wants," Kit murmured.

Belle squirmed. What she wanted and what she was bold enough to ask for were two entirely different things. "What the lady wants," she said firmly, "is to know more about you."

He shrugged. "There isn't much to know."

She slanted him an exasperated look. "Of course

there is. I know little about you save your name and the fact that you are conversant with all the latest fashions. Surely there is more to Kit Stanhope than that."

He gave her a sardonic look. "A bit, I suppose. What do you want to know?"

"Everything—where you're from, who your parents are, how many siblings you have. . . ."

"My family has an estate in Sussex, which is where I grew up. I have one mother, one father, one brother, and two sisters."

What a dry recitation of facts. It told her nothing about him, really. "And your father is a lord?"

"He is Viscount Stanhope, or Lord Stanhope, yes."

"What does that mean your title is?" she asked curiously, having heard various opinions on that subject.

"It means I am the son of a viscount, but have no title myself other than 'Honorable.' Nor does my brother."

He said that with a curiously flat inflection which made her think there was more to it than he let on.

"And when your father is gone, will you be a viscount?"

"No, my older brother has that honor," he drawled. "I am only a younger son." Casting a sideways glance at her, he added, "Before you ask, no, I won't be a viscount when my brother is gone, either. Not unless he dies without issue. And since his wife has already honored him with two sons, there is little chance of that." Now his gaze turned curious. "Why? Disappointed that I won't be a lord someday?"

"Of course not—why should I care?" It's not as if

she were expecting to be his bride, after all. "I told you—I just want to know more about you." And she wondered how he felt about what he had just revealed, though he was careful to keep that to himself.

He gave her a wary glance. "So you said. But I don't understand. Why the sudden interest?"

Belle felt her face warm and hoped he didn't think this meant she was trying to secure his interest in other ways. "No reason, really. It's just that it was pointed out to me that you know a great deal about me, but I know very little about you."

"I see," Kit said, and indeed, he did look enlightened. "You feel guilty."

"No, not really," she snapped, then relented. "Well, perhaps a little." But she admitted it only because she was unwilling to reveal her true motives.

He relaxed. Evidently, guilt was a motivation he could understand. "What else do you want to know?"

"You seem to miss your home." Or so she assumed from the longing that came into his voice whenever he spoke of it. "So why have you come here?"

He shrugged again, though she could see this subject bothered him more than he let on. "It is the duty of the younger sons to go out into the world and make money for the family coffers. And, since Colorado Springs is known as Little London, I hoped I might find an opportunity and congenial company here."

"So that's why you're looking for an investment?" she asked, finally beginning to understand.

"Yes, of course." He glanced at her, curious. "Why, what did you think?"

It was her turn to shrug. "I didn't think anything. I had no idea." And she hadn't wondered about it at all. How incurious of her. "Some people call you a remittance man, but you seem so different from the others."

He clenched his jaw, though his tone was mild. "I am and I am not. I receive remittances from home like the others, but unlike them, I refuse to squander the money. I use it to keep myself in funds until I can find a suitable investment." He grimaced. "My father has ensured that."

Oh, my. There was a great deal of bitterness in that last sentence. "Your father?"

"Yes. If you must know, he insists on seeing some return on his investment in me—rightly so," he added in a grudging tone, "and has given me until the end of next quarter to do so. Unfortunately, I have had no success so far."

"Why not?"

He grimaced. "Several reasons. First, my father's expectations constrain me to invest only in those things a gentleman of his stripe would consider, which narrows the field considerably. He does not understand how different the opportunities are in America. Second, I don't understand this country well enough to recognize a good opportunity, and too many have taken advantage of my countrymen's ignorance. And third, there has been an unexpected drain on my resources."

Well, she had hoped for a few revelations and she got them—though it wasn't quite enough to satisfy her curiosity. From his clipped tone, it sounded as if the third was very important to him, but she didn't quite understand why. "Drain on your resources? How?"

He slanted her a glance that said very clearly that it was none of her business and he regretted revealing himself in this way. "It is unimportant," he said, though his tone belied his words.

So she fell back to his second reason. "I don't understand. If you aren't familiar with this country, why didn't you just stay in England, where it would be easier to find an investment?"

Tight-lipped, he said, "Because I prefer it this way." Then, pointing off to their right, he said, "Look, do you see that patch of lavender flowers?"

So she was getting too close to home, was she? Good—that was just where she wanted to be. "They're dwarf irises, and you're changing the subject," she accused.

"Yes, I am," he admitted. "And I'd appreciate it if you'd cooperate. Didn't you come out to see the flowers?"

"Not really. You're keeping something secret from me and I'd like to know what it is."

"It doesn't concern you," he said flatly. "Let it be."

"Can't you just trust me?" she asked plaintively.

He gave a derisive bark of laughter. "Why should I? You hardly trust me."

Again, she was surprised by the bitterness in his tone. "But I do trust you," she assured him.

"That's not entirely true," he pointed out, "or you would tell me the name of the man you are trying to attract with these lessons I've been giving you."

She colored. "I can't tell you that."

He nodded with an ironic grin. "As I thought."

"But it's not the same," she protested. It wasn't because she didn't trust him, but because if he knew what she was really after, he would do everything in his power to stop her.

"Yes, it is," he said firmly. "Until you trust me with

the name of the man you care for, how can I trust you with the more intimate details of my life?"

Belle had no answer for that. Quite obviously, this matter of trust was far more important to him than she had imagined. Well, there was more than one way to learn his secrets.

And she had a good idea where to start. . . .

Eleven

The next day, Kit was still railing at himself for revealing so much to Belle. What was it about her that made him open up like that? She was just like a dozen other young women he had met—attractive, well-dressed, naive. It wasn't as if she were a well-practiced courtesan skilled in extracting information from a man. So why had he told her so much about himself?

He didn't know, but by God, he wasn't going to let it happen again. He'd be on his guard from now on.

Today he wasn't up to giving Belle a lesson in winning some other man's affections or to dealing with any member of the fairer sex, so he passed Madame Aglaia's and went straight to the El Paso Club, where women were not allowed.

But just as he settled in with a paper and a good cup of coffee, Daltrey slithered into the seat opposite him.

His grip tightening on the newspaper, Kit didn't take his eyes from the article he'd been reading. "What do you want?" he growled.

"What do you think?" Daltrey challenged.

Kit lowered his paper to get a good look at the man. Just as he thought, Daltrey was looking both smug and belligerent—a very bad combination. "It's too soon," Kit reminded him. "My remittance isn't due for another few days."

Daltrey shrugged. "I know that, old man, but I just thought I'd check."

Kit gritted his teeth at the familiarity but chose to ignore it. "All right, you've checked, then." He snapped his paper back in front of his face, hoping the blackmailer would get the hint.

No such luck. Using a pencil-slim dagger that he no doubt carried concealed on his person, Daltrey dragged down the top of Kit's paper until their gazes met. "Do pay attention, won't you?" Daltrey said, the threat evident.

So as not to draw attention to their discussion, Kit slowly lowered the paper to the table. "You asked, I answered. Aren't you through?"

"Not quite." Using the dagger to clean his nails, Daltrey added in a nonchalant tone, "I have a few debts to settle."

"And how does that concern me?"

Daltrey continued to lavish attention on his nails. "They're gambling debts—debts of honor, you know."

Kit grimaced. It was a peculiar kind of honor, but he knew many of his acquaintances felt the same way, that paying gambling debts to peers was somehow more important than reimbursing mere tradesmen. "The honor would lie in not incurring debts in the first place," he drawled. And in not blackmailing one peer to reimburse another.

"Shall we speak of honor, then?" Daltrey said with a bite in his voice. "What honor is there in fathering a bastard child on an innocent young girl?"

"None," Kit said in a clipped tone. "But then, I didn't do it."

"Funny," Daltrey mused. "Your family thinks you did."

"They are mistaken."

Daltrey shrugged. "Then you won't mind if I whisper the rumor into a few ears . . . ?"

Kit glared at him, feeling impotent. If Daltrey chose to spread his rumors, there was nothing Kit could do . . . and unfortunately, many people would choose to believe those lies. While Americans admired British gentility, beneath their fawning ran an undercurrent of resentment.

Daltrey grinned, knowing he had Kit cornered. "I've seen you quite a bit about town lately, escorting a certain young heiress. Tell me, what would Miss Sullivan think if she knew you had ruined a young girl in England? Or, better yet, how would her very worthy father react?"

"I wouldn't know," Kit bit out. He almost said he didn't care, but he knew it for a lie, and so would Daltrey.

More confident now, Daltrey sheathed his dagger in its slim holder, then slid it into his jacket pocket. "And all those stupid Americans who fawn over 'Lord' Stanhope . . . what do you think they would say if they knew what you have done? It would be quite difficult to find an investment if no one could trust you."

"You're a fine one to be talking about trust," Kit said with a sneer. But inside, he worried. Was there anything Daltrey didn't know about him?

The man didn't know about the indiscretion with Belle, Kit was certain of that. If Daltrey had known, he would surely have played that card by now. No, he knew only what any other interested party would be able to ascertain—that Kit was in the market for an investment. But that was already too much.

Ignoring Kit's insult, Daltrey asked, "And just what did you plan on investing *with*?"

"With whatever little money I have left after you're through with me," Kit ground out. He wasn't about to let Daltrey know about his secret cache.

Daltrey gave him a feral smile and said softly, "Oh, but I plan on taking it all."

Frustrated fury seized Kit. How the devil was he supposed to get anywhere with this man bedeviling him? "Impossible," he declared. "I must have some to live on."

Daltrey grinned. "What good will it do you if your reputation is in shreds?"

"What good will it do you if I must return home in disgrace because I've run out of funds?" Kit countered. "It isn't wise to kill the golden goose, you know."

Kit knew he had scored a hit when Daltrey's eyes narrowed. "You have other ways of making money. You said so."

"Yes, but it isn't that much." And he couldn't count on Belle's generosity forever. It was time to explain the situation to Daltrey. "And if I don't show a return on an investment soon, my father has promised to cut me off." In case Daltrey didn't fully comprehend, Kit spelled it out for him. "That means you would be cut off, too."

Daltrey rose from the table and scowled. In a low, menacing tone, he growled, "I don't give a damn about your personal problems. And I don't care how you get the money. Just get it, or the whole town will hear of your sordid past." With that, Daltrey abruptly left.

Kit wanted to refuse, wanted to tell Daltrey he couldn't meet his blackmailing demands. But it would be a lie. Sooner or later, he would have to comply.

Damn it.

Belle closed the door to her bedroom so no one could overhear. "So, what did you find out?" she asked her sisters eagerly.

Tired of being on the outside looking in, Grace and Charisma had wanted to do their part in helping Belle learn more about Kit. Belle had agreed to let them help and was glad she had when they came up with an excellent idea. Who, they reasoned, would know more about him than his former neighbor, John Daltrey?

Though Kit had warned Belle away from Daltrey, Belle had a sneaking suspicion that he had done so only so she wouldn't learn more about Kit's past. And since she was becoming known throughout town, it made it difficult for her to learn John Daltrey's habits so she might approach him. Instead, she had asked Grace and Charisma to spy on him for her.

Charisma shrugged as she sprawled in a chair in a manner Mama would certainly object to if she knew of it. "It wasn't much of a challenge. The man is rather predictable."

Grace's eyes sparkled. "Oh, don't be so cynical. It was fun—admit it."

A small smile curved Charisma's mouth. "All right, it was fun—at first. We pretended to be nothing more than silly schoolgirls, and it worked like a charm. You know, it's amazing how little attention anyone gave us. It's as if we were invisible. I'm sure Mr. Daltrey never knew we were watching him."

Grace giggled. "And Mama has been so busy with her new friendship with 'Cousin Cora' that she hasn't paid much attention to what we've been doing either."

"But what did you find out?" Belle asked.

Grace frowned. "I think Mr. Stanhope was right. I don't think Mr. Daltrey is a nice man."

"Why do you say that?" Belle asked in an apprehensive tone, hoping her sisters weren't going to try to talk her out of questioning him.

"Well, he sleeps the morning away," Grace explained. Then, in a lowered tone, she added, "I think he must stay up all night drinking and . . . and carousing."

Belle laughed. "Most bachelors his age do."

Charisma nodded. "True, but not Mr. Stanhope. We often see him out and about in the early morning hours."

But Belle already knew that about Kit—she wanted new information. Especially since he seemed to be avoiding her of late. "But did you learn where Mr. Daltrey spends his time? Is there a place where I might approach him casually for a conversation?"

Shaking her head, Charisma said, "Grace is right—Mr. Daltrey isn't the sort of man we should know. He spends much of his time gaming or drinking . . . or in the El Paso Club."

Well, the El Paso Club didn't admit women, and even Belle wasn't courageous or assertive enough to brave the terrors of a gaming establishment or saloon.

"Surely there's some place he frequents that is suitable for ladies," she said in exasperation.

Grace and Charisma exchanged concerned glances. "There is one . . ." Charisma admitted.

Belle brightened. "Wonderful. What is it?"

"Well, he has luncheon every day around noon in the dining room at his hotel."

"Which one?" Belle asked eagerly.

"The Cascade Inn," Charisma said, frowning. "But I don't think it's really respectable. . . ."

Belle waved away her objections. She didn't know much about the Cascade Inn, save that it was a little shabby, but it couldn't be that bad if so many young gentlemen stayed there. Could it? "Surely there will be no harm in visiting a public dining room?"

"It's just barely respectable," Charisma said, and Grace nodded in agreement. "How are you going to convince Mama or Miss Keithley to take you there?"

Belle chewed on her lip. She hadn't thought that far ahead, but they were right. If the Cascade Inn was even a little shady, neither Mama nor Alvina would agree to a visit there, for any reason.

"I'm not sure. Perhaps Madame might help?" The dressmaker had been very helpful so far, so maybe she would assist Belle in this one little thing.

"She might," Grace conceded. "But what are you going to tell her is the reason you want to go there?"

An excellent question, though Belle was getting a little annoyed at the constant obstacles her sisters kept throwing in her path. "I don't know—why don't you two help me figure it out?"

"Why not tell her the truth?" Grace asked.

"The truth? How will that help?" Belle was of the mind that people didn't need to know all of the truth all of the time.

"Well, part of the truth anyway," Grace said. "Why don't you just tell her you want to know more about Mr. Stanhope, and that Mr. Daltrey is the most likely person to have that information?"

"And if she asks why I want to know more about Mr. Stanhope?"

Charisma grinned. "Then tell her you're in love with him. Now *that* she'd find believable."

Belle shot Charisma a quelling look, but didn't deign to respond to the provocation, especially since it might be more true than Belle was willing to admit to herself.

"It's a good idea," Grace said eagerly. "And what woman her age doesn't fancy herself a matchmaker? I bet she'd love to help if she thought she was furthering the cause of true love." To punctuate her statement, Grace made a sweeping gesture and managed to knock everything off the small table beside her.

After Belle cleaned up the mess, she allowed her sisters to persuade her. Then, later that day, she found it rather easy to blush and stammer enough to make it appear to Madame Aglaia that she was interested in Mr. Kit Stanhope in a very particular way.

Madame cocked her head to regard Belle thoughtfully, as if she were searching the very depths of her heart. For a moment, the woman's shrewd expression made Belle believe she hadn't fooled her a bit.

But soon, Madame nodded. "I see why you want to learn more about Mr. Stanhope, but why do you feel you must approach Mr. Daltrey?"

"They were neighbors back in Sussex, and there seems to be some bad blood between them. Kit—Mr. Stanhope—is keeping some secret from me, and I'm certain Mr. Daltrey might know what it is."

Madame nodded. "But are you certain you *wish* to know what it is?"

"Of course. After all, he knows the most intimate details of my life and I hardly know anything about him. How do I know I want to . . ." She couldn't quite say 'marry him' out loud. ". . . further our acquaintance if I don't know what he's hiding?"

"And if it's something truly horrible?"

Belle shrugged, but she doubted Kit had done anything so bad that she couldn't overlook it. "I'll deal with that if it happens."

"All right," Madame said, smiling.

Belle's heart lightened. "You'll do it, then?"

"Yes. I've been wanting to learn more about Mr. John Daltrey myself," she said cryptically.

Not wanting to change Madame's mind, but wanting the dressmaker to understand exactly what they were getting into, Belle said, "It appears the only way to get close to Mr. Daltrey is to find a way to join him for lunch at the Cascade Inn."

Madame nodded thoughtfully. "That can be arranged."

Her confidence had the opposite effect on Belle. "But how are we going to do that?" She suddenly realized it might be more difficult than she thought to invite herself to eat at his table, and doubt filled her.

"Hmm," Madame mused. "We must ensure the

dining room is full, and assure the waiter that we are so hungry, we do not mind sharing a table."

"But how can we do that?"

Madame Aglaia smiled. "Don't worry about that, dear. I'll take care of it."

"But how?"

"Oh, I have my ways. . . ."

No doubt she did, but Belle refrained from asking for more information, fearing Madame would actually give it to her.

The next day, Belle waited nervously outside the Cascade Inn for Madame Aglaia to join her. Charisma and Grace, saying they were still a little apprehensive, had insisted on escorting her to the hotel and waited with her.

"Oh, look," Grace exclaimed with a bounce of excitement. "There's Madame now."

And Madame, beautiful as always, looked dressed for battle in a tailored walking dress of a rich shade of brown. Belle, too, had felt the urge to dress conservatively, and had chosen a plainly cut outfit to wear. She at least wanted to *look* respectable.

Madame eyed Belle approvingly. "An excellent choice. Now, just follow my lead."

She led the way and Belle followed, but so did Charisma and Grace, Belle noted with dismay as she heard Grace trip over something behind them.

Madame stopped short. "Oh, no. This won't do at all. Miss Charisma, Miss Grace, you must not go in with us."

"Why not?" Charisma asked with a belligerent tilt of her chin. "If Belle can do it, so can we."

"I'm not questioning the propriety of it," Madame said sternly. "But I don't think Mr. Daltrey will speak as freely in front of two young girls."

Charisma scowled. "But—"

"Madame is right," Belle said sternly. "Besides, he might recognize you since you've been following him about, and wonder what you are up to. It would be best if you were to just go home."

"But we want to know how it turns out," Grace said.

"You will," Belle promised. "I'll come home straight away and tell you all about it."

Charisma folded her arms, looking stubborn. "All right then, we won't go inside, but we will wait right here. You can't make us leave."

Belle supposed she would have to be content with that. Once Charisma had set her mind to something, she could be as unyielding as Papa. "If you insist. But stay out of sight—don't let anyone know you're loitering here."

"Don't worry," Charisma said with a grin. "We know how to be invisible, remember?"

Belle turned back to Madame, who looked amused. "Are we ready now?" the older woman asked.

"I hope so," Belle muttered.

"Then let us go. And, once we get inside, just follow my lead."

Belle followed Madame into the dining room and her hopes rose when she noticed that the room was as full as Madame had promised . . . and Mr. Daltrey was there, eating alone. Perfect. Now they just had to find a way to join him.

The host rushed over to greet them. "I am so sorry," he gushed. "But we have no place to seat you at the moment. If you ladies would care to wait . . . ?"

Madame frowned. "I think not." With a vague wave in Belle's direction, she said, "My young charge is feeling rather faint and requires sustenance immediately. Isn't there something you can do?"

The man gave Belle an apprehensive glance and she tried to look pale and ill, as if she might faint at any moment. She must have been successful, for the man wrung his hands and said, "Of course, of course. If you wouldn't mind sharing a table . . . ?"

"That would be acceptable," Madame said crisply. Then, directing her parasol in Mr. Daltrey's direction, she said, "That one, I think."

"Of course, of course." Swiftly, he obtained Mr. Daltrey's concurrence, then fluttered around them until he seated them with profuse apologies for the inconvenience. No doubt he served few ladies here, especially of their degree of respectability.

Madame ordered a light luncheon to be served up immediately and the man left to do her bidding.

Sharing a table must have been a fairly common occurrence at the Cascade Inn, for Mr. Daltrey barely registered their presence, and he returned his attention to his soup.

How were they going to question him if he wouldn't even acknowledge their existence? Dismayed, Belle shot a pleading glance at Madame.

Undaunted, Madame cleared her throat, rather peremptorily, Belle thought.

Mr. Daltrey raised his gaze warily, then the light of recognition shone in his eyes. "Ah, Madame Aglaia, the dressmaker, is it not?" he said in an accent reminiscent of Kit's. But there the resemblance ended. Compared to this man with his devilish dark eyes and even darker hair, Kit looked positively light and angelic. "And Miss Sullivan?"

"Indeed," Madame said frostily, as if his

recognition wasn't her goal all along. "But I'm afraid you have the advantage of us, sir."

"Daltrey. John Daltrey," he said with an insincere smile. And the conversation seemed to die there.

Quickly, Belle said brightly, "You have a wonderful accent, sir. Why, it sounds just like Mr. Stanhope's." She made an abortive move to use her fan, but decided against it almost immediately. There was something about this man she didn't like, and she didn't want to give him any sort of encouragement— especially not the sort the fan seemed to promote.

He raised an eyebrow. "It should. We were neighbors in Sussex."

"Really?" Belle said with an appropriate schoolgirl gush. "Why, then, we have a mutual acquaintance. Madame is related to him and he is a good friend of mine."

Mr. Daltrey's lips curved in a faint smile, but the expression didn't reach his eyes. "How nice for you."

The waiter brought their soup then, along with Mr. Daltrey's meal, and Belle was obliged to let the conversation languish.

Before the silence became unbearable, Madame smiled with determination at Mr. Daltrey and said, "I know so little about my young cousin. And he's so modest, he refuses to regale us with stories of his youth. Perhaps . . . you know some?"

Mr. Daltrey eyed them with calculation. "I know a few, but nothing flattering. Nothing fit for a lady's ears."

Belle bristled, but let Madame speak for both of them. "Now, now," she said. "We'll be the judge of what is appropriate and what is not. Surely it can't be that bad . . . ?"

He shrugged. Too casually, Belle thought. "Well, it's nothing but rumors, mind you, but the word is that he's a womanizer and a philanderer."

No, it couldn't be. Not the man she knew. Belle opened her mouth to protest, but shut it quickly enough when Madame trod on her instep under the table.

"Oh dear, is it so?" Madame said with just the right amount of dismay in her voice. "I had heard something to that effect, but no details. Do you know . . . could you tell us . . . why he left England?"

As Belle waited anxiously for his reply, she caught sight of some movement in the doorway. It was Charisma and Grace, frantically trying to get her attention. Good heavens, couldn't they follow simple instructions? Angrily, Belle shook her head at them and turned her attention back to Mr. Daltrey.

He smiled wolfishly. "I might know. What's the information worth to you?"

She knew it—there *was* a secret. Belle was willing to pay whatever he asked, but Madame placed a restraining hand on her arm. She reached across the table to touch Mr. Daltrey's arm as well, but they were all distracted by the sound of crashing china and shattering glass.

Glancing in the direction of the din, Belle saw Grace covering her mouth in consternation as a waiter sprawled facedown at her feet, covered in what looked like the luncheon Madame had ordered for them.

Grace's doing, of course. Belle should have known.

And Charisma was still frantically trying to convey some sort of message to her.

"Why, whatever are they doing?" Madame asked in surprise.

A man behind her answered. "They're trying to warn you that I am here."

Belle whirled around to see Kit standing there, glaring down at them all impartially. Guilt filled her as she stared in horror at his angry visage. She had never seen him so haughty, so remote. How much had he heard? Did he know she was trying to pry information about him out of Mr. Daltrey?

Darn it, if he'd only waited just a minute or two longer, she would have that information by now.

Mr. Daltrey's grin widened. "Ah, Stanhope," he said in a false jovial tone. "Do you have something for me?"

"Later," Kit growled. "For now, I need to escort these ladies to a more . . . suitable location. You will excuse us?"

"Of course," Mr. Daltrey said. "But do return soon, won't you?"

Kit answered him with a glare, then pulled Madame's chair out for her, staring at them with a tight-lipped expression that left no doubt in Belle's mind that he expected them to leave, and at once, or they would suffer the consequences of his ire.

Belle stiffened, but realized there was nothing more she could learn here with Kit hovering over them. And since her luncheon was all over the floor—and the waiter—she might as well leave. She stood in a huff and refused his arm, marching out the door with her head held high.

As they passed through the doorway, Kit deserted them for a moment to speak to the head waiter and pass him some bills.

Grace caught Belle's arm, saying, "I'm sorry. We tried to warn you."

"I know," Belle said in chagrin.

"Did you learn anything?" Charisma asked.

Belle shook her head. "Nothing useful. And we were so close, too."

Madame patted her arm. "It's all right, dear. I'm sure whatever that man said would have been a lie anyway."

Would it? Then why did Mr. Daltrey look so smug . . . and Kit so very angry? There was still a mystery here, and Belle was even more determined to learn what it was.

Twelve

After Kit had reimbursed the Cascade for the meals and damages, he stood for a moment, undecided whom to strangle first—Daltrey or Belle.

Daltrey would be there when he got back. Belle was likely to take off to avoid the consequences of her actions if he didn't speak to her immediately. Decision made.

He strode out the door and came to an abrupt halt in front of the gaggle of females. Conscious of their potential audience, he curbed his natural inclination to have it out with them then and there. Instead, he made an effort to school his expression.

But before he could say anything, Belle raised her chin with defiance and said, "How much was it?"

What? "How much was what?"

"The damages," Belle said, avoiding Grace's guilty glance. "How much did you pay the waiter for the meal and broken dishes?"

He waved that away as irrelevant. "It doesn't matter."

"It *does* matter," Belle insisted. "I know you are having some pecuniary difficulties."

"Not today," he said abruptly. "I received my remittance from home. And don't change the

subject. Let's discuss this little incident at
Madame's, shall we?"

Belle's gaze dropped. "I don't think so," she said
in a forced nonchalant tone. "I have another engagement."

"Break it," Kit said. He would brook no argument
today. "I think you owe me an explanation."

Belle's gaze slid toward Madame, and the dressmaker said, "He's quite right, dear. Come, it won't
be so bad. You'll see."

Having ascertained that they intended to follow
his instructions, Kit turned on his heel and
marched off to the dressmaker's establishment.

What with Grace tripping over something every
few steps or stopping to apologize to people she
had run into, the ladies couldn't keep up with his
long, ground-eating stride. After a short time, they
stopped trying.

And Kit couldn't slow down to match theirs. His
frustration and anger had to go somewhere. Just
what the devil had Belle been doing with Daltrey?
And why had Madame Aglaia countenanced it?

He covered the three blocks in record time and,
rather than loiter in front of the establishment, he
went around to the rear to await their arrival.

But it seemed an age until Madame opened the
door to him. She glanced up at him with a stern
expression and held the door as if to bar him
entry. "You will be reasonable, won't you?"

He raised his chin a fraction. She dared question
him? "I am always reasonable."

She raised a disbelieving eyebrow. "See that you
are."

Inside the shop, Belle awaited him with a defiant

expression, flanked by her sisters who looked both mulishly protective and frightened at the same time.

Some of Kit's ire abated at the sight. "Am I such an ogre?" he asked in a bemused tone.

"We didn't think so," Belle conceded as her sisters seemed to relax. "Until now."

"You made me very angry," Kit said more as a reason for his behavior rather than an apology.

"Obviously," Belle snapped. "What I don't know is why."

Surely she couldn't be so ignorant. "Why were you at the Cascade Hotel with Mr. Daltrey?"

She shrugged. "We went there to dine. What's wrong with that?"

"You know quite well it is not a place ladies usually frequent. No tricks, Belle. Tell me the real reason."

Her evasive gaze and silence were his only answer.

"You went there to speak to Daltrey, didn't you? You deliberately sought him out after I told you to avoid him."

Belle didn't answer him in words, though the self-conscious and guilty expressions she and her sisters wore were answer enough. Turning to the dressmaker, he asked, "Why did you accompany her on this meeting, ma'am? Surely you knew better."

Madame had the grace to look apologetic. "Belle was so determined," she murmured. "I thought it would be better to ensure she was chaperoned than to deny her and have her seek him out on her own."

Very true. And no doubt Belle would have been stubborn enough to accost Daltrey alone if Madame hadn't gone. The thought of what might have happened made him ill.

Belle shrugged. "There was no harm done."

Kit turned on her furiously. "No harm? Perhaps

this time, but you were lucky. You have no idea what kind of man you were dealing with."

Belle, equally angry, said, "Of course not. Because you never tell us anything. No wonder we have to go to other people to learn the slightest detail about you."

"Is that what this is all about? Your desire to learn more about me?" He should have known, after her insistence on learning his "secret."

Belle nodded. "Yes." And Charisma and Grace's expressions verified her assertion.

Kit thought furiously for a moment. Should he tell her? It went against the grain to reveal the intimate details of his life, but if he didn't tell Belle *something*, she was likely to waylay John Daltrey again to try to worm information out of him.

He glanced at the four eager faces turned up to him. Well, he'd find something to tell Belle, but he didn't want the whole world listening in. "All right, but may we speak alone?"

Belle's belligerence turned to eagerness. "Of course."

He ignored the disappointed expressions on her sisters' faces and pulled Belle aside into another room where they couldn't be heard but could still be seen by Madame Aglaia. After his one little slip-up, he was more determined than ever to observe the proprieties.

All traces of her apprehension now gone, Belle turned her face eagerly up to his. A pang of conscience shot through him as he remembered another time when she had turned her face to his, then with a young girl's desire to taste what it meant to be a woman. And he had been only too eager to show her.

He stepped back a fraction to remind himself to keep his distance. And to keep his mind on the subject at hand. "What did Daltrey tell you?"

"Nothing—you showed up before he could say anything."

He believed her—Belle didn't lie well. Relief filled him. At least he didn't have to answer false accusations.

"Why?" Belle asked curiously. "What would he have told me, given the chance?"

"Nothing but lies," Kit said with a bitter twist of his mouth.

"What sort of lies?"

Kit hesitated, wondering how much to reveal.

With exasperation, Belle said, "Never mind. If it's too much trouble, I could just go back and ask him myself."

Kit narrowed his eyes at her. So she would blackmail him as well, would she? "I wouldn't recommend it," he drawled, and was as surprised as she apparently was to hear the threat in his voice.

Though her eyes were wide, Belle still persisted. "What sort of lies?"

"He knows the purported reason why I left home."

Eager now, Belle asked, "And why was that?"

He sighed, unwilling to sully her ears or his reputation with the false accusations. "It doesn't matter. Suffice it to say that I was accused of something I did not do." Something he would never do.

"Obviously, it does matter. What did they say you did?"

"Isn't it enough to know I was banished from my home for something of which I was innocent? After all, if I didn't do it, what good does it do you to know what it is? Can't you trust me?"

Belle considered for a few moments that left him feeling on edge, but it must have seemed reasonable to her, for she said, "I suppose."

Thank heavens. "And you won't seek out Daltrey again?" he persisted. He hated the thought of what the man might do or say to her if he got her alone. "He is an evil man."

"Really? If he's so evil, why are *you* going back to see him?"

"What makes you think I am?"

"You said so—back there in the dining room."

So he had. "That's different—that's business."

"What sort of business would you have with a man—" She broke off suddenly and her eyes widened. "The secret, the lack of funds, meeting him again today . . . Suddenly, it all fits. He's black-mailing you, isn't he? You're going back to give him money!"

Damn. Kit had hoped she wouldn't put those facts together, but she had, all too readily. He didn't say anything.

But she must have taken his lack of denial as confirmation, for she said, "No wonder you need money. That's why you agreed to tutor me."

He shrugged, choosing not to confirm or deny her guess.

She eyed him speculatively. "But if you're innocent, how can he blackmail you?"

Disappointment filled him. So, she still didn't trust him, no matter how much she might protest otherwise. "Just the suggestion of impropriety might jeopardize my chances of finding a suitable investment. Until I find one my father will approve, I need to keep my reputation spotless."

Belle nodded thoughtfully. "Well, you can continue to tutor me, of course. That will help with your funds."

So she fancied herself his savior, did she? His pride wouldn't let him stomach that. "I do not need your charity," he muttered.

She opened her eyes wide at him. "Who said it's charity? With the Founders' Day Ball coming up next month, I need to learn how to dance, how to talk, how to behave. . . . You wouldn't want me to make a fool of myself, would you?"

"Of course not. But you hardly need my help. Madame Aglaia and Miss Keithley are more than capable of teaching you anything you want to know. Besides, I am not sure your father would approve, now that he knows you've been paying me."

"He has no objections and . . . and . . . I want *you*, " Belle said with an innocence that set his blood heating to a slow simmer. "Won't you let me help you in this way?"

But he was supposed to help her, not the other way around. "I cannot," he said stiffly.

"Oh, have I offended your pride?" Belle asked with contrition. "Would you rather I lent you the money for your investment? You can pay me back when it pays off."

That was even worse. How lowering to think he might be dependent upon a schoolgirl for his livelihood. And didn't she realize an investment was just as likely to lose money? "No," he choked out. "I prefer to give value for the money I receive."

"Then you'll just have to continue my lessons,"

Belle said with a sensual undertone he couldn't miss.

"I suppose so," he conceded. It was the only way to prove to his father that he could make good on an investment, especially since Daltrey was so adamant about taking a great deal of his money.

"Good. I'll expect you at the house tomorrow afternoon at two o'clock. We have a ballroom upstairs where you can teach me how to dance."

He bowed briefly. "Very well." But *he* was going to control the lessons . . . and do his damnedest to eliminate that erotic undertone Belle seemed so intent upon. For both their sakes.

The next day, Belle waited anxiously for Kit to arrive so she could begin her dancing lessons. Mama had employed a dancing master to teach them a few things the previous year, but the man had been hopelessly old-fashioned and so horrified by Grace's lack of coordination that they had all parted on mutually satisfactory terms.

But Belle had learned precious little from the man and she really did need to learn to dance if she weren't to disgrace herself at the Founders' Day Ball.

She had told her sisters everything Kit had told her the day before. If she hadn't, they would have hounded her until she did. Besides, he had revealed little enough.

Of course, she still wanted to know exactly what lies had made his parents banish him from his own home . . . and why his family had believed those lies. But she would have to give up on that for the present. She really had no desire to have another discussion with Mr. Daltrey, and she had other concerns to worry about.

Namely revenge.

Though she had been successful in routing Harold, she had yet to determine how she was going to punish George and Kit. She just knew she needed all the ammunition in her arsenal to get Kit to fall in love with her.

She glanced down at her bosom. It was really too bad that day wear required she cover her chest clear up to her throat. Kit did so seem to enjoy the sight of her exposed flesh.

Well, she might not be able to ensnare him that way, but proximity might do the trick—and there was nothing like dancing for enforced public proximity. And if she were very lucky, and very clever, she might even be able to get Kit to tell her himself what attracted him to a woman.

She had enlisted Grace and Charisma into her scheme, telling them truthfully that she needed Kit to fall for her before she could punish him. But what she didn't reveal was the excitement and anticipation she felt at the thought of being in his arms once more. If only she could figure out a way for them to be alone. . . .

She couldn't at the moment, but hoped the time might come when she could persuade him to repeat that sense-stealing kiss. She became quite giddy at the thought, but felt no remorse. After all, why shouldn't she enjoy the process?

Belle heard a commotion downstairs and realized Kit must have arrived. Grace and Charisma escorted him upstairs to where she had uncovered the piano and moved the chairs all to one side.

Kit glanced around, one eyebrow raised. "And your mother is . . . ?"

"With her newfound cousin, Cora Bell," Belle explained. Nothing would make Mama give up an afternoon with the leader of Little London society.

Kit frowned. "Aren't we to be chaperoned?"

Belle shrugged. She hadn't asked Alvina, knowing that proper young woman would be rather too strict in observing the proprieties, and though she sensed Madame Aglaia would be less so, Belle didn't want to test that assumption.

"Charisma and Grace are here. Isn't that good enough?" she asked innocently. They would be far more likely to give Belle a little leeway, especially if she convinced them it was in the interest of furthering her revenge.

Kit looked doubtful, but said, "I suppose." As the four of them stood uncertainly about in the large room, he asked, "Where would you like to begin?"

"What dances are we most likely to encounter at the ball and elsewhere?"

"The cotillion is still popular, along with the schottische, the polka, and the waltz."

The waltz would do perfectly for her purposes. "Our dancing master taught us the first three," she said, exaggerating only slightly. "But we never learned the waltz. Could you show me how it is done?"

"Very well." Kit glanced at the piano. "Does one of you play?"

"Charisma does," Belle said, and shooed her sister toward the instrument. "And Grace can turn the pages for her."

"That won't be necessary," Kit said with a smile.

"I'm sure Miss Charisma can turn her own pages. We'll need Miss Grace here."

"We will?" Belle asked, puzzled. "For what?"

"Why, to be your partner, of course," Kit said smoothly. "Come, let me show you."

Smiling at Grace, he said, "I'm sorry, but for this purpose, you must be *Mr.* Grace so you can take the lead . . . and pretend you are taller than your sister."

Grace giggled, but nodded happily as Belle scowled. This wasn't at all what she had in mind. But she didn't know how to change their positions without giving away her intentions, so she allowed Kit to show Grace how to place one arm at Belle's waist and hold her hand with the other.

Once they were in the proper position, Kit asked Charisma to play. Smoothly, he demonstrated the steps for them as he danced with an invisible partner. "Now you try it," he said. "Slowly."

Did he really think he could impart instant grace to her awkward sister? Belle thought about saying something to that effect, but didn't want to hurt Grace's feelings. And perhaps Grace would surprise them all and do just fine.

They tried waltzing in small steps as he suggested, but it resulted in nothing but a great deal of stumbling. Kit frowned and gave more instructions, but nothing seemed to work.

"These small steps seem to be the problem," he said. "Perhaps you need to try it at full stride. Miss Charisma, if you would?"

Charisma launched into a sprightly waltz and Grace took off like a horse out of the starting gate, ungainly propelling Belle into a row of side chairs, then glancing off the piano.

"Please, slow down," Belle pleaded.

But Grace was having too much fun. Gaining more confidence, she surged into the center of the room, whirling and hauling Belle along with her, willy-nilly.

Amused by Grace's enthusiasm, Belle had a moment to thank heaven that at least there were no obstructions there, but her thanks were short-lived as Grace somehow managed to get one of her legs crosswise between Belle's. The resulting scissor action sent them both off balance and tumbling to the hard floor.

Grace landed atop Belle, who couldn't help but let out an "Oof" of surprise and pain.

"Oh, I'm so sorry," Grace said with an apologetic expression as she scrambled off her sister.

Yes, she always was. But it was usually other people who ended up sporting the bruises. Belle lay sprawled there for a moment, trying to catch her breath, and glared up at Kit, who had a look of unholy amusement in his eyes. Oh, wonderful. Just the way to make him see her as a desirable woman.

He reached down to help her up, and as she rose he murmured, "I'm sorry, I forgot Miss Grace . . ."

Wasn't graceful, obviously. But she was glad he didn't finish that statement out loud. "No harm done," Belle said gamely, though she winced as several sore spots, notably on her backside, made themselves known. At least nothing seemed broken.

But she wasn't about to give up her advantage. Giving him a challenging look as she dusted off her skirt, she said, "Perhaps it would be better if *you* were to partner me."

"What about Miss Charisma?"

"I don't think so," Belle said. "She's better at the

piano." Then added softly, "You don't want to hear Grace's playing. Truly."

He conceded that point with an ironic nod. "Very well, then." He bowed slightly and held out his hand. "If I might have the honor . . . ?"

She smiled and dipped in a small curtsey. "I would be most pleased, sir."

And, finally, Kit took her into his arms once more. He nodded for Charisma to play as Grace pouted at being relegated to turning pages.

He whirled Belle effortlessly around the room, making her giddy with pleasure. Dancing with Kit was so much easier than with Grace. Not to mention infinitely more pleasurable. She didn't even have to think about her feet or the steps, and the resulting sensation was like floating through the room, anchored to the earth only by her handsome partner.

She closed her eyes to enjoy the feelings rippling through her, loving the warm feel of his arms around her, the way he made her feel safe and protected, yet extremely feminine at the same time. And he smelled wonderful, the scent of his soap and cologne combining in a manly fragrance that evoked memories of their intimate embrace at the Opera House.

Did he feel it, too? Would he want to kiss her if they were alone?

She opened her eyes to glance up at him, but his expression was rigid, giving nothing away. And, all too soon, the dance came to an end. He released her immediately, as if she were too hot to handle, bringing an abrupt end to their lovely time together.

On the sidelines, Grace and Charisma applauded furiously. "That was wonderful," Grace said. "So beautiful and elegant."

"I don't know," Belle demurred. "I think I stumbled a time or two." Holding out her arms, she said, "Let's try it again."

"Nonsense," Kit said. "Your dancing was flawless. You, Miss Sullivan, are a natural. You don't need any more lessons. Simply follow your partner's lead as you have been, and you will do wonderfully."

How stupid of her. Belle should have thought, should have arranged a misstep or two. And now her lack of foresight had resulted in another lost opportunity to get Kit to notice her as a woman. But perhaps she could still salvage something from the day, she thought as she remembered her intent to learn more about what Kit found attractive in a woman.

Carefully, she wondered how to word it. "But isn't it customary to speak to your partner while dancing the waltz?" It was difficult during some of the more strenuous dances, but the closeness of the waltz gave the two dancers more opportunity to talk to one another.

"Customary, perhaps, but not required," Kit said as Grace and Charisma wandered over to join them.

"And if we do converse, what should we speak about?"

Apparently baffled, Kit said, "Why, whatever you wish. The normal things, I suppose—a compliment on your partner's prowess, your enjoyment of the function, the weather. Why do you ask?"

"Well, *we*"—Belle cast a significant glance at her sisters to include them in the conversation—"want to know what to do to attract a . . . *particular* man."

"That's right," Charisma said, entering the conversation as Belle had hoped. "Can you tell us how to make a man fall in love with us?"

Kit's expression turned wary. "I don't think so. No one could. It is different for each person."

"Is it?" Belle asked in an innocent tone. "Yet there are some things that seem to be commonly attractive to all men."

Charisma nodded. "Like a pretty face, charm, elegance, and high, rounded bosoms."

Grace covered her mouth, looking scandalized.

And Kit definitely looked uncomfortable now. "Well, you needn't worry about those, Miss Sullivan. You possess all these . . . attributes in great abundance. And more."

She would have been flattered if she didn't believe he said so only to still her tongue—and Charisma's. "Really?" she asked ingenuously. "What others do I possess?"

At his flustered look, she added, "I ask only so that I can use my attributes to my best advantage."

He glanced around as if looking for escape, but the three Sullivan girls surrounded him, watching him eagerly and waiting for his wisdom. "You need no help in that area, I assure you," he said, looking desperate.

"Then why is it that . . . a particular man is not yet in love with me?"

He gave her a desperate smile, obviously intent on being gallant. "It can only be because you have not yet tried to ensnare him. If you would but put your mind to it, I'm sure you could have any man at your feet."

But she didn't want just any man—she wanted Kit. "I *would* put my mind to it," she explained, "if only I could determine what it is I should do."

"Yes," Charisma said, not constrained as Belle was to be discreet. She stepped forward, pinning him with a penetrating stare. "For example, what do *you* find attractive in a woman?"

Kit ran a finger around his collar, as if it had become suddenly tight. "I am certain that's irrelevant."

As Belle enjoyed his discomfort, Charisma cocked her head and eyed him seriously. "Not at all. If we know what you find attractive in a woman, we could extrapolate it to other men in general."

"Yes," Grace said. "You see, we have no brothers to ask."

"I, well, I—" He paused, then seemed able to regain some of his lost composure. "Wit and beauty, of course. Good breeding, a sunny disposition."

Charisma nodded thoughtfully. "I see. Yet these are very general characteristics. What, specifically, would make you fall in love with one woman and her alone?"

His gaze skimmed all three sisters, evidently hoping for some sort of reprieve. He found none. "I really do *not* think this is a suitable conversation—"

"All right, then," Belle interrupted. "Then let's turn it around. What would make you turn away from a woman? What would give you a disgust of her?"

"Questions like this," he blurted out. Then immediately said, "I apologize. That was uncalled for."

Actually, he had been provoked, and Belle was surprised he hadn't complained more vociferously earlier.

"I'm sorry," Grace said. "Were we too forward?"

"A bit," he said with a sigh and a longing look toward the door.

Cocking her head once more, Charisma asked, "Just what constitutes being too forward? Is plain speaking offensive? What if a woman takes the initiative? May she touch a man's arm? His hand? His—"

"It depends," Kit said quickly, evidently not wanting to know how Charisma planned to finish that sentence. He gulped visibly. "A great deal depends on the circumstances."

"I don't quite understand," Charisma persisted. "Could you perhaps demonstrate for us?"

"No, I cannot," Kit said firmly. "And today's lesson is at an end. Farewell, ladies." And without further ado, he strode swiftly toward the door with the obvious intention of seeing himself out of the Sullivan house as soon as possible.

As soon as he was out of earshot, Grace laughed. "I don't think he appreciated your questions, Charisma."

Charisma's mouth twisted in an answering smile. "Or your dancing. But we did learn something, nonetheless."

"We did?" Belle asked.

Charisma nodded. "We learned that Mr. Stanhope finds you attractive."

"He does?" A warm glow filled Belle at the thought. *Details. I want details.* "Why do you say that?" she asked in her most nonchalant tone.

"Why, he said so," Grace exclaimed.

Oh, was that all? "He was just being gallant. Polite."

"I don't think so," Charisma said. "There was something in the way he looked at you. . . ."

"What way?" Belle asked, trying to pretend that it didn't matter.

"The same way you looked at him," Charisma said with a knowing grin. "As if he wanted to eat you up."

"Oh." Had he really looked at her like that? What did it mean? Did he want to kiss her again? Run those marvelous hands over her body? Use those decadent lips to do delicious things to her breasts? She desperately needed to know the answers to those questions.

"That's right," Grace concurred. "I don't think you'll have any problem making him fall in love with you."

"Only one question remains," Charisma drawled with a raised eyebrow. "Once he does, will you be able to follow through on your plan to spurn him?"

"Of course," Belle said with a confidence she didn't feel. She never went back on her word, especially to her sisters.

But rejecting Kit Stanhope's advances would be one of the hardest things she would ever do.

Thirteen

A few days later, Belle was back in her bedroom, talking to her sisters again. Kit had pretty much avoided them after they scared him away, so it was time to concentrate on George once more.

Belle sighed. "The problem is, I haven't been able to get near George lately. It's difficult to get him to fall in love with me, or to get any sort of revenge, if he won't even talk to me."

"Do you think he's avoiding you because he knows what you did to Harold?" Grace asked.

"No, George is affable enough when I see him."

"It *is* springtime on his father's ranch," Charisma said. "I'm sure they have a lot to do. He may just be busy."

"I don't think that's it," Belle said in a distracted tone. "He still manages to make the most of the social events in the evenings."

Charisma shrugged. "He probably thinks you are nearly engaged to Mr. Stanhope. After all, you are often in his company."

"That's because I pay him to squire me around," Belle protested, not wanting them to think she actually preferred Kit's companionship.

Even if she did.

Charisma raised an eyebrow. "We know that, but

no one else does. Imagine how it appears to the rest of society."

"Yes," Grace chimed in, "I imagine they think you two will be making an announcement very soon."

Belle frowned. Her sisters were right. No doubt George thought he didn't have a chance against Kit's breeding, family connections, and good looks. And under any other circumstances, he'd be right.

"Then how can I get George to talk to me, to invite me to a function?"

"You could stage a public fight with Mr. Stanhope," Charisma suggested.

No, that was more Charisma's style than Belle's. Belle shook her head. "Kit is too much a gentleman to squabble in public. Remember, he waited until we were in private before he had words with us over the Cascade Hotel incident."

Grace shook her head. "There's no reason to make everyone think you've had a falling out with Mr. Stanhope. You just have to find a way to make George believe it—and to believe you like *him* instead."

"But how am I to do that?"

Grace exchanged a glance with Charisma that Belle couldn't interpret. "You know George's sisters?"

Vaguely. "Carrie and Susan?"

Grace nodded. "Carrie is my age, and Susan is two years younger, so we saw them at the Applebaums' party. We learned there that they are . . . well . . . not very discreet."

Charisma rolled her eyes. "What Grace is trying to say is that they are gossips of the worst kind. Whisper a secret anywhere in their vicinity and the next thing you know, the person you least want to hear it is fully aware of every syllable you uttered."

Belle nodded slowly. "So we only need to get

them to believe I'm on the outs with Kit, and they'll pass the information on to George."

"Exactly," Charisma said. "Even better, make them believe you are enamored of George so he's predisposed to believe he could win your hand."

What a wonderful idea. Belle rather liked the poetic justice of doing George in with gossip after he had denigrated Charisma for speaking her mind. "Good—we'll do it. Let's figure out how."

Charisma and Grace were soon able to ferret out the information that Carrie and Susan Winthrop visited the town's lending library every Tuesday afternoon.

So the following Tuesday, the three Sullivan sisters set off for the library with a plan in mind. True, the last time they had made plans, they hadn't turned out very well. But this time, Belle felt more confident. After all, fooling two young ladies was bound to be easier than trying to extract information from one disreputable gentleman.

Charisma and Belle lurked in the aisles while Grace peeked through the stacks, hands held carefully behind her back as she searched for the audience for their little drama.

After an hour or so of waiting, the pretty blond Winthrop girls hadn't appeared yet and the proprietor had thrown several frowns their way. If Carrie and Susan didn't show up soon, the Sullivans were likely to be booted out of the library.

But finally, Grace whispered, "Here they come."

When the girls were in position on the other side of the stack, Grace grinned and nodded at Charisma to begin.

In a whisper loud enough to be heard on the other side of the shelves, Charisma said, "For heaven's sake, Belle, why did you turn down Mr. Stanhope's invitation to Mrs. Palmer's concert? It's the event of the season."

Belle tried to imbue boredom in her voice. "I don't know—I'm just weary of going everywhere with him."

"I thought you liked him," Grace piped up, on cue.

Belle risked a peek through the space at the top of the books. As she had hoped, Carrie and Susan were listening avidly.

Belle nodded and smiled at her sisters to let them know their scheme was proceeding as planned. "I do like him—as a friend. But he's Mama's choice, not mine. I'd really like to have the opportunity to get to know"—she paused for dramatic effect—"some *other* young gentlemen."

"And I'll bet you have one particular young gentleman in mind," Charisma said in an arch tone.

"Well, perhaps," Belle said with feigned reluctance.

"Who?" Grace asked eagerly.

"I'd rather not say." It wasn't in the script, but Belle could almost feel Susan and Carrie leaning in to hear her answer on the other side and couldn't resist teasing them a little longer.

Giving her an exasperated look for deviating from their plan, Charisma said, "I know who it is— it's George Winthrop. I've seen the way you've been looking at him."

Twin gasps, quickly stifled, sounded on the other side of the shelves.

"What was that?" Belle asked, trying to sound horrified, but in reality hardly able to contain her amusement. "Do you think someone overheard?"

Grace's eyes danced with merriment at the ad lib. "I don't know, but I'll find out."

She turned too fast and her elbow caught a row of books, pushing them through the shelves to tumble onto the floor on the other side. The resulting blank space between the stacks revealed Carrie's and Susan's wide-eyed expressions staring back at them.

Carrie recovered first. "Really, Grace Sullivan, can't you be more careful?"

Grace placed her hands on her hips. "Really, Carrie Winthrop," she mimicked, "can't you stop eavesdropping?"

"Eavesdropping?" Carrie blustered. "Why, we were doing no such thing. Come, Susan, let us leave before Grace brings the shelves down around us."

They left hastily as the proprietor hurried over to assess the damages.

Grace would have helped him pick up the books, but Belle and Charisma restrained her, fearing her efforts would prove more detrimental than helpful. With apologies to the harassed man, they fled into the street.

"Do you think Carrie and Susan heard everything?" Grace asked.

"Oh, I have no doubt," Charisma said with a gleeful grin. "I'll bet they are giving their brother an earful even as we speak."

"They heard, all right," Belle confirmed. "Now, let's hope George takes the hint tonight at Alvina's dinner party and asks me to attend the concert with him."

"What do you plan to do to him there?" Charisma asked curiously.

"I don't know," Belle admitted. "But I'll think of something."

She always did.

Belle declined Kit's escort to Alvina's, saying her father would be happy to escort her there and take her home. She hoped Kit would take that as an excuse to pass on the entertainment, but no such luck. He appeared at Alvina's, looking as handsome as always.

Belle's pulse quickened when he gave her a slight smile from across the room, and she felt that odd sensation in her middle again. Why did her body react so strangely when she saw him?

It didn't matter—she would not give free rein to her body's impulses tonight. Instead, she must avoid Kit so as to give George the opportunity to invite her to the concert.

Though she was lucky enough to avoid sitting by Kit at supper, unfortunately, her hostess had placed her at the opposite end from George as well. Belle had no choice but to endure indifferent conversation with the callow young men Alvina had seated next to her, waiting for supper to be over so the dancing would begin.

She entertained herself by throwing the occasional wistful glance in George's direction. He intercepted two of them, and both times, he colored-up and looked self-conscious, as if he weren't quite sure what to do. Ah, very good—it seemed their little playlet in the library had gotten the word to the right ears.

After the meal was finally over, Alvina led them into another room where most of the furniture had been removed to allow for dancing. This was more like it. Now Belle could circulate.

She wanted to use her simple ivory lace fan to communicate with George, but unfortunately, many others in the room could read her message as well. Especially Kit. She tried to maneuver so that George was the only one who could see her fan, but she was continually thwarted by intervening guests and Kit's watchfulness.

When the band struck up a waltz, Kit crossed to her side. "May I have this dance?" he asked with a smile.

Belle hesitated. She didn't want George to think Kit was monopolizing her attention, but she didn't want to be rude to Kit either. "Of course." But she must somehow contrive to let George think she wasn't enjoying it.

As the music swelled and Kit whirled her onto the dance floor, Belle's traitorous heart leapt with joy. They fit together like two halves of a puzzle. Sighing with pleasure, she thought, *This is where I should always be—in Kit's arms.*

Wait a minute. What am I thinking? Kit Stanhope might be handsome and charming, but there was no way she could spend the rest of her life with him, no matter how pleasant it might be. Not only did he have some dark secret he wouldn't share with her, but he obviously thought of her only as a pupil. Besides, she had promised her sisters she would somehow get even with him for calling her homely.

That did it. The memory of that humiliation was enough to remind her of her primary purpose and stiffened her spine. She looked about for George.

"Is something wrong?" Kit asked.

"No, of course not," Belle prevaricated. "Why, should there be?"

He stared down at her. "You seem preoccupied tonight."

"Ridiculous," Belle said, but she had spotted George on the sidelines watching her and wanted to take advantage of the situation. She frowned at Kit, hoping George would get the idea that she wasn't pleased with her partner. "I'm just trying to mind my steps, is all."

She glanced back at George and noticed he was still watching her, looking concerned. Not sure if that was a good sign or not, Belle decided this was the best time to give him a signal.

She wanted to use her fan to ask, "When may I be allowed to see you?" but that required that she place the shut fan over her right eye. How in Sam Hill was she going to do that with her right hand held securely in Kit's?

"You *are* preoccupied," Kit said accusingly. "You haven't heard a word I said."

Guilty. "I'm sorry," Belle said. "I have a great deal on my mind of late."

"I was asking you if you would like to attend the outdoor concert Mrs. Palmer has arranged for Friday evening."

She would, but not with him. "I'm afraid I can't," she said, hoping he wouldn't pursue the matter.

Kit didn't press her further, but he looked surprised. Well, it would do him good to be turned down every once in a while, Belle thought. Let him wonder what she was up to.

Then, finally, the dance was at an end. While George was still watching her, Belle gave him a significant look and brought the closed fan up swiftly to her right eye.

A little *too* swiftly, she realized as she jabbed herself in the eye. "Ouch." Darn it—that sort of thing was usually Grace's problem, not hers.

"Are you all right?" Kit asked solicitously.

"Yes." She was now. Through her smarting eye, she had seen that George's face had brightened and he had given her a slight nod.

In fact, he was on his way over right now. Frantically, she wondered how to get rid of Kit. "I just need a moment or two, and I'll be fine," she said dismissively.

And with raised eyebrows, Kit took the hint and left.

The band struck up another waltz just as George made it to her side. "May I have the honor of this dance?" he asked with a self-conscious look.

Belle beamed at him, feeling like a teacher bestowing favor upon a prized pupil. He *had* gotten the message. She murmured the appropriate response and was on the dance floor once again. Only this time her partner wasn't nearly as graceful or athletic. Nor did he make her limbs weak with longing.

This was a good thing, she assured herself. She didn't need any distractions. She smiled up at George. "I hoped you would ask me to dance."

He reddened. "I thought . . . that is, I thought you were trying to convey a message . . . ?"

She laughed lightly. "When I poked myself in the eye, you mean?"

"Oh, no," he assured her. "I'm sure you could never be so clumsy."

Oh? Yet he had had no problem in condemning

Grace as hopelessly awkward. "You're too kind. And a wonderful dancer," she gushed.

Uh-oh, was that too much? No, apparently not. He puffed up like a pouter pigeon and essayed a more vigorous step. Oh, dear, she hoped they wouldn't come to grief this way. Especially since she still had the bruises from when Grace had tried the same thing.

"Oh, my," she said, batting her eyelashes at him. "You're making me dizzy."

Obligingly, he slowed down and her fears abated. Though she wouldn't mind *him* being humiliated publicly by sprawling on the floor, she didn't want to join him in that embarrassment.

But either he hadn't gotten the message that she wanted to go with him to the concert, or he didn't have enough nerve to ask her out. It must be the latter, so Belle found herself making small talk and hoping the dance wouldn't end before he had screwed up the courage to ask her.

Using the band's playing as an excuse, she led the conversation around to music. "I do so love a good concert, don't you?" she asked, hinting as blatantly as she could.

He gulped and stared down at her with a sick expression. "Oh, yes, I do. Love it. Good music."

"And outdoor concerts are so much fun," she prompted.

"Er, yes." He stretched his neck, as if his collar had suddenly become too tight. "I say, have you heard that Mrs. Palmer is giving such a concert?"

Finally. "Oh, yes." Belle gazed up at him with a sad expression. "But I have no one to escort me."

Come on, take the bait, she urged him silently.

"Uh, er, would you . . . that is . . . would you like to go with me?"

Hooked! "Why, I'd love to," she said. And not a moment too soon as the dance came to an end.

"Marvelous," he exclaimed. "I'll see you then." Then he escaped as if that were all he could manage for one evening.

"Well, that was interesting," came a drawl behind her.

Belle whirled around to see Kit regarding her with a quizzical expression. Oh, dear, how long had he been there? What had he heard?

"What was interesting?" she asked with a challenge in her voice. "Seeing another man ask me to dance?"

"No, seeing you accept an invitation to a function you 'couldn't' make with me." He didn't word it as a question, yet the query was implicit in his tone and expression.

Unfortunately, Belle didn't have a good answer for that. She raised her chin. "I don't have to explain myself to you."

"Perhaps not," he said in a dangerous tone. "Yet I find myself continually rescuing you from the folly of your actions nonetheless."

He glanced around, saying, "No one's looking," and drew her into a dark, secluded alcove, the dancers shielding their exit as they took their places for the polka. Lowering his voice, he asked, "Is Winthrop the man you are trying to attract?"

How could he think she would be interested in such a gauche young man? Then again, why not let him believe what he wanted? "Why would you think that?"

"Why wouldn't I? What foolishness do you have planned now?"

"I don't have any *foolishness* planned, as you put it. I simply wanted a different escort to the concert." And if Kit hadn't been right there when the dance ended, he would have never known about it.

He narrowed his eyes at her, and all of a sudden the small alcove seemed infinitely smaller . . . dangerously so. She retreated a step and came up against a wall. No escape there, especially since Kit closed in to stare down at her, only a breath away.

Her pulse quickened, responding to his nearness, the light touch of fear adding an edge of excitement. What did he intend to do?

"What are you playing at?" he muttered.

"N-nothing. I just heard rumors that everyone has been expecting us to announce our engagement soon and I, uh, thought it would be better if we weren't seen so much together."

He pursed his lips in thought and her stomach went all fluttery again. She couldn't help but stare at them—those lips had been featured prominently in many of her dreams of late.

"I see." He gazed at her curiously. "Why do you stare at my mouth so?"

"Because it's so very mesmerizing," she blurted out before she could stop herself. Then she immediately covered her own mouth, her heart pounding as his gaze turned dark and unreadable.

"Is it now?" he drawled, low and seductive as the small space became charged with energy, sending little prickles of sensation over the bare skin on her arms.

He lowered that sensual mouth closer to hers, drawing her hands away from her face until he was only a kiss away and she could feel his warm breath on her cheeks. "Do you wonder how my lips would feel pressed to yours in a kiss?" His voice deepened, becoming husky. "A long . . . deep . . . satisfying kiss?"

"Oh, yes," she breathed, but her heart was thumping so hard, she was sure it could be heard above the polka.

"Good," he said . . . and kissed her.

He took his time about it, sliding his soft, mobile lips against hers, tasting, teasing, making her head swim with forbidden wonder.

She slid her arms around his neck to draw him closer and felt his arms go around her. *Oh, my.* She opened her mouth to get a breath and stilled in shock as he slipped his tongue inside.

Oh, my goodness!

A surge of warmth invaded her, oozing to every part of her body, pooling wetly in the crevices. How . . . thrilling.

More—she wanted more.

She pressed herself up against him, emitting an inarticulate sound of pleasure, but he broke the kiss off abruptly and pulled away.

What? No. . . . She reached for him again, but he held her off.

"Pardon me, I—I should never have touched you."

On the contrary. He never should have stopped. . . .

He backed off even more, looking as shaky as she felt. "The music has started again. I'll . . . go now. Wait a few moments, then follow me." Without waiting for her agreement, he left abruptly.

Feeling bereft, Belle watched him leave and took a few moments to compose herself, her hands to her cheeks. Oh, dear Lord, what had just happened here? Had she really begged him to kiss her? What must he think? That she had fallen in love with him?

The truth hit her like a cave-in. The problem was, he'd be right.

Joy filled her at the realization that she was in love; then her world bottomed out again as she realized her love wasn't returned.

Oh, Kit might kiss her and make love to her, but he wasn't *in* love with her. Nor did he intend to marry her, or he would have asked her after the first time he had kissed her. Mama had often told her men didn't treat their future wives with such disrespect.

And what would the son of a viscount want with the daughter of an Irish miner—especially a *homely* one—when he could do so much better?

So, he was just dallying with her. The thought hurt, and a sudden suspicion blossomed within her. Was Kit the womanizer Mr. Daltrey claimed?

If so, he was uncommonly good at it. . . .

She loved the way he touched her, kissed her, used his mouth on her. The only problem was, he always broke off before he got to the really interesting parts. What else might he have to teach her?

Her resolve firmed. No matter what anyone else said, she was going to enjoy every minute of their association . . . right up until the moment she made him pay.

Belle felt a little low as she dressed for her evening with George Winthrop. She wished it could be Kit instead . . . and yet she didn't. In some ways, she wanted to be with him as much as possible, to soak up his presence and commit his every movement to memory so she could cherish it forever.

But . . . she was also afraid that he would see her love in her face. And, perhaps, pity her. She didn't think she could bear that.

"What's the matter?" Grace asked.

"Oh, nothing," Belle said with a sigh, and voiced the only concern she felt she could share with her sisters. "I'm just not sure the method I used with Harold will work with George."

"What do you mean?" Charisma asked.

"Well, I know I said I wanted to make all three men fall in love with me . . ."

"Yes, we know," Charisma said. "So you could spurn them in revenge. Have you changed your mind?"

Charisma looked disappointed, and Belle remembered how much George had hurt her sister with his insults. "Oh, I still intend to make him pay for what he did," Belle assured her sisters. "But I don't want him to offer for me. I . . . don't want to be alone with him."

Grace nodded wisely. "He might attack you like Harold did."

"Exactly," Belle said, relieved that she didn't have to explain. "I don't want to go through that again." And Kit might not be so handy to the rescue this time, either.

"So you're not going to make him fall in love with you?" Charisma asked.

"No—I don't want to take that chance." Besides, she couldn't wear a low neckline to this entertainment, and she wasn't sure of her ability to make him fall for her without those twin inducements.

Grace squirmed in excitement. "Then what are you going to do?"

Yes, that was the question. "I'm not sure," Belle admitted. "But I do have a few ideas. We'll just have to see how they pan out."

Her escort arrived then, and Belle went down to meet him, pleased that George had chosen to join Miss Mattingly's party to attend the concert. With eight people in the party, she didn't have to worry overmuch about George becoming too familiar.

When they arrived at the park, they found that the concert area had been covered with a large tent in the event of rain. It was a good thing she hadn't planned on pulling George aside—there just wasn't any place to do it.

George was very solicitous as he insisted on finding a choice spot for her to sit, asked her anxiously if she required refreshment, and generally acted the perfect escort.

His kindness made her wonder if she should really go through with her plan. Then she remembered what he had said about Charisma and the subsequent wounded expression on her sister's face. Belle steeled herself. She had promised her sisters she would do this, and she would. She just had to find the best opportunity to do so.

As various members of the town played musical instruments or regaled the crowd with song, Belle tried to formulate a plan. She knew the music should have elevated her, should have sent her into transports of rapture or some such thing, if the other female members of the party were any indication. But Belle found it all rather boring. She was not musically inclined, and listening to amateurs wasn't her idea of fun.

She glanced around to determine who else was present, and was surprised to see many of the town's social elite. No doubt she was alone in thinking this a rather boring entertainment. Even Madame Aglaia was there.

Then Belle's heart skipped a beat as she saw Kit's fair head in the audience, bent toward the woman next to him. A stab of jealousy assailed her. Who had he brought tonight? And did the woman know she was his second choice?

When the woman turned her head to answer him, Belle recognized his companion as Alvina Keithley. Belle's jealousy eased. That was all right— she knew they were merely friends.

Not that Belle had any right to approve or disapprove Kit's choice of companion when she herself had declined his invitation, she reminded herself. In Kit's eyes, she was only a pupil, a short-term dalliance, if that.

Eventually, a murmur rose in the audience when one particular performer rose to sing and Belle roused herself from her lethargy to ask, "Who's that?"

"Queen Palmer," George whispered back.

Oh, the wife of the founder. No wonder everyone was so interested. The woman dubbed "Queen" sang a few popular ballads for which she received resounding applause; then an intermission was announced. The members of the audience rose to stretch their legs and obtain refreshment, to gossip and wonder, to see and be seen.

Once more, George became a solicitous host and went in search of refreshment for her. Madame Aglaia made her way to Belle's side and said, "You're in fine looks tonight, dear. How are you doing?" Her words were innocuous, but the questioning look that accompanied them was penetrating, as if she were trying to read Belle's mind and soul.

Belle answered her spoken question, unsure how to deal with the unspoken ones. "Thank you, I am doing just fine."

Madame nodded, but looked concerned as she placed a hand on Belle's arm. "You will be careful tonight, won't you?"

How odd. "Of course. Is there something in particular I should be careful of?"

"No, just . . . think before you act, won't you?"

"All right," Belle said, puzzled.

Apparently satisfied, Madame took her leave when George and the other male members of their party returned with lemonade.

Now what was that all about? Belle wondered. But all else fled her mind as she chatted in a circle with the members of her party and pondered how to carry out her promise to Charisma.

At one point, George leaned down to whisper something in Belle's ear about Mrs. Palmer, likening her voice to a songbird in springtime, or some such nonsense. Belle stiffened at the familiarity, then realized he had just presented her with the perfect opportunity for revenge.

"Really, Mr. Winthrop," she protested. "I wonder you would say such a thing."

George looked puzzled, but Belle had garnered the attention of the rest of the party, which was exactly what she wanted. With pretended disgust, she said, "It is most unkind of you to compare Mrs. Palmer's voice to that of a wounded feline."

George was so taken aback, he couldn't say anything.

Miss Mattingly, of course, had no such trouble. With a glare at George, she said loudly, "George Winthrop, I am ashamed of you for saying such horrible things about Mrs. Palmer."

One of those odd lulls that happen in company fell at that moment throughout the tent, and Miss Mattingly's penetrating voice effortlessly reached the far corners. Shocked silence reigned as everyone present turned to stare in condemnation at George.

With a gulp, he opened his mouth, apparently to defend himself, but no words came out. Instead, he turned red and, with a strangled sound and clenched fists, strode away.

Revenge at last, and in a manner fitting the original crime.

Belle should have felt triumph, but that emotion eluded her as guilt filled her instead. She hadn't thought about how carrying Miss Mattingly's voice could be, nor had she intended for all of Colorado Springs to witness George's humiliation. She'd just wanted to embarrass him in front of the few members of their party. Now he'd never be able to hold his head up in society again.

Darn it, she hadn't wanted it to be this bad. How could she set it right?

Fourteen

Across the tent, Kit watched the sordid little scene play out and frowned. Though Belle's escort had been embarrassed and hastily departed, Belle looked exceedingly guilty. What had she done? Murmuring his apologies to Miss Keithley, Kit threaded his way toward Belle and her party.

When he reached them, Miss Mattingly was still holding forth on Winthrop's perfidy and was causing so much commotion that apparently no one else had noticed Belle's guilt-stricken countenance. Or perhaps they just didn't know her as well as he did.

Kit schooled his face to politeness and greeted the people clustered around Belle and Millicent Mattingly. Lowering his voice so they would have to be silent to hear him, Kit said, "This has been a most unfortunate occurrence, but perhaps you could return to your seats? It appears the entertainment is about to begin again." And the sounds of the small orchestra tuning up confirmed it.

But Miss Mattingly had the bit in her teeth and was not about to let go of it. "Really, I don't see where this is any concern of yours," she said in frosty tones.

But it was. He didn't doubt for a minute that Belle

was behind the current mess, though he didn't understand quite how yet. Kit smiled at Millicent and said in a deceptively mild tone, "You have made it everyone's concern, have you not?"

Miss Mattingly appeared taken aback that anyone would question her, but before she could say anything else, Kit added, "I'm sure Mrs. Palmer would appreciate it if you would spare her further embarrassment by forgetting this ever happened."

Miss Mattingly colored, apparently unaware until that moment how the object of everyone's gossip might feel about the topic of discussion . . . and Miss Mattingly's tenacious pursuit of it. "Of course," she said faintly, or as faintly as she was capable of with that voice of hers.

Kit nodded, then turned to Belle, who had apparently tried to lose herself in the crowd. "Miss Sullivan? Would you care for an escort home?"

Miss Mattingly puffed up again. "She is a part of my party, sir, and I shall see her home."

Kit censured her with a glance. "Mrs. Palmer is not the only person who has been embarrassed this evening. May I remind you that Winthrop was Miss Sullivan's escort? I don't think she would care to sit through the rest of the concert with everyone's eyes upon her."

"I quite agree," Madame Aglaia said, coming to stand beside him. "Let us take her home and you can get on with your enjoyment of the evening without having to worry about Miss Sullivan."

Everyone looked at Belle, who appeared decidedly uncomfortable at all the attention. She colored and looked down at the ground.

"Well," Miss Mattingly said bracingly to Belle, "is that what you want?"

"Yes, please," Belle murmured.

"All right, then," Millicent Mattingly said as if bestowing a great favor. "I'll allow the two of you to escort her home."

The music was about to begin again, so Kit merely nodded and offered his arm to Belle. Followed by Madame Aglaia, they made their way swiftly out of the tent.

Once outside, Belle seemed to relax a bit. "B-but what about Miss Keithley?" she asked.

"What about her?" Kit asked, puzzled.

"Didn't you bring her to the concert?"

"No, I came alone." Though musicales weren't his favorite form of entertainment, he had suspected Belle might be up to something and wanted to know what it was. But rather than sit alone for the evening, he had attached himself to Miss Keithley's party.

"Oh," Belle said, then fell silent.

Kit allowed that silence to continue until they reached the small buggy he had rented for the evening. "I apologize for the crowded conditions," he said as he assisted Madame Aglaia inside, "but I had no idea I would be sharing the conveyance with anyone else this evening."

"Quite all right," Madame murmured.

Kit smiled at her. "But I do want to thank you for coming so swiftly to Belle's aid." He took Belle's arm to assist her in as well. "Between the two of us, we might be able to save her from the folly of her actions."

Belle paused, half in and half out, and gave him a disbelieving look. "The folly of *my* actions?" she repeated. "What have I done?"

"That is what I'd like to know," Kit said.

As Belle settled herself and he joined her in the buggy, he asked, "What have you done, Belle?"

She turned defensive immediately. "I? Nothing. Why would you assume I did something?"

Kit steered the vehicle out of the park. "Because disaster seems to follow you," he said wryly.

Belle gave a bitter laugh. "You're thinking of my sister, Grace."

"No, I'm not," he said firmly. "I'm speaking of emotional, not physical, disasters. What did you do?"

Belle turned to Madame Aglaia in supplication. "Can you please make him understand?"

Madame raised an eyebrow. "I did warn you to be careful. I'm afraid Mr. Stanhope is correct—you look quite guilty. What did you do, Belle? You know we shall find out sooner or later."

Belle hung her head. "Well, I might have . . . misinterpreted something Mr. Winthrop said. . . ."

"Oh?" Kit said in an uncompromising tone.

"Yes," Belle said in a rush, "but I didn't know Miss Mattingly would repeat it quite so loudly."

Kit stared at her in disbelief. "You know Miss Mattingly's voice. How could you think she would repeat it any other way?" Then her phrasing suddenly struck him as odd. "You mean . . . you planned this?"

"No, of course not," Belle said hastily.

It was too dark to see her expression, or Kit would have been able to determine if she was telling the truth or not. It didn't matter—he suspected she was prevaricating.

If she was, that meant she *had* planned it. But why? Why humiliate George Winthrop in public? He narrowed his eyes suddenly as he realized she had also been involved in Harold Latham's disgrace. Had that been deliberate as well?

Suddenly suspicious, he said, "I find it odd that two of the three men who insulted your sisters have received their comeuppance at your hands."

Madame said nothing, tacitly letting him continue with his questioning.

Belle stiffened beside him. "Is that what you think?" she asked in an innocent tone.

"Yes," he said baldly. "I assume that means I'm next?"

"Don't be ridiculous," she said sternly, and once more he wished he could see her expression. "I assure you I had no intention of publicly humiliating George Winthrop."

"Just privately, eh?" Kit asked, and was rewarded with a small jerk of startlement from Belle. Apparently, he had hit upon the truth. "So, am I to assume that Latham wasn't really manhandling you at the opera—that it was all just part of your plan to embarrass him for insulting your sisters?"

Belle shuddered. "No! He . . . he really did attack me. I hate to think what might have happened if you weren't there."

Kit remembered his own folly that night, how he had taken this innocent into his arms and attempted to take full advantage of her. And again at Miss Keithley's. He was no better than Latham.

But . . . wasn't that Belle's plan? She had made it very clear from the beginning that her goal was to be beautiful so she could make men fall in love with her.

The hell of it was, she was achieving that goal all too easily. A sudden thought struck Kit. Was it part of her plan to make *him* fall in love with her so she could spurn him?

Suddenly disgusted with her and himself, Kit was glad they had come to Belle's home. He walked her to her door, promising, "We shall speak of this later."

Belle said nothing, but went meekly into the house.

Madame was not quite so shy. "Don't you think you were a bit hard on her?" she asked from the darkness.

"Not if I am correct in what I suspect," Kit bit out.

"Even if you are correct," Madame said mildly, "do you think the two men deserved to be taught a lesson?"

"Not in that way," Kit said.

"Perhaps not," Madame conceded. "But I wonder . . . would you be so very angry with her if you didn't suspect you were the third target on her list?"

Kit scowled. Damn it, she was right. He cared nothing for Winthrop or Latham, but he had developed a great deal of fondness for Belle. In fact, he had begun to think she was someone rather special. Her plucky behavior and loyalty to her family made her stand out from all the silly girls her same age.

It was lowering to think that all the time he was becoming ensnared by her charms, she had simply been luring him into a trap.

Well, now that he was aware of the danger, he wouldn't let himself be lured. And if Belle tried any of her tricks on him, he'd just turn them back on her. Kit Stanhope was not about to let a woman make a fool out of him.

* * *

Grace and Charisma accosted Belle in her bedroom the next morning before she even got out of bed, demanding to know how the concert went. Belle had been so worried about that same subject the night before that she hadn't gotten much sleep. She sat up in bed and said in groggy accents, "Horrible."

Charisma slouched in disappointment. "You mean you didn't follow through?"

Belle rubbed her eyes. "Yes, I did."

"So what happened?" Grace asked eagerly.

"It went horribly wrong. I humiliated him in front of the entire town."

Charisma looked puzzled. "Wasn't that your plan?"

Belle shook her head ruefully. "Not exactly. The embarrassment they afforded us was private, and I intended for his to be not quite so . . . public. Instead, quite by accident, he was disgraced in front of everyone at the concert, and I'm sure word of his *faux pas* is all over Colorado Springs by now."

Especially if Millicent Mattingly had anything to do with it.

"What did you *do?*" Grace asked, wide-eyed.

Belle winced—that was the same question Kit had repeatedly asked her. She explained the situation, finishing with, "I should have known Miss Mattingly would screech it to the entire world, but I wasn't thinking. I just saw the opportunity and I took it."

Charisma waved a hand in dismissal. "It wasn't your fault the situation got out of your control."

"Yes, it was," Belle insisted, feeling remorseful. "I should have thought first, should have surveyed the company to ensure there were no tattlemongers present before I said anything. Now George won't be able to show his face anywhere in town. It is too much."

"Are you sure?" Charisma asked. "Perhaps you are blowing it out of proportion."

"I don't think so. Even Mr. Stanhope and Madame Aglaia are displeased with me . . . and they don't even know I did it on purpose. What shall I do?" Belle wailed.

"That does sound bad," Grace agreed. "But what can you do?"

"I must make it right." Belle hit her pillow. "Darn it, whenever I try something clever or try to be beautiful, it misfires. But when I am myself, things seem to work out just fine."

Charisma arched an eyebrow at her. "So what can you do to salvage this situation?"

Belle sighed. "As much I hate the thought, I shall have to apologize to George, and make sure I set the record straight with the town."

"Apologize?" Charisma repeated in dismay. "After what he did to us?"

"Yes," Belle said firmly. "After having the whole town discussing him last night and probably this morning, I think he's been punished enough."

"She's right," Grace said with a frown. "It went too far. An apology is the best way to correct it."

Charisma sighed. "I suppose you're right. But at least you *did* get revenge."

And now she would have to pay the consequences for it. Reluctantly, Belle got out of bed to dress. She couldn't ask Madame Aglaia or Alvina to assist her in such a delicate task. And Mama wouldn't understand why Belle had to apologize. For this, she needed Papa.

Papa was in his study. At her knock, he called for Belle to come in. She did so, not sure how he would take what she was about to say. But she was sure her apprehension and reluctance were clearly evident in her expression.

"What's the matter, Belle?" he asked kindly.

Tears filled her eyes. She could take any amount of yelling or condemnation, but let one person be kind to her and she turned into a watering pot. "I did something very bad," she admitted. There. Blurting it out made her feel better already.

He nodded gravely. "Do ye want to tell me about it?"

Not really, but she had to. Haltingly, she explained what she had done, leaving out only that she had intentionally set out to punish George. "I— I think I misinterpreted what he said," she explained. "And now he's going to be ostracized by the whole town and it's all my fault." She stared anxiously at her father, hoping he could put it all right with a word, or tell her it wasn't as bad as she thought.

But Papa wouldn't lie to her. "That *is* a serious matter," he agreed. "And ye came to me because . . . ?"

"Because I want to make it right, Papa. I want to apologize to Mr. Winthrop and set the story straight. Could you . . . escort me to his house?"

"That I can do."

As Papa drove her to the Winthrops' house in town, Belle worried about what to say, and if George would even agree to see her. But she needn't have worried—Papa took care of the latter, insisting to the butler that Mr. George Winthrop would want to see them.

George came in with a hollow-eyed look and a haughty, distancing expression that showed more clearly than words that he hadn't slept at all the night before and was prepared to thumb his nose at the world.

"You wished to see me?" he asked coldly.

He addressed his question to Papa, who nodded at Belle. "Me daughter has something to say to ye."

George raised an eyebrow at Belle, who felt even worse than she had before. "I-I wish to apologize," she said, trying not to stutter. "I think I may have . . . misinterpreted something you said last night."

Something unidentifiable flickered in George's eyes. "I am *certain* you did," he said stiffly.

She glanced at Papa, who nodded at her, clearly telling her to get on with it. "Then I fear I may have done you a great disservice and I would like to set it right." She paused, swallowing hard when his stony expression didn't change. "What exactly did you say to me?"

"I said Mrs. Palmer had a voice like a songbird in springtime," he said with a fierce glare. "*Not* like a wounded cat."

"Oh," Belle said in a small voice, though she remembered what he had really said quite well. "I'm sorry. I'm afraid I misheard."

Apparently angry now, George said, "How could you mistake it so? They sound nothing alike."

Belle hung her head. "I don't know . . . there was so much noise all around us, so much chatter. I fear I must have heard two conversations and they jumbled themselves in my head as one."

But George still looked angry, rightfully so. "You do realize I did not insult Mrs. Palmer?"

"Of course." He was far too obsequious for that. "And in . . . in reparation, I shall visit Miss Mattingly and others of my acquaintance to set the record straight."

Something like relief flickered in his eyes, but there was no forgiveness anywhere. "I would be obliged to you," he said, though his eyes insisted it was more a debt than an obligation.

She nodded, knowing better than to ask for his forgiveness or friendship. He wouldn't give the first and she didn't really want the second. With another muttered, "I'm sorry," she took her leave.

Papa said nothing once they were in the carriage about what had gone on. Instead, he merely asked for their next destination. With trepidation, Belle directed him to Miss Mattingly's.

But when they were shown into the parlor, she halted in dismay. It appeared half the town was there before her. Not only were most of the guests present who had made up her party the night before, but so were Kit, Alvina, Madame Aglaia, and a few others she didn't know.

When she was announced, all eyes turned to her, but she noticed only Kit's—accusing and disappointed. Her heart sank at the sight. Would she ever get back in his good graces?

"Oh, do come in, Miss Sullivan," Miss Mattingly shrilled. "And tell Mr. Stanhope exactly what Mr. Winthrop said last evening. He is trying to convince me that you were mistaken in what you heard."

Avoiding Kit's condemning gaze and Madame Aglaia's concerned one, Belle murmured, "He is correct."

"What?" Apparently, that was the last thing Miss Mattingly had expected her to say, for she appeared quite shocked.

"Yes, I realized later that I must have misheard what Mr. Winthrop said. He actually likened Mrs. Palmer's voice to a songbird in springtime . . . but there was another conversation going on in the area about cats, and I'm afraid I confused the two."

Miss Mattingly looked indignant. "Really." But it wasn't a question—more of an exclamation of disgust.

"Yes. I've just apologized to Mr. Winthrop and came directly here to set the record straight . . . and to apologize to you as well."

Millicent seemed mollified by the offer of an apology. "Well, I'm sure it does you credit to admit to your mistake," she said firmly, evidently unwilling to acknowledge responsibility for her own part in humiliating George Winthrop.

"Yes, it does," Kit said.

Belle peeked at him and was relieved to see that he was regarding her approvingly.

He continued softly, "It does you credit and shows great courage. I commend you, Miss Sullivan."

The relief that filled her was tremendous, and she felt tears pricking at her eyelids. She hadn't done this to gain his approval, but to regain his regard was an unlooked-for bonus.

Madame, too, looked pleased with her, and Belle felt infinitely better. Especially since the fierce whispering occurring in the rest of the group assured her that the word would be all over town very soon.

Not knowing what else to say, and fearing she would start bawling in public if Kit continued to be kind to her, Belle took her leave.

Papa handed her into the carriage and gave her a hug. "Ye did a good thing there. I'm proud of ye, lass."

Belle did burst into tears then. Everyone else might be pleased with her, but she was not at all pleased with herself. She should never have gotten into this situation in the first place.

Fifteen

A week after the debacle at the concert, Kit was glad to see that the furor and gossip had finally died down. A new scandal had taken its place, and George Winthrop was once more welcomed in drawing rooms around Little London.

Apparently Kit was the only one who suspected Belle had intentionally embarrassed Winthrop, for he realized Belle's social standing had never been called into question. Instead, she emerged as the heroine of the affair.

He smiled to himself. Belle was a heroine in his eyes as well. She had made the right decision without any prompting from anyone and refused to let people give her credit for it. It had taken a lot of courage to stand up in front of people like Millicent Mattingly and admit she was wrong, but Belle had done it without shirking.

Even if her original intent had been to embarrass Winthrop, she had made up for it by apologizing.

As a result, Kit had been more than happy to continue their lessons at Madame Aglaia's. They had proceeded nicely, and Belle was fast becoming a model pupil. Today, he was demonstrating how to converse with diverse dancing partners.

To amuse her, he had played the roles of several

gentlemen who might ask her to dance at the Founders' Day Ball, such as a retired major, an avid horseman, and the genial founder himself, William Jackson Palmer.

Belle laughed at him throughout each impression, but still managed to maintain her poise and aplomb no matter what conversational ball he threw her.

Kit dropped his impression of a stuffy business-man and grinned at her. "I don't think you'll have any problem in this area, Miss Sullivan. You are doing quite well."

Belle bobbed him a curtsey. "Thank you, sir. But I have an excellent teacher, and it is all to his credit."

"You flatter me. Really, you are becoming quite skilled in all your lessons."

She smiled at him. "Thank you. And thanks *to* you, each day I'm becoming more and more confident in my ability to attend the Founders' Day Ball without mishap."

"Ah, yes, the ball—and the end of your lessons. I'm sure you can't wait. I know I can't." It would be Belle's triumph, the moment she brought every-thing she had learned together to be the belle of the ball. And it was less than a week away.

She gave him an odd look, one he couldn't inter-pret. "Of course," she murmured, then glanced into the parlor where her sisters were waiting. "But it is time for me to go. Mama is expecting me at home, and my sisters are here already to escort me."

Kit watched her leave with a smile as Madame Aglaia came to stand next to him.

"She has certainly blossomed, has she not?" the dressmaker asked.

Kit smiled. "Yes, she has come a long way from the awkward girl I first met. It is odd how improving her appearance a fraction has increased her self-confidence tenfold." She was truly a beauty now.

"You have done well there," Madame said. "She is quite a young lady."

"And I shall be sorry when our lessons are over."

"You won't see her any more after that?" Madame asked in surprise.

It was a shame, but . . . "No, she won't need any more lessons." In fact, Belle didn't need them now, if she but knew it. "She needs to move on, to use her newfound confidence to find the man who will be right for her." And, sadly, Kit needed to let her do that.

Madame regarded him oddly. "I was beginning to think you might be that man. . . ."

"I?" Kit said in surprise, though the thought had crossed his mind a time or two. Or twelve. "No, she is interested in another."

"Are you certain of that?"

"She has said so repeatedly," Kit reminded her. "And I have the impression she is harboring a secret from us. Do you not think so?"

Madame shrugged. "Perhaps. Many girls do."

"I mean with regard to me."

Madame Aglaia nodded wisely. "I see. You still suspect she is setting you up for revenge."

Frankly, yes. Though he was surprised she had guessed his mind so accurately. "Do you think it likely?"

"Perhaps," Madame conceded. "But you know her better than I. What do you think?"

"I hope not." He hoped his friendship with Belle had progressed beyond that point, but from some of the things she had let slip, he feared she had something . . . devious planned for the ball.

No matter. After it was over, he would be able to get back to his own life, to continue pursuing his investment.

As if she had read his mind, Madame asked, "Have you had any luck in finding an investment?"

"Not yet." And it was becoming rather frustrating.

"Well, instead of looking blindly for opportunities, perhaps you should concentrate on areas you are interested in," Madame suggested.

Kit turned a questioning look on her. "What do you mean?"

"Well, what sort of things interest you? In general terms, what you like to be a part of?"

Kit thought for a moment. "I have come to like this country, despite its rough edges, and to admire its citizens. I believe I would like to invest in its future, in good and honest men like Patrick Sullivan and General Palmer who are shaping this country into something noble and fine." Though how he was to do that, he had no idea.

"And where do you see the future going?"

"West, of course." Everyone knew that. The future lay in continuing to civilize the wild frontier.

"And how are people going to get there?"

What an odd question. "They have traveled by wagon train, on mules, horseback, however they could. And, to the more civilized areas, by train."

Wait—that's it. The future of western America would depend on good transportation, and that meant more trains. And hadn't Kit heard that General Palmer was seeking to expand operations on the Denver and Rio Grande Railroad? It was perfect. Even his father would approve.

Suddenly enthusiastic, Kit took his leave of Madame with a hearty "Thank you" and hurried out the door.

Unfortunately, Daltrey was waiting for him on the other side. "I thought I might find you here," the man said with a sneer.

"How very perceptive of you," Kit said impatiently. Why did Daltrey show up *now*, when everything seemed to be going his way?

Kit tried to move past him, but Daltrey stopped him with the simple expedient of stepping in front of him. "I'd like a word with you," he said in a menacing tone.

Kit sighed. He was becoming weary of this whole sordid blackmailing scheme of Daltrey's, not to mention extremely annoyed. "I gave you money already," Kit said in a low tone. "What more do you want? Blood?"

Daltrey scowled. "That is a distinct possibility, old man, if you don't open your pockets."

"I have very little left," Kit explained impatiently. "You've taken most of my remittance."

"But you have a bank account," Daltrey said with narrowed eyes. "I overheard someone mention it. You've been holding out on me."

Damn. Kit had mentioned his account to a few potential investors when they asked for references, but he had no idea the word would get back to his nemesis. He had set the money aside when he first arrived in Colorado Springs, never touching it, holding it in reserve for a potential investment. Now that the perfect investment was so close to becoming a reality, he didn't want to give it up.

"There's not much in the account," Kit explained, hoping Daltrey hadn't heard speculation as to the amount as well. "Just enough to get me home if I fail here."

Daltrey shrugged. "Whatever it is, I'm sure it's enough for me." His eyes narrowed. "No more excuses. I need that money and I'm going to have it, or I'll make sure all of Colorado Springs knows of your secret—especially that Sullivan girl you've been spending so much time with. What would she think if she knew you had a reputation as a womanizer and a cad?"

Damn. What could Kit do? He didn't want Belle's ears sullied with this man's lies and he needed to keep his name clean until he had established himself with his new investment.

Time. I need time.

Ignoring Daltrey's comments about Belle, Kit lied, saying, "My funds are in New York. It will take some time to send for them." Though Daltrey had somehow learned about his account, it appeared he wasn't aware just how much money Kit had there. Perhaps he could placate Daltrey with a small amount, keeping the bulk for the railroad investment.

"How long?" Daltrey growled.

Kit thought furiously. If Daltrey wasn't happy with the amount Kit was willing to turn over to him, he might be angry enough to reveal Kit's secret immediately. If he did so before the Founders' Day Ball, Kit would be obliged to forego the ball and Belle would be very disappointed. He needed to put Daltrey off until after that. "I'll have to send them a letter because they won't release the funds without a signature. It should take a week."

"All right, then," Daltrey said ungraciously. "I'll be back in a week—and you'd better have the money then, or else."

Kit nodded shortly and strode off, thinking furiously. The stalling tactic would gain him a little time, but would it be enough?

It would have to be. He couldn't fail now when he was so close to getting exactly what he wanted.

Though it had taken a great deal of soul-searching, Belle had come to a decision and wanted to tell her sisters immediately, before she lost her nerve. So she asked them to come to her room after breakfast.

Grace breezed in as usual, setting things topsyturvy, and Charisma closed the door behind her. "What did you want to see us about?" Charisma asked curiously as she calmly set things to rights in Grace's wake.

Belle twisted her fingers together in her lap, uncertain how her sisters were going to take what she had to say. Well, there was only one way to do this. Get it over with, fast.

"I don't want to get revenge on Kit anymore," she blurted out.

"I knew it," Charisma said. "Why not?"

"I punished Harold for Grace and made George pay for insulting you, but since Kit is the one who insulted me, I guess I can change my mind if I want."

"That makes sense," Grace said.

Encouraged, Belle added, "Besides, he apologized long ago—and he's the only one of the three who did."

Grace nodded. "Very true."

But Charisma wasn't satisfied. "There's more to it than that," she insisted.

"Of course there is," Belle said. "The first time I sought revenge, I was almost ravished and the second time I had to apologize for overdoing it. I'm not at all sure how it will turn out if I try a third time." Something even more horrid would probably happen if she tried to punish Kit.

"Well, I just think you're making excuses," Charisma said with a flounce.

"Nonsense." Well, maybe. But even if they were excuses, they were legitimate ones.

Charisma wasn't appeased. "You're sweet on him, admit it."

Why not admit it? Charisma figured she had it all worked out anyway. "Yes, I am," Belle said with a defiant tilt of her chin. She wasn't ashamed of it.

Belle could have laughed at the expression on Charisma's face—she looked so surprised, she was momentarily speechless.

"You are?" Grace said in delight. "You're really in love with him?"

Belle nodded ruefully. Yes, she was in love with him, for all the good it did her.

"What does it feel like?" Grace asked in eager tones.

"It feels . . . horrible. Every time I see him, I get a sinking sensation in my middle, like there are hundreds of butterflies flying around in there, beating against the walls and trying to get out. And if he speaks to me, I feel weak and light-headed, as if I'm going to faint."

Not to mention what happened to the other parts of her body when he used that sinful mouth on her.

Charisma scowled. "That doesn't sound like love. It sounds like you have a case of the flu."

No, Belle had been ill with influenza, and it was nowhere near as bad as this. "This feels worse, only I'm not sure there's a cure."

"But you don't need a cure," Grace said with a smile. "You two are perfect for each other."

Belle agreed, but . . . "Kit doesn't think so."

Grace's smile faltered. "Are you sure? Has he said so?"

"Not in so many words."

"Then what makes you believe that?" Grace asked in a puzzled tone.

Too many reasons. "The way he looked at Miss Downs . . ."

"You said 'looked,'" Charisma said. "That means he doesn't anymore, right? After all, what could he find to like in such a boring lady?"

Belle grinned—Charisma's bluntness was good for her sometimes. And it was true, Miss Downs's milk-white skin wasn't enough to overcome the inanity of her conversation. But that wasn't the only reason. "We aren't of the same social standing," she protested. "Kit is the son of a viscount, and, much as I love Papa, he's only a miner."

"But a rich one," Charisma reminded her. "And that makes him equal to any number of viscounts."

"That's right," Grace declared. "And with all these lessons Mr. Stanhope has given you, you can hold your own with anyone in society."

Belle felt tears prick her eyes at their support. She couldn't ask for two better or more loyal sisters. But they didn't have all the facts. "He treats me like nothing more than a prize pupil."

Charisma snorted. "Right. That's why he's constantly underfoot and ogling you when you're not looking. Because you're a 'prize pupil.'"

"He doesn't ogle me," Belle protested. Except that once. But she wished he would. . . .

"None of that matters," Grace said. "I'm sure he loves you, too. I just know it. Why, it's only a matter of time before he offers for you."

"No, if he was going to offer for me, he would have done so by now," Belle said.

Charisma raised an eyebrow. "You mean . . . ?"

Belle sighed. She wasn't sure she wanted to explain this to her sisters, but Charisma had figured it out for herself. "Yes."

"Yes, what?" Grace asked, confused. "What are you talking about?"

Charisma shrugged. "He must have crossed a line somewhere—the line that says 'beyond here you must ask the girl to marry you.'"

"Line?" Grace said. "What line? No one said anything about a line."

Charisma cocked her head at Belle. "I would guess that he kissed you. Is that right?"

Belle nodded, not trusting herself to speak at that moment.

Grace gasped, her eyes wide. "Really? How was it? Did that make you sick, too?"

Belle smiled. "No, it was wonderful. Like heaven on earth. He has the most incredible lips. . . ."

"I don't understand," Grace said. "How is a wonderful kiss crossing some sort of line? Why is that bad?"

"It's not bad," Charisma explained. "At least, if he asks her to marry him immediately. You know Mama says a man won't buy the cow if he can get the milk for free."

"Oh," Grace said in a small voice. "And Belle has been giving away free milk. . . ."

Belle winced. It sounded so . . . vulgar, put that way.

Charisma regarded Belle speculatively. "What else did you give him besides milk? A little cheese, perhaps?"

What the devil did she mean by that? "I am not a cow," Belle reminded them, even as she felt her face heat. And she wasn't about to answer that question honestly. There were some things she wouldn't share, even with her sisters. "And of course I didn't give him any 'cheese.'"

Charisma wiggled her eyebrows. "Not even a little Roquefort?"

"No." Belle made her tone uncompromising to discourage further questions.

Grace giggled. "Now you're just being silly." She turned to Belle. "And there's still time for him to ask you to marry him. It's not as if he's left town or anything."

"I'll only see him until the ball." Belle sighed. "He's a man of his word, and he's promised to escort me there . . . but nothing beyond that." He had made it very clear he was looking forward to the end of their association. "He might as well be gone." Sudden sadness assailed her at the thought that she would no longer see him, share his friendship, laugh with him . . .

"Nonsense," Charisma said bracingly. "That's only if you do nothing to keep him."

Keep him? "What do you mean?"

"If you want him, fight for him," Charisma said.

"How?" But it made her think. What could she do to keep him by her side? The only things she could think of were not at all honorable or noble.

She shook her head. "If I tried anything, it would probably misfire on me again."

"So, you're going to just let him go?" Charisma asked in disbelief. She snapped her fingers. "Just like that?"

Even Grace frowned at the thought.

"What else can I do?"

Charisma shook her head in disgust. "Well, if you don't know, I won't tell you. Come on, Grace. Let's leave Belle to her moping."

They left and Belle scowled, suspecting she knew what Charisma had in mind. But Belle had had enough of schemes and revenge— she wasn't about to try to trick Kit into offering for her.

Besides, it wouldn't mean anything if she had to fool him into it. She wanted him to love her as much as she loved him, to want her with a depth of passion she could only dream about.

She sighed. Unfortunately, that wasn't about to happen. Mama would be sorely disappointed— Belle would never find a husband now who could possibly compare to Kit. Since she wouldn't settle for second best, she would probably dwindle into an old maid.

Sadness filled her at the thought. Never to know a man's touch, the intimacy only a man and woman could share? The thought was depressing. She'd had a few tastes of what it meant to share that most intimate of acts, and she wanted more. Before she embarked on a life as an old maid, she needed— just once—to know what it was like to be a woman. After all, shouldn't she know what she was giving up before she decided to remain forever celibate?

Surely Kit would oblige her in this. Plans spun through her head. The ball would be the perfect opportunity. It was the last time he would be her escort, the last chance she would have to dance with him, feel his arms about her, experience his lovemaking.

Yes, Kit would just have to give her one last lesson. . . .

On Mount Olympus, Euphrosyne set her teacup down with an elegant flair and dabbed at her mouth with her napkin. "Belle seems to be coming right along. You are doing an excellent job there, Aglaia."

Aglaia inclined her head in appreciation. "Yes, I am quite pleased with her progress."

Thalia nodded. "You should be. Your penchant for creating beauty has worked wonders," she said. "Do you think you shall be done soon? I am anxious to get started on Charisma's wish."

"Yes, it should be done soon," Aglaia said. "Belle's choices at the Founders' Day Ball shall tell the tale, one way or another."

But would Belle choose wisely?

Sixteen

The evening of the Founders' Day Ball, Kit drove over to the Sullivans' to escort Belle and her parents to the event. He was glad to see that the heat, never very oppressive in Colorado, had dissipated and the evening was clear and cool, with a light breeze. Perfect for Belle's special night.

He arrived precisely on time, but the whole house was in an uproar, apparently all emanating from Mrs. Sullivan. When Charisma rushed past on an errand, he snagged her. "What is all the fuss about?" he asked, worried that Belle might have decided to wear her pearl powder again or do something else that might offend her mother.

Charisma rolled her eyes. "It's just Mama. You know our parents received an invitation to the ball tonight?"

"Yes." Probably as a result of their "relationship" to Dr. and Mrs. Bell. That was why they were able to dispense with other chaperonage this evening.

"Well, attending the Founders' Day Ball has always been one of Mama's dreams, and she wants to make sure everything is perfect—even if she has to drive us crazy to do it."

Mrs. Sullivan bellowed down the stairs, "Charisma, where is my shawl?"

Charisma rolled her eyes again at Kit. "Coming, Mama." Then in a softer voice to Kit, she said, "I'll tell her you're here. That's sure to hurry her up."

She rushed up the stairs and Kit made himself comfortable. Having had experience with primping mothers before, he was certain that nothing would be able to dislodge Mrs. Sullivan from her boudoir until she was satisfied with her entire party's appearance.

But to his surprise, Belle appeared first without any fanfare. She almost seemed to float down the stairs in a beautiful gown of deep gold that shimmered in the light, matched only by the sparkling citrines she wore at her ears and neck. The gold material made Belle's cosmetic-free face, framed by soft curls, glow with radiance. And her freckles, rather than detracting from her appearance, were so natural and appealing as to look like inspired beauty marks rather than despised blemishes.

Kit's gaze was drawn inexorably to where her neckline dipped to a decorous vee in front, and the part of her skin that was exposed gave testimony to the high, firm young breasts that lay beneath the gold material.

"You are beautiful, Belle," he said sincerely. And the heating of his blood made him realize he had never been more aware of her as a woman. A desirable woman. How could he have ever thought her homely?

Belle smiled at him. "Do you really think so? You're not just saying that?"

She had arrived at the bottom of the stairs by now and he reached for her hand, then raised it to his lips and kissed it, gratified to see her blush at the simple action.

"I not only think so, I know so. You shall truly be the belle of the ball."

Belle's fingers tightened upon his as she stared with rapt attention into his eyes. Then her gaze turned serious, and there was another emotion there he couldn't quite read, though he sensed it was very important. "Kit, I—"

The sound of his first name on her lips had an odd effect on him, as if it suddenly sounded very right. But he didn't hear what she had to say, for her parents descended the stairs at that moment.

Belle snatched her hand away from his, but her parents hadn't noticed anyway—they were too involved in a low-voiced argument. Mrs. Sullivan was attired in a gown he was certain owed much to Madame Aglaia's influence, and as she reached the bottom of the stairs, Belle's mother abruptly cut off their conversation and greeted Kit effusively.

Kit much preferred Mr. Sullivan's grunted greeting. The man didn't look comfortable in his finery, and Kit rather suspected that was the crux of the problem between him and his wife.

Then again, perhaps not. They maintained a strained silence all the way to the Colorado Springs Hotel.

Once inside the glittering ballroom, Mr. Sullivan muttered an excuse and made for the smoke-filled room at the side where Kit knew he would find congenial male companionship and conversation more to his liking.

That reminds me. Kit patted his breast pocket, suddenly realizing he had forgotten to bring the bank draft to give to General Palmer as promised.

"Is something wrong?" Belle asked as her mother looked eagerly around the ballroom.

"I have forgotten something rather important," Kit said. "Would you mind if I ran upstairs to my rooms to get it? I promised General Palmer I would give it to him tonight." Thank heavens the ball was being held in the same hotel where he was staying.

"Is this in regard to your investment?" Belle asked.

"Yes—I've finally found a suitable one." He grinned, happy to be giving an affirmative answer to that question at last.

She smiled. "Then by all means, please do. I can wait a few minutes longer."

"Thank you," he said with a glance full of gratitude. "I won't be long, and I promise I'll tell you all about it when I return."

He hurried up the stairs to retrieve the draft, then tracked General Palmer down in the smoke-filled room and handed it over.

"Excellent," the founder said. "I'm happy to have you as an investor in the railroad. You won't regret it, son."

Kit smiled at him, relieved that the money was finally safe from Daltrey's clutches. "I'm sure I won't, sir."

He made his way back to Belle's side, but her mother didn't even seem to notice he had been gone. She was too interested in seeing who was present and identifying various local and regional celebrities such as the Palmers, Rose Kingsley, and Helen Hunt Jackson.

"I apologize," Kit said in a low tone to Belle as he whisked her into a waltz. "I should not have deserted you on your special night."

"Quite all right," Belle assured him. "I know how important this investment is to you, and you weren't gone that long. I assume you found something appropriate?"

"Yes—an investment even my father will find unexceptionable." He bowed and smiled at her. "May I have this dance?"

She agreed and he told her about the investment as they danced, waxing enthusiastic about railroads and the country's future. Then, when the dance ended, he suddenly laughed at himself. "I see your lessons served you well—you managed to be polite even as your dancing partner bored you to tears."

Belle waved away his apology. "I wasn't bored," she assured him. "And I'm glad to see you so enthusiastic about something. Does . . . does that mean there's nothing keeping you here anymore?"

"Nothing but the friends I've made," he said gallantly. But he could keep tabs on his investment from anywhere, which would come in handy if he had to leave town suddenly to escape from Daltrey's blackmail. Leaving Belle, however, would be a great deal more difficult.

"I see," she said in a small voice.

Wondering what had made her spirits suddenly deflate, he returned Belle to her mother's side, where Mrs. Sullivan was chatting animatedly with Mrs. Bell.

Cora Bell laughed. "Our menfolk are holed up in that nasty, smoky room, so we have no dancing partners. Won't you join us in the card room?" she asked Mrs. Sullivan in a cajoling tone.

Mrs. Sullivan cast a regretful glance at Belle. "No, my daughter needs a chaperone . . ."

"Oh, no harm can come to her here," Cora Bell said. "And I'm certain there is someone who would be more than happy to watch your lovely Belle for you."

Mrs. Sullivan cast a doubtful glance at Belle, but it was obvious she dearly wanted to join Mrs. Bell and her cronies in the card room. And, no doubt, Belle wished her mother there as well.

"Please, enjoy yourself," Kit said to Mrs. Sullivan, adding his entreaties to Mrs. Bell's. "I'll have the next dance with Belle, then take her immediately to Miss Keithley's side."

"There, you see?" Cora Bell exclaimed. "The perfect solution."

Mrs. Sullivan allowed herself to be persuaded, and Belle and Kit took the floor in another dance, this one a vigorous polka that gave them little opportunity for conversation.

During the dance, Kit watched Belle, wondering if he would finally learn which man in the ballroom was the one in whom she was interested. He assumed she would try to catch his eye, but either she already knew where he was, or had such utter self-confidence that she didn't need to look to see if he was aware of her. It had Kit baffled.

When they finished, Kit looked around for Miss Keithley but Belle stayed him with a hand on his arm. "Wait. Before we find Miss Keithley, may I talk to you . . . alone?"

He raised an eyebrow. "I doubt your mother would approve. It's not exactly proper."

Belle stared at him with a challenge in her eyes. "Well, what I have to say isn't exactly proper either."

She had managed to surprise him. For a moment, he just stared at her, not certain what to say. What was this all about? Had she formulated a plan for revenge tonight?

Disappointment filled him. He had hoped their friendship would exempt him from her plans, but if revenge was what she wanted, he'd let her have it. He had promised this would be her night, and he didn't want anything to spoil it.

He didn't have to make it easy for her, though. "I thought you wanted to be the belle of the ball. How can you do that if you spend so much time with me?"

Belle shook her head. "I don't want that, not really. That was more for Mama than me. She's happy now with Mrs. Bell, so I've changed my mind. I want . . . something else."

Her vagueness made him even more certain this was one of her plans for revenge. Hadn't she learned her lesson yet? Well, he'd play along. For a while, anyway. "And what is it you want?"

She glanced around at the busy ballroom and lowered her voice. "Can we find somewhere to talk privately?"

He raised an eyebrow, remembering what had happened each time they had found someplace private to "talk." Frankly, not much talking had occurred.

The memory of exactly what had happened when he had taken her into his arms, and the thought of doing so again, made him thicken with desire.

Suddenly, he needed a private place as well before the entire population of Colorado Springs was able to read what was on his mind from the tightening in his trousers. "The balcony?" he murmured as he led her to the side of the room.

She glanced uncertainly at one nearby, but it was occupied by people seeking fresh air. "No, too crowded. I want someplace where we won't be overheard."

What could she have to say to him that needed that much privacy? "Perhaps another time, then? I could stop by tomorrow."

"No," she said with a vehement shake of her head. "It must be tonight."

"But those are the only options I can think of that would ensure we are still within sight of a chaperone."

Belle lowered her head and her voice. "But chaperones are exactly what I am trying to avoid. Could we . . . use your rooms upstairs?"

"No," Kit said quickly, though he suddenly began to throb at the thought of having her within the confines of his rooms. "It's too risky. If we were found, it would ruin your reputation."

"I don't care," Belle said with a defiant tilt of her chin. "It must be there or nowhere."

"Then it will be nowhere." If she had any idea what sort of things were running through his mind right now, she'd run like hell in the other direction.

Tears filled her eyes as she gazed up at him pleadingly. "Please, Kit, I don't care about any of that. This is very important to me."

The sound of his name on her lips and the tears in her eyes made him waver. "What could be so important? What is it you want that would cause you to risk your reputation so?"

She licked her lips, then said earnestly, "I want one last lesson. You owe me that."

"Lesson? In what?"

"In . . . love."

He didn't think it was possible, but she had managed to shock him. He pulled her out to the balcony anyway, hoping no one would overhear *this* conversation.

He thought he knew what she wanted, but could she really be so bold? "You have no idea what you're asking," he said in an urgent tone. Or did she? Was this all part of an elaborate revenge scheme?

"That's the problem," Belle said in a bitter tone. "I have no idea what I'm asking . . . and I want to." She lowered her voice so only he could hear. "I want you to make love to me, to take me the way a man takes a woman."

Kit swallowed hard. Dear Lord, she did know what she was asking. And she was asking it of *him*. His member throbbed and he resisted an urge to gain some relief by rubbing himself up against her softness, burying himself deep inside her, sliding in and out—

No. He desperately wanted to accommodate her request, but knew it wasn't prudent or wise. He must be firm.

Damn—wrong word choice. He was past firm and far into gradations of hardness only a rock enthusiast could recognize. No, he must be adamant. That was it—adamant.

"That is a pleasure you should reserve for your husband," he managed to say. "He will expect you to be . . . untouched on your wedding night."

"But I'll never have a wedding night," Belle said with soulful eyes and a trembling lip.

Despite his struggle to gain some sort of control, her unhappiness penetrated his fog of absorption. "Why not?"

"Because the man I love doesn't love me. If I can't marry him, I will marry no one."

Jealousy rampaged through him at the thought of her loving another man. "Who? Who do you want to marry?"

She lowered her eyes again. "That's not important."

"The devil it's not," Kit ground out. She asked him to perform such an intimate act and still wouldn't trust him with the name of the man she loved?

She looked a little shocked at his language, but said gamely, "Please, I want to experience lovemaking just once before I become an old maid."

He shook his head, not trusting himself to speak. *I can't believe I'm having this conversation . . . and with such an innocent.*

"We'll be seen," he protested. Much as he would have liked to accede to her request, he didn't see how it could be done without getting caught.

"No, we won't. No one's watching me now, and we can slip away and do . . . it . . . then return right away. We won't be gone long enough for anyone to notice."

He gave her a wry grin. "You certainly have a poor idea of my lovemaking skills."

She blushed. "What?"

He lowered his voice to whisper in her ear, "Done properly, lovemaking is a slow, sensuous undertaking." Though the way he was feeling, he was afraid he wouldn't last long.

"Oh," she said in a small voice. "Then, can we do something in between? Something that will get us back to the ball before it ends?"

He couldn't help but chuckle. Sweet, innocent Belle. Sweet, *seductive* Belle. Who could resist her? Not Kit. In fact, he absolutely adored her.

The realization hit him right between the eyes.

I love her.

He didn't just desire her, he wanted her by his side for the rest of his life, to be his lover and helpmate, his companion and friend, the mother of his children. She was everything he could ever want in a wife—witty, charming, beautiful, brave, and, at times, entirely unexpected. With Belle by his side, life would never be dull.

But she doesn't trust you, a small voice reminded him.

Yes, that was a problem. She didn't trust him enough to reveal the name of the man whose attention she had tried to snare. The man whom she loved, but who didn't love her. Could Kit live such a life? Could he stand to marry her, knowing she loved another?

Pain stabbed through him, but he ignored it. The thought of losing her was even more painful. Besides, if he didn't oblige her in her desire to learn what it meant to make love, another man might not be so reluctant.

More doubts assailed him as he remembered that her desire to make love to him might just be a ploy to get revenge. Could it be? He doubted it, but had to test the waters. "It would be dangerous to tempt a man with such forbidden fruits unless you are absolutely certain you wish to follow through," he said in a low tone.

"I do," she said earnestly. Her face brightened. "Does that mean you'll do it?"

God help him, but he would. "Yes," he said and was gratified to see pleasure spread across her countenance. But he knew his duty. He would let Belle feel wicked and wild for one night, but after he made love to her, he would insist she marry him.

Once they were wed, however, he would have to find a way to make her love him. Somehow.

Relief and pleasure filled Belle when Kit finally agreed to give her a lesson in lovemaking. She had been afraid she would have to seduce him, but had no idea how to go about such a thing. It would be so much easier with his cooperation.

"Shall we go to your rooms now?" she asked and was embarrassed when her voice emerged in a squeak.

"We shouldn't leave together," he cautioned.

"I know—I have a plan," Belle confided eagerly. "They have a room set aside on the second floor where ladies can withdraw. I'll just pretend I tore my hem and go there. You head straight on up to your rooms, and I'll wait a suitable interval, then join you there."

He raised an eyebrow. "I see you have it all planned out."

"Well, yes. Is there something wrong with that?" Surely he wouldn't back out now, would he?

"No, it's just that a man likes to have some . . . say in these things."

Botheration. "Well, you'll have your say once we get there," she assured him. "I—I have no experience in these matters."

"Really?" he drawled. "I never would have guessed."

Was that sarcasm in his tone? "What do you think about my plan?" Time was wasting. At this rate, she'd never get her lesson in love.

"It's a good one," he said. "I shall await you in room three-twelve." He gave her directions to his room that would make it easy to avoid prying eyes.

She memorized them carefully, then said, "I'll go now." She paused as a sudden thought struck her. "You will be there, won't you?" She would be mortified if she were caught knocking on a man's door and no one answered to let her in.

He gave her a short bow and said with a smoldering look, "Never fear. I shall be there."

"Good." With her heart tripping in double-time, Belle made her way up the stairs, keeping her fan beating close to her face, hoping she wouldn't meet anyone she knew. Not only did she fear her intentions would show clearly in her expression, she didn't want anyone to know where she had gone in case there were inquiries.

Once inside the withdrawing room, she was chagrined to realize she wasn't the only woman present. Several others had congregated there, either to repair their toilettes or escape from the gaiety below. Belle made her way to a corner and tried to look inconspicuous as she pretended to mend her hem.

Good heavens. How could she leave without being noticed? She sat there for a while, but as some of the women left, others joined them. She had hoped to find a time when she had the room to herself in order to put her plan into action, but now she feared it would be impossible.

Giving up was not an option. She would just have to revise the plan. She rose to her feet and made her way slowly to the door, once more covering her face as much as she could with her fan. Good—no one inside was looking. But once she was outside, there were several people on the stairs. She hovered in the hallway, pretending to study a particularly ugly painting, as she waited for the area to clear.

It took much longer than she expected, but finally, there was no one else around and Belle slipped up the stairs as fast as she could and made her way to Kit's rooms.

Once there, she halted with her hand raised. Butterflies roamed freely in her midsection, and her pulse beat wildly in anticipation. *Dear Lord, what am I doing?*

I am meeting the man I love, she reminded herself. For the first and last time. And if she didn't work up the gumption to knock on the door right now, she would never have the opportunity to learn what it was like between a man and a woman. Either that . . . or someone would come along soon and wonder what she was doing here.

That did it. Taking a deep breath, she pounded firmly on the door.

Kit opened it immediately and pulled her inside, then closed it behind her. "Did anyone see you?" he asked.

"I—I don't think so," Belle stammered.

"I was beginning to think you weren't going to come."

"Of—of course I was," she said with a gulp. "I just had a hard time getting away."

She looked around and felt the blood drain from her face. Her plan had seemed so reasonable when she had first thought it up, but the reality was so much more . . . intense. Though she was sure his rooms were large by any standards, they didn't feel that way. Instead, they felt close and intimate in the dim lighting. She could smell the scent of his shaving soap, see his coat draped over a chair, catch a glimpse of the bed in the other room. . . . Somehow those simple things made what they were about to do seem so very sinful.

He ran a hand down her arm in a caressing motion and she jumped.

He removed his hand. "Nervous?"

She nodded wordlessly.

He stared into her eyes with a serious expression. "Have you changed your mind?"

"No, of course not," she said swiftly. She still wanted—needed—to do this.

He lifted her chin with his fingers. "You needn't, you know. You don't have to do anything you don't want to."

"But I want to," she assured him. And wished like the devil that he would just get on with it before she expired from an excess of nerves.

He stared into her face, but must have been satisfied with what he found there, for he said, "All right. But you can stop me at any time if you don't feel . . . comfortable with what we're doing. All right?"

"Yes, thank you," she said in relief. She didn't really think she'd want to stop, but it was nice to know she had the option. "Wha-what do we do first?"

He smiled. "There are no rules, except that it helps if we are both . . . unclothed."

"That sounds . . . appropriate," she said with her heart in her mouth, then chastised herself. Could she possibly sound any more stuffy?

He grinned. "Shall I go first, then?"

She sighed in relief. "Yes, please." It would be much easier to disrobe herself if he were already unclothed. She sank into a nearby chair and watched him.

She had expected him to shed his clothes quickly, but he took his time about it, his blond hair gleaming in the dim lighting as he turned his back, apparently to save her modesty, and removed everything but his nether garment, folding the rest carefully over a chair. The sight of his bare back and legs made her heart beat faster . . . an introduction for things to come.

He turned around then and she gasped. She had never seen a man's bare chest before, and the sight was rather stimulating. Light blond hair sprinkled his chest, making her wonder what it felt like to touch it. And his naked limbs were strong and lean, nothing at all like the pale softness of hers or her sisters'.

But her eyes were drawn inexorably to the area below his waist that was still clothed. The material did not lie flat, but was distended in an interesting bulge.

Oh, my. She felt her face heat and raised her hands to cover her cheeks, then closed her eyes in mortification. She shouldn't be staring at him so.

"Do you want me to stop?" he asked softly.

"No. Please, I just . . ."

"It's all right," he said in gentle tones. "I'll stop right here for now, and we'll work on you."

"M-me?" she repeated, and hated the way her voice came out in a squeak again. What did he mean, *work* on her?

"Yes," he said with a smile. "It takes two, you know."

He was teasing her. "I know," she said, but that was as far as her knowledge went. And if she wanted to learn more, she would have to expose her body to him.

She stood up, trembling, eager yet afraid. But she wasn't too frightened, remembering how he had made her feel the last time he had touched her.

She desperately wanted to feel those sensations again.

And he obliged. Cupping her face in both his hands, he kissed her gently at first, then with more fervor as she responded eagerly. Her senses reeled and she put her hands against his chest to steady herself.

Oh, my. The feel of his short, coarse chest hair against her hands was intriguing, and a bit exciting. As he deepened their kiss, she ran her hands over his chest, loving the manly feel of him.

She wanted to explore further, but was too shy to do so. Kit, however, had no such problem. "May I undress you now?" he asked softly.

"Yes, please," she said in a small voice, wanting to feel his hands against her skin once again. "But quickly." He was going too darned slow.

Chuckling, Kit turned her around and made short work of the hooks at the back of her dress, then her corset, leaving only the thin fabric of her chemise to cover her as he carefully laid her clothing on a nearby chair.

He returned to where she stood, still trembling with unexpressed emotion and need, feeling a little vulnerable clad only in her unmentionables. She crossed her arms over her breasts, not quite knowing why, but feeling the need to protect herself.

But Kit didn't leer or laugh at her. Instead, he came up behind her and kissed the back of her neck.

She sighed in contentment and relief even as goose bumps chased their way across her skin. Her breasts tightened with need and warmth pooled deep within her, making her relax a fraction. As if sensing her capitulation, Kit ran his hands down her arms and hugged her to him, his front against her back, his arms crossed beneath her breasts.

Her heart beat faster as she felt the hardness between his legs nestle against her backside. She gasped and couldn't help but stiffen. Was this it? Was now the time?

"It's all right," Kit murmured. "I won't do anything you aren't ready for."

But she *was* ready. Wasn't she? Was there some sort of signal she was supposed to give? Something she was supposed to do? Darn it, why hadn't her mother taught her these things?

Kit cupped her breasts in both hands and squeezed them lightly through the material. Belle nearly gasped aloud again at the pleasure, and her knees almost gave way. "Oooh," she breathed on a contented sigh.

"You like that?" he asked in a throaty voice, the warmth of his breath tickling her neck.

"Oh, yes."

"Then let's take it one step further." He slid the chemise down to puddle at her waist, baring her breasts, making her feel wanton and wicked. He cupped them again, squeezing them lightly, and ran his fingers over the tips.

She didn't think it could get any better, but he proved her wrong. She felt moisture pool in that secret place between her legs and the tips of her breasts hardened even more. He rolled the tips between his fingers and the sensations were so exquisite, she involuntarily gasped again—she almost couldn't stand it.

But when he took his hands away, she pleaded, "More."

"In a moment," he said gently, and, lifting her into his arms as if she weighed nothing, he carried her into the other room to set her down next to his bed.

Her heart beat faster as she wondered what would happen next, but Kit surprised her by leaning down to take the tip of her breast into his mouth. He suckled lightly and her knees almost buckled. Dear Lord, she didn't think she could stand much more pleasure. But she realized she could as Kit slid the rest of her underthings down her body to lie at her feet.

As she stood there, feeling shaky with need and rather vulnerable, he laid her on his soft bed and ran his hand down over her stomach to gently stroke the curls between her legs. Embarrassed, she tried to close her legs, but he gently parted them and slid his finger inside to the slick wetness that had somehow appeared within.

The intimacy shocked her, and she was on the verge of asking him to stop when he suddenly found and stroked a small bud inside. Pleasure arrowed straight to her core and she forgot all about stopping him, forgot everything but the pure sensations he was generating with small strokes of his fingers, not to mention his sinful mouth on her breast.

In fact, she couldn't even think at all as a crescendo of blissful feelings surged and ebbed within her, building to some sort of unknown pinnacle she longed to attain.

She lost all sense of decorum as she spread her legs wider to give him more complete access, moving her hips against his fingers and whimpering with need. Then, finally, that nebulous event she sought was upon her and she peaked with shuddering ecstasy as wave upon wave of pure pleasure washed over her, leaving her weak and replete.

Oh, my. No wonder they kept this secret. If they were to reveal exactly how wondrous it felt, every young maiden would be eager to try it.

Kit leaned down to kiss her softly, and she sighed in pleasure.

"Are you ready for the rest now?" he asked softly.

Her eyes widened. There was more? "Oh, yes, please."

He chuckled. "You are so polite, even in bed."

She felt herself blush, but it appeared he wasn't offended. Instead, he stood and slowly slid his garment down over his manhood.

Belle knew she shouldn't feel embarrassed after what he had just done to her, but she couldn't help it. This was a sight she had never seen in person, though it appeared Kit had much in common with the Adam on her fan. She took one quick peek, then looked away, not wanting him to know how curious she was.

Oh, dear. What did he intend to do with that?

But he didn't seem bothered by her curiosity. Instead, he moved closer, as if inviting her to look her fill. She peeked again and swallowed hard at the forbidden sight, wondering boldly what . . . it . . . would feel like. He had touched her. Could she be so audacious as to touch him . . . there?

She reached out tentatively, and when he didn't pull back, she ran her fingers lightly along his jutting shaft. Kit groaned and his male member jumped and bobbed at her. She pulled her hand back swiftly. Oh, no, what had she done?

"It's all right," he assured her. "It felt good. Please . . . do it again."

Thus reassured, she touched him again, this time wrapping her hand fully around him. She was prepared this time when it jumped and wasn't alarmed. Instead, she wondered at the remarkable feel of it—hard, yet covered in skin as soft as a baby's bottom. And evidently Kit did enjoy it, for she saw him close his eyes in what could only be pleasure.

Emboldened, she moved her fingers to explore the intriguing tip, but Kit pulled her hand away with a gasp.

"I'm sorry—did I do something wrong?" Again, she desperately wished she had a rule book or *something* to tell her what to do next.

"No, you did something very right," he assured her. "But if you touch me that way much longer, I may not be able to hold out."

"Oh," she said knowingly, though she wasn't quite sure what he meant by "hold out."

"Here, let me show you." He knelt beside her on the bed and made her quiver all over when he slid a finger inside her again.

"Ah, you're still wet for me," he murmured. Then he knelt above her and placed his male member at the entrance of her most private place and pushed a short distance inside.

She placed her hands against his chest, and her eyes widened once more. "What-what are you going to do?" she asked in a tremulous voice as she realized his intentions. At least, what she *thought* were his intentions. Did he really mean to put that inside her?

He leaned down to caress her breasts and

whispered, "I'm going to finish making love to you."

"I don't think it will fit," she said in alarm. He was too big.

"Don't worry," he murmured and continued caressing her until she was once more filled with longing.

He pushed in a little farther, and it did seem to go in all right.

He stared with concern into her face. "Now, since you are a maiden, this is going to hurt—just this once."

"Hurt?" No one told her it was going to hurt.

"It'll be brief, I promise. Then it will feel very, very good. Will you trust me?"

"All right," Belle said in a tremulous voice. She had trusted him so far and things had gone quite nicely—there was no reason not to trust him now.

He pushed inside and there was a brief, sharp pain. But before she could even cry out, he was moving deeper inside her. *Oh, my, that does feel good.* And it felt even better when he pulled out a little, then thrust in again, giving her a feeling of fullness, completeness.

So this is what a man and woman did together— and it was wondrous. Satisfied to be finally experiencing the ultimate intimacy, Belle closed her eyes and hung on to Kit for dear life.

He continued thrusting in and out, and she heard herself emitting little sounds of pleasure as that crescendo built within her once more. But this time she knew what to expect and she welcomed it, gasping aloud as she erupted with bubbling bursts of sensation.

Kit, too, seemed to reach release as he arched

above her, pausing once, twice, then a third time before letting out a shuddering breath and collapsing on top of her. But he quickly rolled to the side to bring her within the circle of his arms, keeping them joined together.

Though it was wonderful to cuddle with him like this, Belle felt as if she should say *something*. But what did a lady say after she had been thoroughly ravished? "That was nice," she ventured.

Kit laughed out loud, the first time she had ever seen him so carefree. "Nice?" he repeated, shaking his head. "Only you, Belle. Only you."

"All right," she said, staring into his face to memorize his expression in this special moment, running her fingers across those sensuous lips. "Then thank you for that most marvelous lesson in love. I'll never forget it."

He kissed her gently. "That's better. But I have something rather important to say to you, and I think it's best if we're both clothed for it. Shall we?"

Belle nodded reluctantly. He was right. Though she had lost all track of time, she suspected this lovemaking business had taken longer than she'd expected, and she really needed to get back to the ball before someone missed her.

She dressed swiftly, Kit acting as her maid where necessary. Once she was clothed, she checked her appearance in his mirror and was glad to see she didn't look *too* disheveled. By just looking at her, one would never know that her world had just changed dramatically.

She was even more certain now that she could never marry anyone else. She shuddered at the thought of having another man touch her in that way. Only Kit.

Kit, of course, looked as if he had done nothing more strenuous than take a walk around the park. Carefully, he shut the door to the bedroom, then seated her in the chair in his parlor.

He regarded her with a thoughtful expression, and Belle felt her apprehension grow. Suddenly, they seemed like two strangers, as if their wonderful lovemaking had never happened. And the seriousness of his expression convinced her he was about to say something she didn't want to hear.

Oh, no. He is leaving Colorado Springs forever. I just know it. She clasped her hands tightly in her lap. "What is it you wish to say to me?"

He cocked his head to smile at her. "First, I owe you an apology."

"Apology?" she repeated in disbelief. If he was going to apologize for the most beautiful thing that ever happened to her, she would have to hit him.

He nodded. "I thought perhaps you were leading me on, that this was your way of getting revenge for that horrible thing I said in the Garden of the Gods. I expected someone to burst in here and accuse me of having designs on your virtue. Obviously, I was wrong."

"Oh," Belle said in a small voice. "So you figured out my revenge scheme?"

He shrugged. "It wasn't hard, but I'm glad to see you've given it up."

She shrugged that off, wishing he would get to the point yet dreading it, too. "What did you want to say?"

He smiled. "I just wanted to ask you—"

A sudden pounding on the door made him break off. They looked at each other in indecision, but before Belle could decide whether she should hide or if they should even answer it, the door burst in to reveal her father and mother.

Papa's face was stony with suppressed anger, and Mama looked shocked.

Papa closed the door swiftly, turning a belligerent expression on Kit with clenched fists. "Ye surly knave. What have ye done to me daughter?"

Oddly enough, Kit looked equally angry, but before he could answer, Belle interposed herself between the two men. "He's done nothing, Papa. It was all my fault."

She couldn't see Kit behind her—her eyes were all for Papa. She couldn't let Kit be punished for something she had initiated. And the less her parents knew about what had really gone on here, the better.

Papa's gaze swiveled to her. "Yer fault, ye say?"

"Yes. I—I followed him up to his room. He didn't even know I was here until I shut the door behind me."

Papa's eyes narrowed. "Is that so? And why did ye do such a daft thing?"

But she had no answer that would satisfy him. She lowered her eyes. "I don't know—I just wanted to talk to him, in private. But I see now that it was foolish."

"Foolish? Aye, that it was." Her father turned accusing eyes on his wife. "Ye see what yer carelessness has done? Yer daughter has gone and gotten herself ruined."

Mama looked so horrified, she didn't even attempt to defend herself. She just covered her cheeks with her hands.

Since Mama and Belle seemed suitably cowed,

Papa turned his wrath on Kit once more. "And you, sir, what are you going to do about it?"

Belle turned around to look at Kit, silently beseeching him to go along with her story, but she was shocked to see his face cold and unyielding.

"So, I was wrong about you after all," he muttered. "You still have your revenge."

"No," Belle said in rising horror. He couldn't really believe she had planned this, could he?

But Kit ignored her and addressed her father. "I was just about to do something about it, sir."

Turning to Belle, he regarded her coldly and said in a voice dripping with unconcern, "Will you do me the honor of becoming my wife?"

Belle barely heard her mother's gasp of pleasure and her father's grunt of approval. All she knew was that Kit, the only man she would ever love, was staring at her as if she were a three-day-old dead fish.

Marrying him was the dearest wish of her heart, but she couldn't marry him—not like this. Not with him thinking she had done it for revenge.

Her mother rushed up to hug Kit. "That's a wonderful—"

"No," Belle said, cutting off her mother's enthusiasm.

Mama broke off her hug to stare at Belle. "What?"

"I said no—I'm not going to marry him." Belle raised her chin stubbornly when the other three bore down upon her. She didn't care what they said. She was *not* going to marry a man who didn't love her.

Seventeen

The next day, Belle moped as she was confined to her room. She had managed to remain adamant in refusing to marry Kit—at least so far—but her decision had resulted in angry words all around. Perhaps it was best if she stayed here awhile. It would give people a chance to cool off.

A knock came at the door, and Charisma and Grace entered, looking as if they were visiting a prisoner in jail instead of their own sister.

Grace shut the door behind her and, surprisingly, didn't immediately flop onto the bed. Instead, she stood with her back to the door and stared at Belle wide-eyed. "What did you do?" she asked in accents of dread.

Apparently, their parents hadn't told Belle's sisters anything that happened the night before. Belle didn't know whether to be grateful that they didn't know of her disgrace, or annoyed that she was going to have to field dozens of questions. "I didn't do anything," she said petulantly.

But Charisma didn't believe her. "You must have done *some*thing or Mama and Papa wouldn't be so angry with you."

"All I did was refuse an offer of marriage," Belle

said. Well, perhaps not *all,* but she really didn't want to talk about that right now.

"No," Charisma said. "There's more to it than that. I can understand *Mama* being upset because you refused an offer, but not Papa."

Belle debated how much to tell her sisters. Charisma would poke and prod until she extracted the most possible information, but Belle didn't want her sisters to know everything. What had happened last night between her and Kit was too private, too special. "I did something . . . unwise," Belle said.

Grace came a little farther into the room, apparently now convinced that whatever Belle did wasn't contagious. "Was it that milk and cheese thing again?" she asked.

"In a way. . . . The ball was in the same hotel as Kit's rooms and I . . . followed him to his rooms last night."

Charisma and Grace looked shocked. "You did what?" Charisma asked in disbelief.

Belle winced. Even her sisters knew her actions weren't ladylike.

Grace sank onto a chair, so stunned she didn't even manage to break anything. "Why would you do such a thing?"

Belle shrugged. She wouldn't tell them the whole truth, but perhaps they would be satisfied with part of it. "I had to speak to him privately. I had to find out if he loves me."

"You *asked* him if he loves you?" Grace repeated in disbelief.

"Well, no, I wanted to . . . test the waters, so to speak."

Charisma nodded. "And what did you find out? Does he love you?"

Belle hung her head. Quite obviously he desired her, but love her? "No—he's angry with me. He figured out what I was up to with Harold and George and thought I had set him up for revenge as well."

"What? How?" Charisma asked. "What happened, exactly?"

From some of the comments her parents had made in the carriage on the way home, Belle had pieced together the events that had led to her disgrace. "Apparently, Miss Mattingly noticed we were both missing from the ball last night and tracked Papa down to ask where we were." And she must have done it maliciously, because Papa had been in the smoking room with all the men—not where a young lady would casually run into him.

Charisma nodded. "I knew that woman was trouble."

"Well, he found Mama in the card room with Mrs. Bell . . ."

"Uh-oh," Grace said.

Belle gave a rueful nod. "Yes, I gather there was quite a row when he discovered she didn't know where I was. They looked for us and Papa thought to look in Kit's rooms . . . and they found us."

Charisma raised an eyebrow. "What were you doing when they found you?"

"Nothing," Belle said with a tilt of her chin. Not at that moment anyway. "We were just talking."

"Did Papa hit Mr. Stanhope?" Grace asked, wide-eyed.

"No, of course not. I explained that it wasn't Kit's fault that I followed him to his rooms."

Charisma sighed. "I see why they're insisting on

marriage then. You said you loved him—why don't you just marry him?"

"Because he doesn't love *me,*" Belle said in a small voice. "He just asked me out of duty."

"Oh, Belle," Grace exclaimed and came to give her a hug. "I'm so sorry."

"Me, too," Charisma said and joined in the hug.

Belle felt tears welling in her eyes. Her sisters understood—why couldn't her parents? Even if she told them she loved Kit, they wouldn't understand why she had to refuse him. Especially Mama. She would just see it as another reason *to* marry him.

Charisma pulled away and gave Belle a fierce look. "I'll tell you what. I'll just go to Kit and tell him—"

"No," Belle said, interrupting her. Whatever Charisma had to say, it would just make things worse, not better. "I don't want him saying he loves me just so I'll marry him. If he's going to say it, I want him to mean it." Otherwise, she'd be miserable the rest of her life. "Promise me you won't say a word."

"All right," Charisma agreed grudgingly.

"But if he says he loves you on his own, you'll agree to marry him?" Grace asked eagerly.

Knowing her sweet sister longed for a happy resolution, Belle said, "Yes. If he loves me, I'll marry him." But she wasn't holding out any hope.

A maid knocked on the door then and informed Belle she was wanted downstairs in the library. Her sisters wished her good luck, but Belle had to face this on her own. She headed downstairs, mentally girding herself for another onslaught on her defenses.

Mama and Papa waited for her in the library,

sitting side by side in two chairs that faced Belle's.
With their stern expressions, all they needed were
rifles to complete the picture of a firing squad.
Belle thought about asking for a blindfold, but
knew they wouldn't appreciate levity at this time.
Instead, she said nothing, but sat in the chair,
folded her hands in her lap, and braced herself.

It didn't take long. Mama sighed heavily. "Why
are you being so stubborn? Lord Stanhope is a
great catch—"

"*Mr.* Stanhope," Belle corrected her.

"What?"

"He's not a lord—he's just plain Mr. Stanhope,
not Lord Stanhope."

Mama waved that away as irrelevant. "He's still
the son of a lord. And he's perfect—just what I
wanted for you, Belle. Why won't you take what he's
offering?"

Because he wasn't offering the one thing she
truly wanted—his heart. But Belle didn't know how
to answer that question without making Mama
angry or confusing her more, so she kept her
mouth shut.

Papa scowled at Mama. "He's perfect, is he? And
that's why ye had to pay the man to escort me
daughter? This mess is all yer fault, Bridey. I'm not
forgettin' that if ye hadn't interfered in the first
place, none of this would have happened."

Mama bridled up like an angry dog. "Is it a sin
to want what's best for my girls?"

"'Tis if ye hurt them in the process," Papa shot
back—and the argument was on.

Belle watched in consternation, feeling a little sad
that her troubles had caused a rift in Mama and
Papa's relationship as well. But not too sad—if they

kept at each other long enough, maybe they'd forget about her.

No such luck.

"It's all the fault of that horrible Millicent Mattingly," Mama said in a huff and glared at Belle. "She's a horrible gossip. Why, the news is probably all over town by now that you and Lord Stanhope were missing together."

"I told you nothing happened," Belle said for the thousandth time. Maybe if she kept on repeating it, someone would eventually believe her. Even if it wasn't true.

Mama sniffed. "It doesn't matter. You'll still be ruined if the word gets around."

Belle raised her chin. "I don't care." If Kit didn't love her, she would just remain an old maid anyway.

Papa shook his head and said softly, "I don't understand, lass. I thought ye had a fondness for the man. Did he do something to give ye a disgust of him?"

On the contrary, he had made her love him. "No."

"Then what is the problem?" he asked in exasperation. "Why don't ye just marry the man?"

Because if Kit married her without love, she feared she would end up with a broken heart—and she couldn't stand that. She tried to explain in a way they would understand. "Because I don't want to marry for society's sake—I want to marry for love . . . like you two did." Though from the way they had been quarreling of late, no one would know it.

Mama and Papa exchanged chagrined glances. Papa seemed to understand, but Mama said, "You could learn to love him. It won't be difficult. After all, he comes from an excellent family, and he's very personable and handsome. Not every woman goes into a marriage loving her husband, but it develops over time. And it would be so easy to love him."

I know—that's the problem. Belle had never said she didn't love him—trust Mama to get it confused. But Belle couldn't set her straight. If Mama knew Belle loved Kit, she would be even more perplexed. She would never understand why Belle had to refuse him. "It would be a disaster," she told her mother. "I would never be happy." How could she be, loving a man who didn't love her?

Mama made an exasperated sound and turned to Papa. "Patrick, tell her she has to marry him."

Patrick shook his head slowly. "No, she has the right of it. She should marry for love, as we did."

Belle's hopes rose. Was Papa on her side?

But Mama wasn't giving up. "What? She can't do that—she doesn't have the luxury of marrying for love. Society won't let her."

Papa scowled. "Yer getting a little above yerself now, Bridey."

"I am not," Mama said indignantly. "This has nothing to do with my social aspirations. I just want what's best for my girls, and I know a ruined reputation isn't it."

"But it's yer precious society who would condemn her," Papa reminded her. "Marriage isn't the only solution. There are other options."

"Such as what?" Mama asked. "If she stays in town, everyone will remember her disgrace and she'll ruin Charisma and Grace's chances of finding good husbands."

Papa sighed. "Finding a husband is not the be-all and end-all of existence—"

"No, Papa," Belle interrupted. "Mama is right." Chagrined that she hadn't realize how her actions might hurt her sisters, Belle knew she had to do something that wouldn't jeopardize their chances for happiness. "I don't want to hurt Charisma and Grace."

Mama's face brightened. "Then you'll marry him?"

"No. But Papa's suggestion is good—I'll just have to go away for a while." Maybe a little time away would be good for her, give her a new perspective on life.

"But where?" Mama asked in bewilderment, obviously not quite ready to give up her hopes of having Kit Stanhope as a son-in-law.

"Me sister would be glad to have her," Patrick said slowly.

Belle beamed at him. Just the thing—she would love to visit Ireland and see the place where her parents had grown up. There would be no memories of Kit there to haunt her, either.

"No," Mama said, shaking her head. "That won't do. It's too far away, and too expensive. She'll just have to visit *my* sister. I never wanted any of us to have to go back to that awful place, but you leave us no choice, Belle."

Fussy old Aunt Margaret in Leadville? Oh, no. "But Aunt Margaret doesn't even like me," Belle protested. She didn't like any of the girls. In fact, Belle didn't think the old fussbudget liked people at all. Life there would be horrible.

"Nonsense," Mama said briskly. "She's family—she has to love you." She paused and a militant light came into her eye. "It's your choice, Belle. Either you announce your engagement to Lord Stanhope, or you visit my sister in Leadville."

"But—"

"No buts, girl," Mama said firmly. "You've made your bed and now you have to lie in it."

Belle scowled. "What if I don't choose?" she asked belligerently.

"Ye must," Papa said gently. "Ye can't have it both ways, lass. Ye said it yerself. Ye must choose."

Mama nodded. "Yes. And you have until this evening to do so. Think carefully, Belle, for what you decide now will have consequences for the rest of your life."

What a choice. Either way, she was being punished for the crime of loving a man who didn't love her back. It was too much to bear. Belle burst into tears and ran back to the comfort of her room.

Several hours later, Belle was no closer to an answer than she was before, despite the fact that she'd done nothing else but think about it. The same thoughts kept going round and round in her head. No matter what she chose, she'd be miserable.

Belle heard someone outside her door and raised her head with a meager hope that one of her sisters had come to commiserate with her . . . but it was Mama who opened the door.

"You have a visitor, Belle. Come downstairs."

She wasn't in the mood. "I'm not really up for visitors. Can you ask her to go away and come back another time?"

"Not this visitor," Mama insisted. "It's Lord Stanhope. Maybe he can talk some sense into you."

Despite herself, Belle's hopes rose. Though she

knew she was probably just letting herself in for more heartache, she had to see him . . . just on the off chance that he had come to declare his undying love. Quickly, she checked her appearance in the mirror, then tried to repair the ravages of her tears, but Mama was too impatient.

"Don't keep Lord Stanhope waiting. You look fine. Now, come on downstairs."

Feeling like a frump, Belle followed her mother downstairs to the back parlor.

At the entrance to the parlor, Mama said, "The damage has already been done, so I'll leave you two alone. Maybe he can talk some sense into your head." Her face turned stern. "Listen to what he has to say, Belle. And if you need your father or me, we'll both be in the library." She gave her daughter an admonishing glance. "And we'll be expecting to hear some *good* news."

Belle sighed and entered the parlor as Mama closed the door behind her. Kit awaited her inside, looking splendidly handsome in a well-tailored suit. She blushed as she remembered what he looked like without it . . . and exactly what he had done to her when unclothed.

Unfortunately, he didn't seem to be reliving the same experience. In fact, the forbidding expression on his face didn't bode well for their conversation. He bowed slightly, saying in a formal tone, "Good afternoon, Miss Sullivan. How are you?"

Miserable—especially since he still seemed so distant and cold. Impatiently, she wondered how they had been reduced to this after everything they had done to each other. Belle murmured, "I'm fine. And you?" Were they just going to mouth pleasantries at each other now, for heaven's sake?

"I'm fine," Kit said, then seemed to lose patience. "But I'll ask you once more. Will you do me the honor of becoming my wife?"

Belle studied his demeanor, searching for some sign of caring or fondness, but found none. He was totally unapproachable—a sure sign that he was asking only because it was the expected thing to do. "No," she said baldly, not caring how rude she sounded. Perhaps some of Charima's bluntness had rubbed off on her.

He didn't look surprised. "May I inquire as to a reason?"

Belle shrugged, trying to look nonchalant. "There is no need to play the gallant gentleman," she said, then belatedly added the formula she'd been taught. "But I am very conscious of the honor you do me, and I thank you for the offer."

Kit ran a hand through his hair, looking impatient. "Honor? But it's your honor I'm trying to save. You must marry me."

"I don't care about my honor," Belle said belligerently. Why was he prattling on so about such a stuffy subject anyway, when she longed to hear how much he cared?

"You may not, but I do," Kit said. "I care."

Belle's heart leaped with hope. "What-what do you mean?" she asked. Could he mean what she thought?

"What if a child results from . . . what we did last night?"

She shrugged. "If that happens, I'll deal with it then." But the thought of having Kit's babe was somehow comforting, no matter how much society might despise her.

"I don't want it said that I dishonored a young lady. Not again."

Again? What does he mean, again? Then, suddenly, it all made sense. "So that's why you left England—they think you dishonored a girl."

Kit looked annoyed that he had revealed so much, but said, "Yes. Now you know. And surely you must realize why I can't let it happen again."

That explained why he had asked her to marry him, but not why she should agree. "It isn't a problem," she said softly. "No one will know." She had hurt enough people by her rash actions—she didn't want to hurt him as well.

He shook his head ruefully. "I am afraid that is wishful thinking. The word will get out."

"Not if we both deny it."

Kit considered for a moment. "It would be nice to think so, but while I trust myself and you not to reveal what happened, I am not so sanguine about Miss Mattingly . . . or your mother."

Belle sighed. He was right. "Still, I'm sure we will both do fine. I can live with people thinking I've been compromised."

"No matter how you sugarcoat what happened, Belle, the fact is, I did more than compromise you—I ruined you. What if you are pregnant?"

Ruined her? What an awful way to put the most important experience of her life. She shook her head wordlessly and lowered her head, not wanting him to see the sheen of tears she was sure showed in her eyes. "It doesn't matter."

Kit signed in exasperation. "You're a sensible person, Belle. Surely you know this is the best thing to do. What's the real reason you are refusing me?"

Because I love you and you don't love me, she cried silently. Then sought for an explanation he would believe. "You—you didn't believe me when I told you I didn't come to your room for revenge," she said quietly, then raised her head to see his reaction.

He raised an eyebrow in disbelief.

"Really, I didn't," she assured him, desperately wanting him to believe her. "I didn't plan on Mama and Papa finding us. It's all Miss Mattingly's fault. She saw that we were both missing and decided to start some trouble. I think she's still mad at me for making her look bad after the concert."

Kit said nothing—he just stared at her with a considering expression as if wondering whether or not to believe her.

"It's the truth," Belle said bitterly. Did anyone imagine she wanted this to happen? "I—I learned my lesson after the concert, when I saw how badly I hurt George."

"So you admit you were trying to get back at him?"

"Yes, and Harold, too. I wanted to punish them for hurting Charisma and Grace."

"And what about me? I can't believe you simply decided to pass me by when I'm the one who insulted you personally."

Belle stared down at the carpet, afraid to meet his eyes. "I didn't intend to pass you by at first, but you were the only one of the three who apologized." *And I fell in love with you.*

But she couldn't tell him that. "Even though you said I was plain—"

"Homely. I believe the word I used was homely," Kit said, interrupting her.

Belle winced at the memory. "Yes, but you did everything you could to make me beautiful."

He frowned. "So that's why you were so eager to

become the belle of the ball—because you wanted to have all three of us at your feet to punish us?"

It sounded so bad when he said it aloud. "Yes," Belle admitted. "At first. But after my two attempts at revenge turned out so badly, I realized true beauty comes from within." And she was still working on that part.

"Well, I'm glad you finally realized that," he said flatly, but there was no forgiveness in his voice.

"Won't you believe me?" Belle pleaded. "I didn't want to hurt you. I just wanted—"

She broke off, not sure who might be listening at the door.

"What?" he asked. "What did you want, Belle?"

She lowered her voice. "I told you last night—I just wanted to make love to you. I didn't expect—or want—to get caught. Don't you think I would have made it a little more obvious what we did if that had been my intention?"

He sighed, and she was glad to see that he had dropped his cold, aloof façade. Perhaps he did believe her.

He shook his head. "Regardless of your intentions, we must pay the consequences. You must marry me, Belle."

Pay the consequences? What a horrible way to put it. Well, if he only saw their lovemaking as a mistake that they had to pay for, their marriage would be a disaster. "No, I *don't* have to marry you. My parents told me I have another option."

"And that is?"

"I can go away, visit my Aunt Margaret in Leadville. That way you won't have to worry about me anymore."

"You'd rather go away than marry me?" he asked in disbelief.

Of course not, but that was the only thing she could do to escape a loveless marriage. She said nothing.

Kit threw up his hands in exasperation. "Well, I know my duty. I won't give up until we're married."

Duty? That hurt. Belle wanted his love or nothing.

And it appeared "nothing" was exactly what she was going to get. With a sigh, she realized she had her answer. She would just have to tell Mama and Papa that she had chosen Aunt Margaret.

On Mount Olympus, the normally graceful Euphrosyne wrung her hands. "Oh, dear. This is a disaster, Aglaia. Is this how you grant Belle's wish?"

"Of course not," Aglaia said defensively. "But I didn't want to interfere too much."

Thalia shook her head. "It's so obvious those two love each other. They're the only ones who don't realize it. Isn't there something you can do?"

"No," Aglaia said with real regret. "This is something they must do for themselves or it won't mean anything. At least we know Belle isn't pregnant."

Euphrosyne said, "I suppose. But it's such a shame you can't give them a little push, somehow."

Aglaia started to shake her head, but then a thought struck her. "I don't want to do anything directly, but perhaps I can give a tiny push in another direction. . . ."

Eighteen

Kit stared at Belle, feeling powerless as she crossed her arms and glared at him with a mulish expression. Not one of his arguments had been persuasive. She didn't even seem moved by the fact that he had revealed the real reason why he left England.

How could he make her understand marriage was the best thing—the only thing—she could do? Didn't she understand *she* would be thought at fault if she refused him? That their union might result in a child?

This wasn't how he had imagined asking his future wife to marry him. He rather thought it would involve a visit to her father to ask for her hand and arrange marriage settlements, then a joyful meeting with his intended when he got down on one knee to propose. Instead, Belle was treating him like an idiot child who didn't know what he wanted.

Then again, he wasn't totally enamored of her actions either. Perhaps she hadn't intended revenge when her parents burst in upon them, but she still didn't trust him enough to confide in him. Quite obviously, as husbands went, he was her last choice.

Last, hell. He didn't even make the list.

Still, Kit had to continue trying. He had made love

to her, and though it didn't seem to mean as much to her as it had to him, he knew many others would think he had taken her most precious asset. Kit had to make it up to her somehow, and marriage was the only way he knew to do so. "Belle, I—"

Kit broke off when he heard the door open. Mr. Sullivan poked his head inside and said, "'Tis mighty quiet in here. What's toward?"

Relieved to have someone to express his emotions to, Kit said, "Your daughter is being stubborn." And suddenly, he was too impatient to try to convince her any longer. Shaking his head, he said, "I'll come back later to get her answer."

"I already gave you my answer," Belle said in stubborn tones.

"Yes, but it was the wrong one. Think it over," Kit said curtly. "I'm sure you'll see I'm right."

Belle merely rolled her eyes, and Kit exited the parlor before he became even more frustrated. Mr. Sullivan held the door open and gave him a look Kit couldn't quite interpret. It gave Kit pause. While he was sure Belle's father would agree to their marriage, Kit wasn't quite sure if Sullivan approved of him.

As a result, Kit left the Sullivan house in a foul mood. It became even fouler when he spotted Daltrey lurking outside. "What the devil?" he exclaimed.

Daltrey smiled at him with a feral look. "You know what they say—give the devil his due." He took a menacing step toward Kit and said in a deceptively silky tone, "It's been a week. You should have your draft by now. Time to pay up."

Fury filled Kit. He had had enough of John Daltrey. He was sick of his demands, sick of his blackmail, sick of Daltrey's constant unspoken reminder of how little Kit's family regarded him. Enough was enough. If he didn't stop this soon, the man would hound him the rest of his life. "No," Kit said and turned to leave.

Daltrey caught his arm. "What do you mean, no? You promised me that money and I want it now."

"I've changed my mind," Kit said. "I'm not giving it to you." Besides, most of his cash was now safely invested in the railroad.

"Have you forgotten the consequences of refusing to pay me?" Daltrey asked with narrowed eyes.

"No, I haven't forgotten." But the thought of having the threat hanging over his head for the rest of his life filled him with dread. Even another week was beyond imagining.

Besides, if Daltrey accused Kit to the entire city, Belle would have a good reason to turn him down that would place the censure on him instead of her. Kit crossed his arms and leaned against a post. "Do it and be damned to you."

Daltrey looked taken aback. "You don't mean that."

"Yes, I do." And the simple act of saying it out loud gave him a great deal of relief. Nothing else was going right lately, so why the devil should he care if one more part of his life went to hell?

Daltrey scowled, then gazed at Kit measuringly. "How about if I start here, then? I hear rumors you're going to marry the oldest Sullivan girl. Shall we see what her father says about this?"

Kit shrugged, trying to act as though he didn't care, but he didn't think Daltrey was convinced. He couldn't even convince himself that he didn't care what Belle or her father thought of him. Apprehensively, Kit watched as Daltrey knocked on the door.

Sullivan answered it himself and Daltrey sneered, obviously seeing Sullivan's act of opening his own door as a sign of weakness.

Sullivan glanced at them both with a questioning look.

Giving him a supercilious smile, Daltrey said, "I have something to say to you that I think you'll be very interested to hear."

Daltrey glanced at Kit, as if expecting Kit to do something to stop him. But Kit refused to give him the satisfaction. To hell with the consequences—he wasn't putting up with any more of Daltrey's blackmail.

"Is that so?" Sullivan said with a raised eyebrow. "And what is it ye would like to talk to me about?"

Daltrey jerked his head in Kit's direction. "I have something you need to know about Stanhope, here."

Some passersby were looking at them oddly. Sullivan must have noticed it as well, for he glanced up and down the street and said, "Perhaps 'twould be best if ye came in, then."

Kit hesitated, not certain he wanted to deal with this right now, but Sullivan said, "Stanhope, you'd better come, too."

Kit sighed. Perhaps the man was right. And Kit didn't want to insult the Sullivans by enacting a scene on their doorstep. Reluctantly, he followed the men into the house.

Belle was there in the hallway and gave Kit a questioning look, no doubt wondering what Daltrey was doing there with him after Kit had so explicitly warned her away from him. Kit shrugged. She would learn soon enough, along with everyone else.

Daltrey leered at her, then gave Kit a sly look.

"You know, it might be a good idea if Miss Sullivan sat in on this conversation, so she can get a good idea of what kind of man her prospective fiancé is."

Belle looked surprised, but said, "All right." Wanting, no doubt, to get ammunition for her refusal to marry him.

Kit frowned. "I wouldn't recommend it," he said to her father. "This man isn't—"

"I know what sort of man he is," Sullivan interrupted. "And I'll be the judge of what is suitable for me daughter." He thought for a moment, then said, "This is probably something ye should hear, lass."

Belle gave Kit a triumphant look and he scowled, wishing he had the right to tell Belle to leave, to run away as far as she could get from this man's lies. But Belle hadn't given him that authority, and Kit wouldn't insult her father by pushing the point. She would learn what Daltrey had to say sooner or later anyway.

They went into the library, and Daltrey took a seat before he was offered one—a move calculated to insult Sullivan, whom Daltrey obviously considered a social inferior. Lounging insolently in the chair, Daltrey turned to Kit with an expectant look, as if he expected Kit to change his mind and say something to stop him.

Kit, however, had no such intention. For one thing, he wouldn't be able to call himself any sort of man if he continued letting Daltrey put the screws to him. And for another, Sullivan was acting oddly and he wondered what the man was up to.

Balked of his blackmail, Daltrey turned to Sullivan and said, "Before you allow your daughter to consider marrying this man, you should know he has been ejected from England for being a womanizer."

"Is that so?" Sullivan said in a dry tone.

Kit wasn't certain if he intended to show disbelief or ask for more information. And he didn't seem surprised at all. Damn it, did the man have so little opinion of him?

Apparently Daltrey wasn't satisfied with his reaction, for he added, "He dishonored a young lady."

"Did he now?" Sullivan said, but it was more of a statement than a question, as if he were merely encouraging Daltrey to continue.

Daltrey scowled. "Yes." He glanced back and forth between Sullivan and Kit. "Let me be more specific. He fathered a bastard on a young girl, then abandoned her and the unborn babe with no acknowledgment."

Sullivan continued to look noncommittal, but a protest came from an unexpected quarter. "That's not true," Belle said hotly, and Kit felt a little warmth at her immediate championing of him.

Daltrey's frustration turned to smugness as he finally achieved a reaction. "Why? Because you think he's too good to do such a thing?"

Belle glared at him. "That's right. I know a decent man when I meet one." And her tone and gaze left no doubt that she didn't consider Daltrey to be one of their number.

Daltrey leaned forward to stare her in the eyes. "Oh, but he's not decent," he said in a malicious tone. "Even his father knows of his depravity. Why do you think his family kicked him out of the ancestral home?"

Belle fired up. "I don't know and I don't care. If you and his father don't know that Kit would never abandon a woman or his child . . ." She floundered for a moment. ". . . Well, you just don't know him very well."

Kit was touched. No one else had stood up for him like this. Not his mother, not his sisters, and certainly not his brother or father. No one else had believed in him . . . trusted him. Especially on so little evidence of his innocence. A surge of feeling rose within him, an unidentifiable emotion that left him a little choked up.

If Belle believed in him enough to fight for him, Kit had to fight back, too. "That's right," he confirmed. "I would never do such a thing."

"See?" Belle said in triumph.

Daltrey sneered. "You think just because he says it, that makes it true?" He turned to Sullivan. "So, who are you going to believe? Me . . . or this bastard-siring cad?"

Sullivan considered for a moment, then said, "I think I'll be believin' Mr. Stanhope."

"What?" Daltrey asked with a stunned expression that mirrored how Kit felt. "It's all true, every word of it. If you don't believe me, just ask his family."

Sullivan raised an eyebrow. "I don't have to—I made some inquiries of me own."

Inquiries? Kit sat up straighter. What was going on here?

Daltrey grinned. "So you know all about Stanhope's little peccadilloes."

"Yer mistaken," Sullivan said grimly. "'Twasn't Stanhope I made inquiries about, but yerself."

Daltrey looked as surprised as Kit felt.

"Me? Why?" Daltrey asked. "I'm not the one courting your daughter."

"No, but while Stanhope is an open book, no one in town was quite sure of yer intentions. So a while back, I sent a man to make inquiries about yer background."

Kit cast a questioning glance at Belle, but she shrugged. Sullivan intercepted their look and gave Kit a reassuring nod. For the first time, Kit wondered if he might actually get out of this situation with his reputation intact.

In any case, Sullivan certainly didn't seem to need any help from him, so Kit decided to stay mum and watch the show.

Sullivan speared Daltrey with a condemnatory look. "What my man found was very interesting."

Daltrey scowled. "I don't see how this pertains to the situation at hand," he protested.

"Ye will," Sullivan said in a matter-of-fact tone. "I received a report last night." He removed some papers from his desk and scanned them. "I take it yer familiar with a young lady by the name of Molly O'Connor?"

Sly triumph filled Daltrey's gaze. "Of course Miss O'Connor is the young girl Stanhope sullied."

Belle opened her mouth to protest, but her father quelled her with a look. Glancing down at the paper again, he said, "That's not what she says."

"What?" Daltrey said in surprise. "But she has named him as the father of her bastard to all and sundry."

Daltrey was right about that—Molly had named Kit as the father, though Kit had never touched the girl. He leaned forward, wondering what Sullivan had up his sleeve.

Sullivan nodded. "Aye, she did name him as the father at first, saying 'twas because he was an honest and decent man."

Belle grinned and cast Daltrey a smug glance, saying, "See, I told you he was decent."

He ignored her and addressed her father. "And he's still the father."

Sullivan shook his head. "Not according to Miss O'Connor. She only named him because she thought he would marry her if she did. She's very sorry for that."

Kit shook his head. He wouldn't be blackmailed into something as important as marriage in that way. She should have known that.

"Ha," Daltrey said dismissively. "A likely story."

"Not as likely as the true story," Sullivan said. "She named another man as the real father."

"Who?" Kit asked eagerly. He had often wondered whose blame he was taking. He glanced at Daltrey with dawning comprehension. Could it be . . . ?

But Sullivan didn't even look at him. Instead, he continued to stare at Daltrey with a hard expression. "That man is you, Mr. Daltrey."

Kit's jaw dropped open in astonishment and disbelief. It all fit. That was how Daltrey knew so much about the accusations and why he had been so thorough in condemning Kit—he was the guilty one all along and didn't want anyone to suspect it.

Daltrey shot to his feet. "Ridiculous. The silly imbecile just wants a peer of the realm as the father of her child. She'll say anything to get one as a husband."

"Ye might think so," Sullivan said. "But me man has proof."

"Proof?" Daltrey scoffed. "What proof? There's no way to prove who fathered a child."

"There are ways," Sullivan said mildly.

"Such as?" Daltrey challenged.

Sullivan shrugged. "The babe has been born and it seems he has brown eyes. Both the mother and yon Stanhope have blue eyes."

And Daltrey definitely had brown, just like the baby.

He laughed. "That proves nothing."

Sullivan nodded as if he expected Daltrey to say that. "Then there is the distinctive Daltrey birthmark."

Daltrey's laughter stilled, and he suddenly looked apprehensive. All of Kit's senses came alert. What was this? Did Sullivan actually have some real proof that Daltrey was the father of Molly's child?

"What birthmark?" Kit asked eagerly.

"Well, 'tisn't a birthmark *per se*," Sullivan said. "More of a hereditary trait. Ye see, it seems some of the Daltrey men have a sort of webbing between their toes. A defect, ye might call it."

Could it be true? Kit glanced at Daltrey and noticed that the man had turned pale. "So," Kit said casually. "Would you mind taking off your shoes, old man?"

Daltrey scowled and ignored him, but looked as if he were about to panic at any moment.

Laying his papers down on his desk, Sullivan said, "Yer son has the same defect."

"No," Daltrey shouted. "I have no son."

Sullivan shrugged. "Whether you admit to paternity or not, yer father has seen the truth. He has acknowledged your son as a true Daltrey."

"Stop saying that," Daltrey said in a panic. "It was Stanhope, I tell you."

"No, it was not," Sullivan said in implacable tones. "I have a signed affidavit from the girl and yer father telling the truth." He glanced at Kit and held up two pieces of paper. "And they've both sent ye written apologies for any sufferin' they and their families may have caused ye."

Relief flooded Kit. The truth was out at last.

But Daltrey wasn't done yet. "You'll never prove it," he said with a sneer. "I can still tell the whole town that Stanhope was kicked out of England for siring a bastard. They'll just think you're trying to cover up the truth to protect your daughter."

But the threat didn't even faze Belle's father. "No, you won't," he said calmly. "We know you've been blackmailing Stanhope here for something he never did, but we know even more about you."

Kit raised an eyebrow, wondering who Sullivan was in cahoots with on this. "We?" he asked.

"A group o' concerned citizens," Sullivan said shortly, giving Kit an admonishing glance that warned him in no uncertain terms to keep out of the conversation.

Since Sullivan seemed to be doing quite nicely on his own, Kit obliged.

Turning back to Daltrey, Belle's father said, "We know why ye left England—because of yer debts."

"So?" Daltrey said belligerently. "Who cares? Everyone assumes a remittance man is in debt anyway. You can't blackmail *me* that way."

"Perhaps not," Sullivan said. "But we aren't quibbling about your debts." His gaze turned hard. "We're doin' this because of yer crime against Molly O'Connor, for blackmailing an innocent man, and fer givin' yer countrymen a bad name."

"Good for you, Papa," Belle exclaimed.

Kit concurred. Sullivan's speech made him want to stand up and cheer.

When Daltrey did nothing but scowl, Sullivan said, "But 'tis yer debts that'll be yer downfall."

"Downfall?" Daltrey scoffed, though sweat had popped out on his forehead.

"We know why yer so insistent on getting money from Stanhope. Though you have conned and swindled several people in town, we're on to ye now. You're not even very good at it. Ye owe a lot of people a lot of money."

"That's none of your concern," Daltrey blustered.

"That's where yer wrong," Sullivan said. And for the first time, he smiled. "We've bought up all yer debts, y'see. We can send ye to jail . . . for a very long time."

Daltrey blanched at the thought of incarceration, and Kit was glad to see that some threat had moved the man.

"You can't do that," Daltrey protested. "You won't do that."

"On the contrary. We can and we will . . . unless ye leave town immediately and never come back."

Daltrey stood in indecision for a moment. Then fury crossed his face as he reached inside his coat and pulled out his slim dagger. Cursing, he lunged for Belle and grabbed her, holding the knife to her neck.

Belle screeched and Kit surged to his feet, his blood boiling. If Daltrey so much as scratched her, he'd have the man's hide tanned and stretched on a barn.

"Stay back," Daltrey warned Kit. "And you," he said, brandishing the knife at Sullivan. "Give me those papers and I won't hurt your daughter."

Sullivan stood for a moment in indecision, but Kit couldn't stand the fact that Daltrey might go free,

that he might perpetrate his crimes on someone else
. . . that he might hurt Belle.

With an icy rage fueling him, Kit waited until Daltrey gestured once more with the knife, then
lunged for his wrist. Pulling the weapon away from
Belle, he squeezed the man's hand in a fierce grip
until Daltrey cried out in pain and dropped the
dagger.

As Belle snatched it up out of his reach, Daltrey
cradled his wrist in his other hand. "You broke it,"
he cried in an agonized tone.

Kit stared at him in contempt. "I'll do more than
that." And with a powerful roundhouse punch, he
hit the bastard full in the face.

Daltrey went down for the count and lay there,
insensible, on the rug.

Shooting his cuffs, Kit said, "I apologize, Belle.
My emotions got away from me."

"Oh, no, that was wonderful," Belle exclaimed
with wide eyes. *"You* were wonderful."

"Not I," Kit said. "You father is the true savior
here." Kit stood and leaned over to shake the man's
hand. "Sir, I can't thank you enough."

For the first time, the masterful Irishman appeared
a little uncomfortable. Kit suspected he was more at
ease dealing with villains like Daltrey than receiving
praise and gratitude.

"'Twas nothing," Sullivan said with a dismissive
wave. "I did it for the town." But he glanced down
at Daltrey's inert body with a look of complete satisfaction.

"But how did you know?" Kit hadn't even suspected any of this.

Sullivan shrugged. "When ye wouldn't explain
why ye left England, I had a feelin' something

wasn't quite right. Then when I learned the two of ye were from the same area, warning bells sounded, so I did a little investigating."

"And I'm very glad you did," Kit assured him fervently. No more blackmail, no more need to pinch pennies, to constantly check over his shoulder to see if Daltrey was watching. It was like a miracle.

"So, did ye ever find an investment to yer liking?"

"Yes, I did. I had some funds set aside that Daltrey didn't know about and decided to invest in General Palmer's railroad."

"Ah, a good choice. I should have thought of that meself."

Kit grinned. "Well, no one can think of everything—not even you. Though I am very grateful for what you *have* done. Please, if there is ever anything I can do for you, you have only to ask."

"Well, there is one thing . . ." Sullivan said.

Taken aback that Sullivan had jumped on his offer so quickly, Kit could do nothing but say, "Name it, sir, and it is yours."

Sullivan smiled at him. "All I want is for ye to tell me daughter how ye really feel about her." Then, clapping Kit on the shoulder, Sullivan called a footman to help him drag Daltrey's limp form out of the room.

When they had left, Kit glanced at Belle, who looked suddenly self-conscious.

"That's not necessary," she murmured. "I know how you feel about me." Then she smiled brightly, saying, "I'm so happy for you. Now you can finally go home."

He was happy, too. Happy that she trusted him, believed in him. Not even his own family would do so. Only Belle—and her father—had believed in him. It was a powerful force, that belief in a person. "No, I won't go home," he said softly. His home was here, with these marvelous people.

"Why not?" she asked, and hope lit in her eyes.

All his doubts fell away when he saw the expression in her eyes. He knew then that staying here was the right thing to do, the only thing to do. She might have kept one small secret from him, but she had shown she trusted him in the ways that really mattered.

"There are too many things here that are important to me now," he said. "My investment, my friends, my heart, and most important . . . you."

Belle inhaled sharply, and for a moment he thought she would forget to breathe.

"M-me?" she repeated breathlessly. "Why would you stay for me?"

"Because I love you," he said simply. As happiness lit her face, he added, "For the last time, will you marry me?"

Belle threw herself into his arms. "Yes, yes!"

They kissed, and Kit allowed himself to feel joy at last.

Belle pulled away and gave him a little shake. "That's all I was waiting for," she said with a little frown. "To know you loved me. What took you so long?"

Smiling down at her, he raised her hand and kissed it. He would no longer hold anything back. "Because my family never believed in my innocence and never trusted in me to do what was right, trust became all-important to me. And when you wouldn't tell me what man you were trying to attract, I was afraid I would never earn your trust. I—I couldn't live with that."

"But—"

He hushed her with another kiss. "It's not important now. After you championed me in front of your father and Daltrey, I can see you *do* trust me."

She slapped him in the arm. "Of course I do, you idiot. I always have."

"Well, not quite always," Kit said. Though he wasn't going to quibble about it now.

"But the reason I didn't tell you who I was trying to attract is because it was you all along. Why else would I insist on spending so much time with you . . . and your lessons?"

Kit suddenly felt like a dolt. He had never suspected, though he had prided himself on being quite an expert on reading Belle. But it was quite evident she was telling the truth. She did trust him—she had all along.

He shook his head at his own obtuseness. No matter—he would have a whole lifetime now to perfect his reading of Belle.

Belle sighed happily. "I can't believe it—my wish did come true."

"What wish?"

"When we went to the Garden of the Gods, Mama wanted us to wish for husbands in front of the Three Graces monument where Papa proposed to her. But after you called me homely, I wished for beauty instead."

"And you *are* beautiful," he said.

She shook her head with a smile. "That's not the wish I'm talking about. Though I made that wish out loud, I held a secret wish in my heart . . . I wished for you."

He kissed her again. "I was a fool," he said. "You could never be homely. In fact, you are the most beautiful person I know . . . both inside and out." And he would be happy to prove it to her for the rest of their lives together.

Epilogue

"Well," Euphrosyne said with a smile. "You must be ecstatic now, Aglaia."

Aglaia beamed and couldn't help but preen a little. "Yes—they finally got together. It was difficult since I had to be so careful, but I finally did it."

"And did an excellent job as well," Thalia assured her graciously. "You should be proud of yourself."

"I am very pleased," Aglaia said. "Especially since I managed to grant all three of her wishes." She smiled at Thalia. "My job is done. Now it's your turn."

Thalia's eyes gleamed. "Yes, and I can't *wait* to get started on Charisma. . . ."

FROM THE AUTHOR

Dear Reader,

This series came about when several of us got together to brainstorm a series based on a monument in the Garden of the Gods. The rock formation known as the Three Graces (yes, it really exists) seemed perfect for our purposes, so we wrote the stories based on it, speculating that the "real" Three Graces might just be listening when three special heroines make wishes at their feet.

If you enjoyed this book and Belle's search for true beauty, I hope you'll return to Little London to learn what happens to the other Sullivan sisters when the Three Graces grant Charisma's wish in *A Touch of Charm* by Karen Fox and help Grace find happiness in *Fallen From Grace* by Yvonne Jocks.

I love to hear from my readers—you can find me on the web at http://www.pammc.com or write to me at PO Box 648, Divide, CO 80814.

Pam McCutcheon

Discover The Magic of
Romance With
Jo Goodman

The Queen of Romance

Cassie Edwards

BOOK YOUR PLACE ON OUR WEBSITE AND MAKE THE READING CONNECTION!

We've created a customized website just for our very special readers, where you can get the inside scoop on everything that's going on with Zebra, Pinnacle and Kensington books.

When you come online, you'll have the exciting opportunity to:

- View covers of upcoming books
- Read sample chapters
- Learn about our future publishing schedule (listed by publication month *and author*)
- Find out when your favorite authors will be visiting a city near you
- Search for and order backlist books from our online catalog
- Check out author bios and background information
- Send e-mail to your favorite authors
- Meet the Kensington staff online
- Join us in weekly chats with authors, readers and other guests
- Get writing guidelines
- AND MUCH MORE!

**Visit our website at
http://www.kensingtonbooks.com**